# HOLLYWOOD PAYBACK

Also available by Jon Lindstrom

*Hollywood Hustle*

# HOLLYWOOD PAYBACK

A THRILLER

JON LINDSTROM

NEW YORK

Quote from "To Althea, from Prison" by Richard Lovelace (1642).



Published in the United States by Crooked Lane Books, an imprint of The Quick Brown Fox & Company LLC.



Library of Congress Catalog-in-Publication data available upon request.

ISBN (hardcover): 979-8-89242-399-1
ISBN (paperback): 979-8-89242-509-4
ISBN (ebook): 979-8-89242-400-4

Cover design by Emily Mahar

Printed in the United States.

www.crookedlanebooks.com

Crooked Lane Books
34 West 27th St., 10th Floor
New York, NY 10001

First Edition: April 2026

The authorized representative in the EU for product safety and compliance is eucomply OÜPärnu mnt 139b-14, 11317 Tallinn, Estonia, hello@eucompliancepartner.com, +33757690241

10 9 8 7 6 5 4 3 2 1

To all those friends who never
hesitate to help.

*"Stone walls do not a prison make, / Nor iron bars a cage."*

*—Richard Lovelace*

# PROLOGUE

# Hollywood

ONE OF THE many ironies of Hollywood is that so much of what's associated with it is imported. The palm trees are trucked in from desert farms to the east. The water is pumped in thanks to the runoff from high in the Sierras hundreds of miles away. Much of its human population has emigrated from origins far removed.

Even its name is misleading. That came about not because holly grows indigenously (no more than the palm trees do) but because the plant, like the illusory four-leaf clover, is said to bring good luck. The holly plant is a strange symbol of fortune. It's not a tree, but a shrub, and with its bright red berries and sturdy, dark green leaves, it is beautiful to look at, especially during the holidays. But, like the city named after it, holly is deceptive.

The berries are poisonous, and its sturdy leaves—rather than its stem like on a rose—are ringed with sharp points. Come at it the wrong way, and those stickers will open your skin as if it was paper. Like the many who come here just to be hammered with bad luck.

Death by a thousand cuts.

Another irony is that Hollywood isn't even a city. It began as a simple neighborhood, and then became a municipality within the city of Los Angeles. Once the area was incorporated into greater LA, it began to take on its own shape and identity. Both alcohol and movie theaters were banned for a time during the early 1900s, the latter of which didn't even exist here when they were outlawed. Tolerance was something that had to be learned.

The American movie industry is said to have migrated from its origins in and around New York City because of the mostly dry and sunny weather, which allowed for countless days of outdoor film production. In truth, many motion picture companies and filmmakers moved west to avoid being repeatedly sued by Thomas Edison's Motion Picture Patents company for violating the patent laws governing the cameras and other equipment that Edison had invented. It was simply easier to evade legal scrutiny three thousand miles away in still-developing California. The weather was more of a value-added situation.

In 1923, some real estate developers erected a sign on the hill above the neighborhood: *Hollywoodland*. The last four letters weren't removed until 1949 as part of an agreement for the city to maintain the sign. Soon, the abbreviated name was established as a symbol of a place of great promise. But, like Disneyland's wonder and secrets waiting to be discovered, behind the scenes you'd find workers operating dangerous equipment for very low pay. The executives in town have always found ways to send the lion's share of the money up to themselves, and then zealously hoard it. Just one result was the lengthy, brutal 2023 writers and actors' strikes.

And then there's the violence. The Chinese Massacre (1871). The Zoot Suit Riots (1943). The Bugsy Siegel Murder (1947). The Watts Rebellion (1965). The Toolbox Killers, The Hillside Stranglers, The Freeway Killer, and The Night Stalker (all between 1977 and 1985). The Wonderland Murders (1981). The Rodney King Beating (1991), and the subsequent LA Riots (1992). The ICE Raids (2025). Most of these made the news, but some did not thanks to the "institutionalized amnesia" prevalent in the media and school textbooks. Much of the cause was racism, but at the heart of each is want, desire, need, and greed. Even the Tate-LaBianca Murders in 1969 were conceived and carried out because Charles Manson felt he'd been cheated of the rock stardom he'd come to believe was his destiny.

It was the movie business specifically that was called "The Dream Factory." And though it's true that it is a place of stunning wealth and grand possibility, it can also be said that it was built on a five-cornered foundation of ambition, avarice, deception, self-deception, and tragedy.

Today, Los Angeles County has eighty-eight cities, is home to ten million people, with over two hundred languages spoken. For many who come here, whether to ultimately succeed or fail, leaving will be impossible. The essence of the city is its pull, its potential, and once it takes hold, it will never leave you.

And a nine-letter sign, for so much of the world, defines the entire region:

Hollywood.

# CHAPTER

# 1

## THEN

## 2000

EVEN AT MY lowest, I never imagined I could kill someone. Then I did.

Before setting out that night I'd packed my nose with blow, and less than an hour later, I was craving another bump. I could have done it—the car was in park—but I was too afraid to take my hands off the wheel. They could come out any second with the money.

The idling engine illuminated the dash cluster, making the clock face easy to read: 3:09 AM.

Downtown LA in the middle of the night has never been a seething hotspot, but especially back then. Pop-up nightclubs would come and go so fast they would shutter in a few months, replaced by a newer club two blocks over. Regardless, under state law, all of them closed by two AM. By three, the streets would be deserted.

Damon and Bill were supposed to be out by 3:05. They were late. What the actual fuck was going on in there? No one should be in the building at this hour. Damon had planned it this way. The week's take was stashed inside, ready to be delivered to the gang's headquarters the next morning. The El Repettos had controlled the downtown drug trade for decades. It was rumored they were pulling down a million a month—meaning that even one week's amount, split three ways, was still enough for each of us to start a new life.

The gang had never had any problem with theft because, well, they were the goddamned El Repettos. Based east of LA in the mostly Asian community of Montebello, they took their name from the main boulevard that snaked through their home base (which was ironically named after a three-hundred-pound Italian immigrant who had owned several thousand acres there in the 1800s). The El Reppettos liked their nickname, the ERs, because they never sent anybody to an emergency room—only the morgue.

You didn't cross them. And you sure didn't steal from them. No one ever had before, but Damon said that would give us the advantage.

As my panic rose, the insanity of it all hit me: We were trespassing in the hiding place of one of the city's most powerful and violent criminal street gangs. We were stealing money made from the illegal sales of cocaine, crack, heroin, weed, speed, and barbiturates. No wonder my knuckles felt like they were about to pop.

I imagined putting the car into gear, stomping on the gas and taking off, leaving my two cohorts to fend for themselves. *Just drive away and keep going.* I imagined making it all the way back home to Oregon, where I would get clean, get a job, and stop selling my dick to horny older women just to feed my habit. A habit I'd never had back home. I'd never had more than a beer back then, maybe a puff or two of weed, but that was it. Now, I couldn't get enough.

It was down here in LA where the cravings began, and once they'd started, they never let go. Fucking Damon. He'd gotten me on this road. It was like he had shown me a shiny, lucrative new world, then left me dumped in a ditch. For about a year before this, I'd ingested just about anything to not feel the way I always did when I woke up. Especially coke. That drug could fool me into believing every hit would feel like the first, so why wouldn't I keep chasing that? I wanted to change my personality, my whole being, into someone other than the piece of shit I'd become. As useless and phony as that was, it felt good. So, I'd pursue that splendid sensation . . . until the coke ran out. Then I'd have to start all over once I'd slept it off, but to do that I'd usually need a coupla' pills. Unless the booze did the trick. What a vicious circle.

My name is Jason, but I always used Jake, even on my headshots. I liked the way it sounded, like a character out of a movie. I'd come to Hollywood to be a movie star, like just about everyone else who wasn't born here. Though it's not like plenty of the natives don't want that, too. Instead, here I was, gripping this steering wheel so tight it made my fingers even more numb than the coke in my nose. This was the car I'd moved to LA in. The one in which I'd criss-crossed this vast city from audition to audition. It had once been my mother's car, a reliable four-door sedan with an easy automatic transmission. A hand-me-down gift from my family, a gesture of their belief in me. And now I'm using it to commit a robbery. Desperately hoping to finance a giant leap to freedom—out of my drug habit, and my even more sordid occupation.

This was my life. A pipe dream if there ever was one.

I stand four inches over six feet tall, but I'd never felt cramped in this car until that night. My eyes, dark brown like my dad's, felt as dry as my mouth. I tried to swallow, but the coke drip made the back of my throat an impassable lump. I thought I might get sick, so I lifted the bottom of the ski mask I had stretched over my head to clear my mouth, and put one hand on the door handle, just in case.

I looked at the clock again. Something was wrong. I'd waited long enough. I hated to leave them behind, but I knew if I got caught, whether by the police or the ERs, my life would be over. I put my foot on the brake to shift into Drive, forced my right hand from the wheel to the gear lever on the column. Then I heard the back door of the building open.

I turned and saw Damon and Bill, also wearing black ski masks, each carrying a pistol in one hand and a heavy-looking black canvas bag with the other. They raced across the alley, and Bill jumped into the front passenger seat, Damon into the rear.

"Go!" yelled Damon from behind me.

I pulled the gear lever, and hit the gas hard. By the time I could focus we were nearly out of the alley, the street beyond coming closer through the windshield. In an instant, we'd be through to the boulevard, then a hard left up the hill and onto the 110 Freeway. From there, we would disappear into the boundless carpet of Los Angeles.

My eyes were lasered past the alley's exit to the four wide lanes of 5th Street, like the border of a country where freedom awaits, when a woman wearing a kitchen uniform and a large purse slung over her shoulder walked across the alley entrance. There was no time to swerve.

"Shit!" I yelled as my car hit the woman.

The force of the impact threw her over the hood and into the windshield, spider-cracking the glass. I could hear her tumble over the roof of the car and across the trunk to land on the sidewalk.

I slammed the brake pedal so hard I thought it might break off and skidded to a stop in the middle of the empty boulevard. The screech of the tires faded, replaced by the night's silence.

The three of us were stock still, as the shock of what had just happened set in. All I could hear was the heaving of my own lungs. Then Damon opened the rear door.

I turned to watch through the rear window as he walked over to the woman. I ripped off my ski mask, as if that would help me see better. The woman lay motionless on the concrete. A can of Mace rolled out of her handbag. Then, miraculously, she moved.

Her head lolled upward. Thin rivulets of blood from a gash somewhere in her scalp ran into her eyes. Her mouth was open, and her head cocked uncertainly from side to side, as if she were searching for a breath. Damon stopped over her and aimed his pistol directly at her.

Whatever amount of blood was in her eyes, it wasn't enough to block her view of the gun being trained on her. She raised her hand in a defensive motion and Damon fired, twice, both shots to her head. The woman's arm dropped as her body jerked from the bullets, then all movement stopped. Next to me, Bill had also removed his mask.

Somehow, he managed to croak, "Oh, shit."

Damon strode back to the car and got in. He closed the door and looked up at the two of us gawking at him from the front seat. He swiped off his own face covering. Sweat had soaked his thinning blond hair, and the jowls forming from his own fondness for dope. His blue eyes were hot in the dark. "Let's go," he said. He looked up at us, still staring at him. "I said, let's *go*!"

I guess my survival instincts kicked in. I turned back to the wheel, gulped hard, then squinted through the spider cracks. I hit the gas and drove up the hill toward the freeway. It was a challenge of maneuvering unlike anything I'd ever done, but we were on our way. I felt a distant hope that I just might get free, after all. But in my heart I knew I wouldn't.

And none of us had figured on the surveillance camera mounted over the alley entrance.

# CHAPTER

# 2

**NOW**

**2026**

I woke to a deep rumble underneath me, a steady crescendo that roused me from sleep. I felt the churning vibration intensifying, like something from Hades, then my whole world began to shake.

It was my first morning as a free man. I hadn't felt an earthquake in a quarter century, and this one was so jarring it may as well have been my first.

I bolted upright, grabbing the edges of the mattress. The lessons I'd learned back when I was new to LA, like jumping into a door frame, or getting *the fuck outside* altogether, had been long forgotten. Not like you could do either in a locked prison cell, but here I was, helpless, the bed shuddering on the carpeted floor of the shabby old building. It lasted less than twenty seconds but, as anybody who's been through one will tell you, it felt like an hour.

I had to pause for a moment, wondering if I'd peed the bed. Thank God, I hadn't. Wouldn't do to begin my freedom so ignominiously.

The reverberation faded into car alarms howling from the street two floors below. Nervous laughter of other hotel guests who *had* made it into their doorways, expressing their relief that the shaking had ended, sounded through my wall. Then some know-it-all out there said something about how aftershocks are almost always less intense. "Don't worry, folks! This place was built in nineteen twenty-four! Survived a lot worse! Hehe."

I lay back down, still grasping the seams of the mattress, my eyes fixed on the ceiling. I wished Hallway Guy would shut the fuck up so I could listen for that aftershock. Despite my certainty that the bed had bounced across the small room, it apparently hadn't moved. The sound and the judder of the bed frame had made the quake seem worse than it was. Only the perfunctory reading lamp next to the phone on the nightstand had tipped over, unbroken. The seismic version of a bark being worse than the bite.

*So this is what freedom feels like.*

I'd told myself if I ever walked out of prison alive, that would be the day I would begin to live again. I was wrong, but I wouldn't come to know that for a while.

The day before, I had been released after serving my sentence for causing the death of Clementine Esperanza. It didn't really matter that we had stolen the proceeds of an illegal drug operation or that I hadn't pulled the trigger; under what was called the Felony Murder Rule, I was just as responsible as Damon. I'd taken part in a robbery that resulted in an innocent person's death.

The prison gate rolling open pushed the air pleasantly across my face. It felt like a cleansing, of sorts. Behind me was over half my life spent inside those walls. Beyond was freedom, and I intended to make the most of it. I just didn't know how.

I turned to the guard who'd escorted me that last morning and extended my hand.

"Just get outta here," he said, his burly thick paw still hovering over the control button, ready to close it. I stepped through before he could lock me inside again.

I made my way to the Greyhound Bus station in Sacramento, used some of the cash I'd earned working in the prison library to buy a few items at the concession stand. Having to make simple choices all of a sudden was an unfamiliar sensation, so I just grabbed what looked good. Sandwiches, chips, water, and soda.

The ride south to LA was an all-day affair that I spent in a window seat. I watched the first sunset I'd seen in a quarter century over the mountains beyond the farmland that lined Interstate 5. An explosion of reds, purples, yellows, and blues. It brought some water to my eyes, and left me feeling hopeful.

I'd stepped off the bus at the downtown station just after midnight hoping for a cab. Finding none, I asked a couple stragglers waiting for late night buses if they knew where I might find a ride to a hotel. One suggested I make my way a few blocks north up Alameda Street into what is now called the Arts District, where nightlife had taken hold since I'd been away. After trudging what had to be five of the longest city blocks ever created, I wandered into a seething street life.

Honestly, the lights and the sounds, the music, the automobiles, it all fairly freaked me out. But I spotted a yellow cab on the next corner and flagged him down. I asked the driver to take me anywhere he thought I might find a room at that hour. The guy brought me to this combo hotel/hostel in the Historic Core, an area built between 1904 and 1937 that, he informed me, was being gentrified. The neighborhood once hosted the world's largest collection of movie palaces, along with major department stores and office buildings. This establishment was priced to be popular with traveling students and young people searching for themselves. *Aren't they always?*

And here I was on a rickety bed frame, gripping a mattress for dear life, praying for a little control for once. I grabbed my jeans off the floor and pulled them on over my briefs.

When I was younger, I loved to sleep naked, but that habit died the night I went inside. I once dreamed of a time I'd feel safe enough to do it again, but last night wasn't it. Not yet. I sniffed the T-shirt I'd had on since yesterday morning; I'd be changing that after a shower.

I stepped across the compact room to the single cup coffeemaker on the desk. I had to use my prison issue reading glasses to make out the lettering of the directions. How is it possible to even print something that tiny? I filled the carafe with water from a tiny oval sink mounted on the wall and started the coffeemaker, then I went to the communal latrine for my morning leak. By the time I came back the coffee was finished.

I wrestled a styrofoam cup from its plastic wrapper and filled it with the coffee, then went to the window and pulled back the gauze curtain. Directly below me, squeezed into the narrow space between a set of opposing car bumpers, was a filthy guy with a filthy blanket draped over him like a serape, attempting to shield the fact that he was squatting to take a dump. He needed a bigger blanket. My first daylight view of Los Angeles as a free man. Suddenly the prison facilities didn't look so bad.

I shook my head, both at the sight and about the cab ride the night before. The driver had taken a winding route passing through the blocks of church missions that serve relief to the homeless—what most people call Skid Row. Both sides of the street were crammed with tents and lean-tos, and piles of refuse. People, a rainbow of ethnicities, lingered around their fabric or plywood housing. It jogged a memory for me.

I'd once worked crew on a music video right on that street, pulling cable for experience and extra cash. We'd arrived in a van and jumped out with a camera and sound equipment and started shooting the tents that lined the streets even back then. The residents were offended about being filmed without permission and demanded payment, and who could blame them? Things got tense, then heated, and we barely escaped by jumping back into the van and locking the doors. The cameraman got behind the wheel and hit the gas, swerving into a panicky U-turn. I could still feel where my skull met the window with a crack. We could hear the angry epithets a full city block away. It looked then just like it had last night, and that was over two decades ago. One of my biggest fears was I might someday become one of them.

If that's what the future had in store for me, I determined it wouldn't happen before I could do what I intended to do: make some amends. State law required that I return here. There's a term for it: County of Last Legal Residence. So, since I had to come back anyway, I was going to make the most of it. Which would begin, and maybe end, with Angela. That desire, that *need*, to make good somehow, was what helped keep me alive all this time. I wondered what she might look like now. Was she married? Was she happy?

Then again, maybe I should just leave well enough alone.

I shook off the sight of Serape Man with a sip of coffee, if you could call it that. It tasted like the watered-down excuse they brewed in Folsom, only weaker. I wanted something better, something that tasted like a choice in a new world of choices.

This was Saturday. Come Monday I would have to check in with my parole agent. Until then, I was on my own.

A shiver went down my spine.

# CHAPTER

# 3

A HOT SHOWER LEFT me feeling cleaner than I had in years. Probably because I wasn't sharing it with twenty hairy, tattooed men. The hostel's facilities were communal but gender-based, and I was the only one using it at this hour. I was happy to have it to myself, as I let the steam rise to envelop me, and only me.

Back in my room I pulled on my one clean T-shirt, then took in my appearance in the streaked mirror over the sink. On the bus the day before, not a single soul had uttered a sound in my direction. I guess the sight of a guy with prison yard muscles and a long beard and ponytail, both well-spotted with gray, had kept people distanced. I noticed a couple of furtive looks, sure, but who wouldn't avoid a guy who looks like he's prepping for a low-budget remake of *The Wild Ones*? I'd gotten so used to hiding my matinee idol handsome under all this hair that it had just become normal to me. *No one's going to take you for a young Clint Eastwood now, are they?* I leaned over the sink and squeezed the last of the water from my beard.

I settled into the one chair, which was fashioned from a thick red plastic in the shape of a hand, with the wrist as a pedestal and the open palm to catch me as I dropped into it. Hotel furnishings had sure changed while I was away. I pulled my cash from my pocket and spread the folded bills with my thumb and fingers. A few hundred dollars. I had several thousand more in an account that had been set up while I was inside, earned mostly in the prison library, but also by doing kitchen and shop work.

I unfolded the paper map of Los Angeles the night clerk had given me when I'd checked in and leaned back to peruse it. I was on Main Street between 6th and 7th. That rang a faint bell. I was tugging mindlessly on my damp beard, a habit I'd had so long I couldn't remember when it started. I wanted it gone: the beard and the habit. A new life needs a new face. But first, breakfast.

Ten minutes later, I was standing in front of a diner that reminded me of the Nite Owl Coffee Shop, site of the massacre that kicks off the plot of *L.A. Confidential*. That happened to be the last movie I saw before my arrest, having watched it on DVD during a coke binge the night before the robbery.

I stepped inside and was greeted by the clattering of plates and spatulas coming from an open grill area. The aroma of sizzling bacon and sausage stopped me in my tracks. I'd forgotten what real cooking smelled like. Under a glass dome atop the greeter's station was a mound of pink donuts sprinkled with crumbled bacon. Next to it was a platter with a colorful assortment of cakes and pastries, most of which I had no hope of identifying, though I did spot some classic apple pie and red velvet cake. It was like a rainbow of diabetes. I wanted to bury my face in it.

A waitress I guessed to be just this side of forty appeared. "Just yourself?" she asked brightly. I nodded, and she snatched a menu from a holder on the wall and led me to a two-top booth, dropping the menu on the table. I took the seat that faced the front door, with my back to the wall. Old habits die hard.

"Coffee?" she asked.

"Yeah," I answered, and she turned to go. "Please!" I called after her, remembering courtesies like that were expected on the outside. She returned a grin and scurried off. Her eyes had a kind of sparkle to them.

The place was about half full with patrons, either in twos or solos like me. Quiet. Deliberate. Relaxed. No one was guarding their plate against a food thief, or had their radar cranked to full in case someone with a beef might get the drop on them during chow time.

The place had been here a long time, and celebrated a 1950s-meets-now vibe. Tile-covered walls were broken up by square columns painted with horizontal lines of light ivory and dark brown. Above the booths was a foot-high molding with diamond-shapes carved into the dark wood. One wall commemorated prices of yore, with vintage signs advertising twenty-five cent burgers that came with a twenty-cent beer. A room dedicated to providing whatever you desired. I felt completely out of place. But I was hungry, so I opened the menu.

I'd thought picking out a sandwich and chips at the bus station was a challenge. This was like that Robin Williams movie about the Russian who defects to America, who finds it so stressful to choose a brand from a literal wall of coffee, he passes out from the pressure. Chilaquiles. Corned beef hash. Breakfast burrito. Chocolate banana jam pancakes. And a house special that made me laugh out loud: the Duck and Cluck (Saturday and Sunday only). I smiled. I'd wanted choice, and I'd gotten it, goddammit.

The waitress returned with a thick white mug filled with very dark coffee, setting it and a small plate loaded with a tiny pitcher of cream and sugar packets of the refined, raw, and substitute varieties on the table. *Jesus, even the sugar demands a choice.* I was surprised she hadn't brought three kinds of creamer.

"See something you like?" she asked. She wore tight black jeans, a yellow T-shirt, and a matching bandana to hold her dark hair back. The shirt had what looked like a washed-out logo for a band I'd never heard of.

"Uh," I said, glancing down at the menu. "What's good?"

She smiled. "It's all good, honey." She was pretty in a simple kind of way, like a cheerleader's plainer younger sister, but that smile made her chipmunk face shine. And man, those blue-green eyes. They didn't only sparkle at a distance; up close like this, I had to turn away.

"Well, the truth is," I said, clearing my throat, "I haven't had a good breakfast in a really long time. And I've never been here before, so I'm in your hands."

"Carla."

"What?"

"I'm in your hands . . . Carla," she said, pointing to the name tag above her ample left breast.

"Carla," I said, nodding, then realized that was my cue. "I'm Jake."

"Nice to meet you, Jake." She extended her hand.

It felt awkward, but I shook it, trying to hide my reaction to how good her skin felt. Warm. Soft.

"OK," said Carla, taking her hand back. "Let's start you with a bacon maple donut." She leaned in. "People come from miles around for those." She winked and straightened up. "A big fella like you could handle the corned beef hash. Or the Duck and Cluck. And some fresh-squeezed orange juice. Then you can say you had all your major food groups."

"Donut sounds great," I said. "And I think the hash and OJ."

"Good call. Coming right up." She spun away toward the kitchen.

I watched her walk away. The way she filled out those jeans . . .

But then, she was the first woman I'd talked to in a while.

I held the coffee mug to my nose. It smelled like toasted nuts. Rich. I took a cautious sip, not wanting to burn my tongue. There was something about it I couldn't put my finger on at first, something I'd forgotten that food and drink were supposed to deliver. *Flavor.* I decided it was the best fucking coffee I'd ever tasted. The best anywhere in the world, as far as I was concerned. I ignored the cream and sugars. I didn't want anything to cut into it.

Before I could down another gulp, Carla returned with my donut on a small plate.

"Now," she said as she set the confection in front of me, "you've never had one of these, right?"

"No."

"Good. I love to watch people their first time." She crossed her arms and waited. "Well?"

I looked down at the circle of pink dough topped with charred bacon crumbles and maple cream. The circular donut was like a bloodshot eye staring back at me. I picked it up and took a bite—the sweet and savory combined into a mess of deliciousness that I chewed slowly, savoring it. I looked up at Carla, who was smiling at me, expectant, but I couldn't find the words.

"Another satisfied customer," she said, then turned and rushed away again.

I took another bite, bigger this time, savoring the mingling of flavors in my mouth, until there was nothing left to chew. Another bite, and it was gone. I felt if I could sip this coffee and eat this donut every day until I died, then my life would not have been in vain.

Soon enough, Carla was back again, this time with the corned beef hash and a glass of pulpy orange juice.

"I think you can manage this on your own," she said. "I've got tables."

For the next twenty minutes, I was in LA Diner Heaven.

* * *

I tallied the check in my head. Twenty-five bucks. I figured a six or seven dollar tip would be appropriate. In all, considering how satisfied I felt, I thought it was a pretty good deal. A far cry from what this would've cost before I went away, probably four to five times as much, but that morning I figured I came out ahead.

Carla returned with a coffeepot in case I wanted a last refill, which I declined. "I haven't seen you here before," she said. "You new in town?"

I wasn't sure how to answer, so I figured less was more. "Yeah, just got in last night."

"When'd you get out?" she asked.

I kept my eyes on the coffee mug for a beat, then looked up at her, as if I'd been caught lifting one of those fancy desserts on my way out the door.

She set the pot on the table and bent closer, leaning on her palms. "I know the look," she said, lowering her voice. "My brother's in the Colony in San Luis."

I pulled on my beard. The California Men's Colony—the state prison Timothy Leary escaped from before his exile to Africa and Europe—was up the coast in San Luis Obispo.

"Drug stuff. And not his first time."

If her brother was in the Colony for "drug stuff," that usually meant smuggling or trafficking. Hardly a difference between those crimes, and they could've been nonviolent, but they're both considered major.

Carla was still waiting for my answer. I cleared my throat, shifted in my seat. "Yesterday," I said.

Carla's tone was matter-of-fact. "How long? And how many times?" No criticism or judgment, but honest curiosity which somehow carried a genuine concern.

I wasn't quite ready to share the details just yet, so I kept it simple. "A long time," I said. "And once." I cocked my head at her. "How could you tell?"

"It's in the eyes," she said. "Soldiers call it the thousand-yard stare. It's like you're always ready for an attack. It's the same with convicts, but that ZZ Top thing you got going on doesn't exactly say 'military' to me." I grunted at how right she was. "It'll settle down, eventually," she said. "But never all the way." I felt a sudden a jolt of sadness, remorse. It must have registered in my demeanor, because Carla said, "If you hit a wall, find it tough to get along, come in and say hi."

I took a long beat as I let her kindness sink in. "Thank you."

She leaned in again. "That pallor could use some vitamins. I suggest a multi for someone your age to make it simple. You might want to think about a shave and a haircut. It can change your whole world sometimes." She pulled off her bandana and shook out her pixie cut. "Just ask any girl."

With that one move, Carla's ranking on the "pretty meter" went off the fricking scale. I realized I'd started pulling on my beard again, and dropped my hand. "Funny you say that. Know a good barber?"

Carla pointed. "Mm hm. Two lights down, make a left, then the first right. You'll see the barber pole." She noticed my eyes had dropped to her chest, and she crossed her arms. "You do remember what those look like?"

My eyes rose to hers. Busted. I cleared my throat. "Oh. Yeah. Two down. Left, then right."

"Come back and show me." She grabbed the coffeepot, then snatched up my check. "This one's on me."

# CHAPTER

# 4

BY THE TIME I left the diner, the tables and counter had filled. Carla, loaded plates balanced on her forearms, was nimbly delivering them to expectant diners. I stepped outside, and found an eager crowd had gathered. Just yesterday, and three times a day before that, I'd had to stand in line for every meal, but never in a sloppy collection like this bunch.

I went to the curb to get a view up the boulevard. The morning sun had cleared the rooftops above and hit me directly in the eyes. Suddenly, I sneezed . . . hard. A Sunshine Sneeze. They'd dogged me those early years in LA, the light being somehow more intense here than anywhere else I'd been. I hadn't had one since I went inside. Sneezes, sure, but not like this. This was like a nasal orgasm. I welcomed it, then worried it might become a recurring event again. I wiped away the wetness that escaped my nose, then looked around to see if anyone had noticed. Not a single look. I raised my head level again . . . and sneezed again. I got hit two more times before I reached the next block.

You'd think a heavy meal like the one I'd just wolfed would make me sluggish, but Carla had kept that coffee coming, and I must've downed five mugs worth. My departing visit to the men's room may have been the longest I'd ever spent over a urinal. Now I was so jacked on caffeine I could practically feel my skin vibrate.

I went in the direction Carla had given me for the barber shop. I hoped the place was open, as I'd like to get this over with sooner than later. The sidewalk was filling with pedestrians who quick-stepped like they were all late for the same thing, but in different places. As they filed around me, I felt a wave of defensiveness, like I had to watch my back. Carla was right. It would be a while before that subsided.

But then I was hit by a different feeling, one I'd completely forgotten: I had a whole day in front of me with nobody dictating where or how to spend it. Of course, I had no idea what I would do, but I still welcomed the opportunity. I'd long ago learned those things we believe we can least live without, that we would miss the most, are creature comforts. But, strangely, it is the truly impactful changes that we adjust to the quickest. The lack of movement, the lack of choice in how you live your life. Those we always somehow adapt to.

I reached 5th Street and made a left. Carla said the barber shop was right around the next corner, which would put it on Spring. The traffic had grown from the bucolic sparseness when I'd left the hostel to a cacophony of engines, tires, and horns. Saturdays were busy here. I walked to the corner, but the first signage that grabbed me was across the street. Block letters in red neon: THE LAST BOOKSTORE.

The "last" bookstore? I hoped not. My years in prison had mostly been spent in the library. Books were the best thing to come out of my time there. That was thanks to Anthony, an old lifer whose job it was to maintain the Dewey Decimal System, collect requested books for inmates, and deliver them to their cells on a rolling cart. It was Anthony who taught me the ins-and-outs of incarceration, and how to escape without actually leaving. He said there was no point in getting shot going over the wall, or buried trying to dig under it, when the entire world was right here, bound between two covers.

I looked to my right. Sure enough, the red, blue, and white candy cane of a barber's column floated behind the leaves of a sycamore tree in need of a trimming. Bingo. When I got there, the place was open for business. I stepped inside.

A fit, casually stylish young man with a short mohawk, tight mustache, and long trimmed goatee hopped up from a row of square cushioned chairs that lined one wall. His open collar and rolled sleeves revealed intricate tattoos on his forearms and neck. "Good morning," he said. "What can I do for you?"

"I'd like a shave and a haircut," I said, though I felt like I had to drag the words out.

The young man sized me up, perhaps figuring an estimate to tackle the jungle around my head. "Are we looking to trim what you have or really go for it?"

I looked in the mirror at the cascade of hair, and the beard that came to my plexus. "Go for it."

"I can do that, but I don't suggest a clean shave just yet."

"Why not?"

"You obviously haven't had a blade on your face in a while. We use straight razors here. If I take it right down to the skin, you could break out. Not a good look." The man's eyes scanned my chin. "Better to take it down to stubble for a couple weeks, then go the rest of the way."

As much sense as that made, it did nothing to mitigate the fact that, for me, anything that resembled a razor was a weapon. My one violent encounter in prison involved an inmate coming at me with a blade fashioned from a kitchen spoon.

The younger man must've read the tension in my eyes, and that I'd suddenly held my breath. "We wouldn't use a razor today," he said. "Maybe after you get some sun on your chin. Give it a chance to breathe."

I exhaled. "OK."

"What were you thinking for the haircut?"

"I don't know." I shrugged. "Shorter?"

The man laughed. "All right. Let's get you shampooed."

An hour later, the young man, whose name was Rhett and had emigrated from upstate New York, spun the chair around for me to face the mirror.

With my hair trimmed to maybe an inch, inch and a half, it was coarse enough to stand up, which somehow made it look thicker. Rhett added a thin pomade to give it some texture. Then he swept it slightly to the side across my even hairline, but without an obvious part. He'd cut it a bit tighter at the sides, and my ears felt their first breeze in a while, thanks to the ceiling fans. As advised, Rhett had left a short, even stubble of beard, so as not to shock my skin. The effect was unexpectedly welcome.

I gave my cheek a light rub. "I look like William Holden in *Stalag 17*," I said.

"Great!" said Rhett. "I don't know who that is."

I met his eyes in the mirror. "The best that ever was." I stood as Rhett pulled off the black barber's cape with a swoosh. "You like old movies?"

"Who doesn't?"

"When I come back for that shave, I'll bring you a list to watch. What do I owe you?"

"On the house."

I looked at him with surprised suspicion. Free breakfast, and now this. *Does everybody give stuff away in this town?* And what if this guy wanted something I didn't want to trade? When I was younger that was nearly a constant, but it had been a while since I'd had to deal with that.

"It's part of our Mission Statement," said Rhett. "We try to do one good deed a day. Today, you're it."

"Mission Statement?"

"Part of the business plan. When we opened, it was still pretty depressed around here. We decided we'd do something to give back. And if I'm completely honest, your case needed a little extra effort. So, Mission Statement." He smiled.

"Thank you," I said, and I meant it. There was a lesson for me in there somewhere, I just wasn't sure what it was yet.

"Come back in a couple weeks when you're ready to finish that shave." Rhett extended his hand.

I shook it. "Deal." I headed for the door.

"And don't forget that list," I heard him say, and waved as I hit the sidewalk.

* * *

Ten minutes later, I was standing at the corner of 5th and Olive. I'd told myself I never wanted to see that intersection again, but when I left the barber shop my feet carried me in this direction. My mind fought them with every step, but my feet won the battle.

From across the boulevard, I stared into the alley where so many lives had changed forever. A vaporous memory formed in my mind, taking shape until it was clear. The desperate act of a robbery gone wrong. The violent death of an innocent woman.

## CHAPTER 5

### THEN

### 1998

"WHAT ARE YOU doing after work?" asked Damon, my coworker and regular party pal, from the end of the bar. A busy Wednesday night was winding down. The high-end eatery where we worked, me as a bartender, Damon as a server, was called Bonetti's. Favored by entertainment executives and luminaries, many of whom were drawn by the clubby atmosphere, and the flattering lighting, but also by the owner's practice of employing very attractive young people. And there were always the lookie-loos who hoped to spot some famous faces.

Damon was an athletic, blue-eyed white boy who'd grown up in the predominantly African-American suburb of Inglewood, and whose hopes of a tennis career were fading along with his overworked knees. Between three sets of tennis every day, and five-to-six-hour shifts waiting tables every night, he was outpacing the average lifespan of any athlete. The coke didn't help, other than to energize him through those long nights, but he had a decent sense of humor and, being blessed with a constitution Keith Richards would envy, he could party with the best of them.

Unlike me, Damon had come from a family for which the description "uninvolved" would be a massive understatement. By his account, his childhood home was filled with lifelike mannequins that moved around silently, never noticing, let alone acknowledging, anyone else's presence. To me, it sounded like something out of a Ray Bradbury story.

One night while still in high school, Damon decided to see what a response of *any* kind from his parents might look like. As they were planted as usual in front of the TV, Damon made a confession, a *There's something I need to tell you* kind of thing, and just started talking. He rattled off all the drugs he'd done in the course of his young life: alcohol, marijuana, mushrooms, cocaine, mescaline, LSD. Even heroin.

His father's blank expression didn't change. He shifted his attention from the TV to his newspaper, as if pretending to read, instead of pretending to watch, would offer better refuge from the truth. His mother at least looked at her son, but didn't say anything, either.

"It was amazing," he told me, alternating between pulls on a joint and a beer. "It was like I never said anything *at all*." That last bit betrayed his mild surfer elocution. Damon left home that night. He doubted his parents noticed.

He dropped out of school and spent a few years kicking around, sleeping in his car or on friends' couches, until he could put away enough to get his own apartment. Considering his youth, he adapted quickly, getting off the street before he turned twenty. But, as I learned later, he was particularly "entrepreneurial."

It wasn't like my own family was full of hugs and deep discussions, but there weren't any real problems. Jessica, my older sister, had moved away long before I'd graduated high school, so we were never really close. Looking back, I realized that there wasn't any real substance abuse in our house, either. My mother didn't drink, owing to the fact her own father was a drunk who shot himself when she was very young. And my dad, whether it was out of respect for my mom, or because he had a weakness of his own, rarely had more than a beer at a time. If there was a tendency to overindulge, I wish they'd told me about it, but again, not a lot of deep talk in our house.

I met Damon at the Hollywood YMCA gym, where all young wannabe actors seemed to go to sculpt their physiques. We'd hit it off and started working out together. It wasn't long before we started hanging out on our free nights and soon discovered a mutual appreciation for partying, which in our early twenties we thought we could handle. A few months later he referred me for the job at Bonetti's.

"How we fixed for bartenders?" the owner had asked his assistant in the bright airy office I was interviewed in.

"We could use one," she'd replied. "Like, tonight."

By that evening I was serving screwdrivers and margaritas to movie stars, studio heads, and top talent agents. And as my handsome-factor passed muster to get the job, I was also getting attention from some of the well-to-do female patrons, especially those with a fantasy to take home a knock-off Clint Eastwood.

And as it was "Hollywood," arguably the plastic surgery capital of the world, it didn't take long to meet someone who was really goddamned attractive. That was true for a lot of the guys. Any given night a staffer might be invited home by a woman twice his age (and with the surgery-enhanced body of an Olympian) for a late-night fuck on her mansion's living room floor.

"What are you doing after work?" Damon called to me from the waiter's station at the end of the bar.

I had just served snifters of brandy to two couples enjoying an after-dinner drink. "Nothin'. Whatcha' got in mind?"

The restaurant had seen good business that night, and the staff would have a nice wad of cash in their pockets to show for it. That had a way of making you feel energized.

"See the two on table six?" Damon said. I looked over to see two bottle-blondes at a prime table usually reserved for four, which meant they'd probably greased the maître d'.

Obviously these young ladies were experienced in the ways of high rollers, knowing how to tip their way to a good table. They were slim and very well but conservatively dressed, almost business-like. An open bottle of Crystal champagne was in an ice bucket next to the table.

"They're from Houston," Damon said. "A couple of rich girls having a good time on Daddy's tab. And their blow is first fucking rate. Haven't had anything like it since that time at MacNeil's."

Jasper MacNeil was the bassist for a hugely successful English rock band, and like many who had struck gold in music or movies, he owned a home in the hills above Sunset Boulevard. His chief roadie, Nigel, lived in the house when they weren't touring. Nigel was a friendly type who liked to bring new friends back to the place and show them a good time . . . at MacNeil's expense.

Nigel had dated one of Bonetti's hostesses, and one night he'd invited her and a few other employees up to MacNeil's house and opened the bar (and the boss's drug stash). We were still there well after the sun rose the next morning. *Who gets the best dope? Doctors and rock stars!* I never did meet the famous rocker, who probably wasn't even in the country while Nigel had the run of his place.

"And," Damon said, twerking his eyebrows, "they got a limo. I say we take a nice long ride after we get outta here."

I never would remember their names, but I never forgot that night. After changing into street clothes, I met Damon and the two ladies out front, where the paparazzi would often lurk on the outskirts of the parking lot for a shot of that week's new celebrity. After intros, we all clambered into the rented limousine, and directed the driver to head for the Pacific Coast Highway.

They could've been sisters. One had blue eyes, the other brown, but their differences ended there, as they definitely shared a taste in makeup, hair color, and clothes. Each wore what I took to be a business suit; dark skirts with matching jackets over lightweight blouses. Nearly identical precious gems hung from delicate gold chains around their necks. The look was countered by the tall spike heels on their feet. And the similar way they wore their long hair, draped over the back of their dark jackets, made it look lush, silky. They were both perky and chatty, friendly Texas Roses.

Suddenly, I was "darlin'" and Damon became "shugah." They reminded me of the Doublemint Twin commercials I'd seen as a kid. I couldn't stop smiling.

The limo sped onto the freeway, and the woman closest to me asked me to hit the power button to the stereo. Bluesy Texas rock filled the car. Stevie Ray Vaughn, Charlie Sexton, Joe Ely. She said something I couldn't hear, so I turned the music down to a dull roar.

"What's that?" I said.

"Like a bump?" she asked with her Texas twang. She held up a small glassine baggie about half full of white powder.

Now, I had done good blow before, but this shit was epic. Clean, didn't burn your nose. And the high was so different from the other times I'd done it. Usually, the stuff was cut with so much animal laxative that you headed right to the bathroom for a number two. But this time, I felt a rush as my bloodstream sped up. My face had a pleasant tingle. And no nerves, none of the shakiness that other strains had given me.

I fully embraced that first rush, then I saw she was staring at my pelvic area. I looked down, thinking I must've forgotten to close the old barn door. That's when I realized my member was pressed against my jeans. As good as the coke was, I didn't expect *that* reaction. Even in the low light of the limo's interior, and despite her sly smile, she seemed to be blushing. I figured the heat on my face meant I was doing the same.

She leaned over to me. "Looks like you've got something that's just dying to get out, darlin'." I returned a dumb smile.

She set her champagne glass in a circular holder, and then flipped a switch that raised an opaque partition between the passenger compartment and the driver. In one easy move, she shifted her weight onto me, pressing me back into the plush seat, and kissed me full on the lips. She held my head as she pressed her face against mine. I reached around her torso to embrace her, but she pulled back and reached for my belt buckle—a Portland Trailblazers souvenir from their 1977 NBA championship I'd picked up somewhere back home. I thought I saw her react to it. Maybe she was a Rockets fan. Once she undid it, she pushed me all the way back, and dropped her open mouth onto me.

I looked over at Damon, who already had his date's blouse open. He spread some coke across her nipples and licked it off. She laughed.

We rode all the way to Santa Barbara and back.

* * *

My eyes opened to near darkness. My head pounded like a hammer on an anvil—my skull being the anvil. I looked around. I was in a king-sized bed, in a very large bedroom, with blackout curtains drawn over a floor-to-ceiling window. A sliver of bright LA sun snuck through a tiny opening where the curtains met in the middle.

A light snore gave away the shapely figure next to me. On closer inspection, I realized it was the other woman from the night before, the one who had taken a liking to Damon. We'll call her Cocaine Tits. I gently raised the sheet. Yep, she was as naked as I was.

I moved slowly, so as not to wake her, and turned to get a look at the clock on the nightstand. Just past

1:00 PM. The digital read out said "TH." Thank God it was only the next afternoon, and that I hadn't lost an entire day and night somehow. Good thing I had nowhere to be today. But there was a blank spot from last night that had obviously involved a trade-off of bodies at some point, though how or who-for-whom I couldn't say. I had to take a wicked leak, and my mouth tasted like a dead rat had taken a wet shit down my throat. *My kingdom for a toothbrush.*

I rose and stepped into a high-ceilinged marble bathroom that was bigger than most of my friends' apartments. I closed the door, turning the knob so it wouldn't click shut. Solid polished brass handles and rods accented the marble's amber veins. I did my business, flushed, then cupped some water in my palm from the faucet and rinsed the crud from my mouth, triggering a thirst I felt all the way to my toes. I bent to the sink, bumping my head on the way to the faucet, and took greedy drinks.

I figured the quickest way to ease the thumping in my head was diversion, so I cranked on the shower, as hot as I could stand at first, then after I was clean, gave myself a good jolt of cold. It helped, but not for long. By the time I'd dried myself, the pounding was back full force. I heard a voice from the bedroom wafting through the wall. I combed my wet hair back with my fingers, wrapped the towel around my waist, and opened the door.

The woman had turned on the lamp next to her and was sitting up in the bed, the sheet pulled over her breasts—*Now we're being modest?*—as she spoke to someone on the hotel phone. I figured her to be a bit older than I was, maybe early to mid-thirties.

She smiled and waved a good morning, then said with a twang, "Yes, service for four. Thanks!" and hung up. Remarkably, last night's makeup was hanging in there. She looked better than I felt. "I hope you're hungry, shugah." Her drawl was soothing.

"I could eat," I said.

"Would you mind tossin' me the robe hangin' on the door in there?" she said, pointing to the bathroom. I fetched the thick robe that hotels like this leave in the room for guests to lounge in. "Thank you. Just give me a few minutes," she said as she rose, now unabashed, and pulled the robe over her nude form.

She headed toward the bathroom, but stopped next to me and planted a soft peck on my cheek. Before moving on, she gave me a flirtatious, knowing grin, and went into the bathroom, shutting the door behind her. Her alabaster skin looked like milk. Even with my pounding head, I felt my body respond to her.

I heard the shower turn on, followed by a flush. I figured I had a few minutes to myself, and went to explore the rest of the place. It was a two-bedroom suite, and judging from the view from the windows, high in the center of Beverly Hills. The door to the other bedroom was still closed, and no sound emanated from inside. Either Damon and Limo BJ were still asleep or had snuck away unheard.

In one corner was a basic kitchenette where I found some mugs and packets of instant coffee in a cupboard. The sink had a dedicated hot water spigot, so I used that to mix a cup. I gulped it as fast as I could get it down, and the throb in my head finally began to ease. I made another black coffee to give Cocaine Tits when she finished her shower, another for myself, and went back to the bedroom.

The bathroom door opened, and she stepped out, her hair wrapped in a towel, the robe tied loosely around her. She looked somewhat refreshed. Maybe she'd touched up her face. I offered her the coffee. "Sorry if you take cream. I didn't see any."

"God bless you, shugah," she said, taking the cup. "This is fine." She sipped. "There's a toothbrush in there with your name on it, if you want."

"God bless you in return. Or the hotel." I found a packaged toothbrush and a tiny, slightly used tube of toothpaste on the counter next to the sink. I brushed vigorously to kill any more rats in there and went back to the bedroom, to find her perched on the bed with her coffee.

"I ordered a lot of food, so I think it'll take a while," she said as she took a sip. Then, "How about we finish what we couldn't last night?"

I felt my face flush. "Is that what happened? Sorry."

"As much my fault, as yours," she said with a wink. She finished the last of her coffee, put down the mug, and patted the mattress next to her. I started for the door, thinking I should close it. "Leave it open," she said, a hint of mischief in her tone. "So I can hear when room service gets here."

I sat next to her.

She shook her head. "I'm sorry but . . . what was your name?"

I chuckled. "Jake."

"Jaaake," she said, letting the vowel linger. "With a name like that, you could be a Texan."

"Just an Oregonian."

"Good enough for me," she said. She reached for my neck, and pulled me on top of her.

* * *

Damon and I left the hotel in the back of another limousine, our stomachs full, our cocks tired, and our noses newly numb.

I dropped one hand on my lap and felt a larger than usual bump in the same pocket where I kept my key ring. I pulled out my keys, plus a full bindle of blow—and a wad of cash. Five hundred dollars even. *Where the hell . . . ?* I scanned my foggy memory. I'd made good tip money the night before, but nothing like this. *Shit.* Did I, in the blur of the long night, pick up something I shouldn't have? I may like to party, but I wasn't a thief. At least not yet. And there was the coke, a good full gram of it folded into this stiff rectangle. No, this was put there by someone who wanted me to have it, and in the crush of goodbyes and thank yous, I hadn't noticed it until now.

"Hey," I said. "You see this?"

Damon looked from the window to my outstretched hand. "Oh, yeah," he said, as if it was nothing. "I got that, too."

"Guess they weren't disappointed," said Damon, and turned back to watch the city pass outside the window. "Wonder what would happen if they were."

Then it hit me. Those two Texans had actually *paid* us for our time. Or more to the point, for the unfettered use of our vigorous young bodies.

I looked down at the cash in my fist. "So, you've been doing this for a while?"

"Yeah," he said. "Shit, I thought you knew!"

*Well, I didn't,* I thought. "How long?"

"A year or two, maybe more. I lose track." He shrugged. "It's easier than those damn drug deals. And a helluva lot more fun."

"You mean those two guys that got fired?"

He looked at me. "Who do you think came up with that idea?"

Things were starting to fall into place. The success of Bonetti's was mainly due to its owner, Pete Bonetti, and what he was *really* good at: image. The "image" was an ideal of beauty, prosperity, and fun, but it hid a darker truth.

A waiter and a bartender had been caught dealing coke to customers because they left an obvious paper trail: by taking payment in the form of gratuities on credit card charges. A bookkeeper noticed that their invoices for two hundred and fifty-dollars' worth of food and beverages had somehow justified a tip of a hundred and twenty bucks. That's an amount an entertainment executive or attorney could easily afford, but not exactly a typical twenty percent tip. And, coincidentally, it was about the same price as a gram of blow in those days.

Damon had skated because he'd stuck to his plan of only taking paper money for the drugs. I had no idea until this moment that he was even involved, let alone the brains behind it all. No wonder he'd gotten off the street so quickly. I didn't call him entrepreneurial for nothing. When his cohorts got fired (not because dealing was illegal, but because it could become a damaging news item), the bar position became available. Even without selling illegal drugs to patrons, a job at Bonetti's was lucrative and therefore in-demand.

"Guess they never got the memo that some enterprises are best run as a cash business." He chuckled and shook his head. "Dumb fucks."

"Why'd you call me? For the job, I mean."

"Because you're not stupid." He said it so matter-of-factly, it was easy to believe. "And I thought you'd fit in."

He had to be referring to my good looks. Hell, the restaurant staff resembled an open modeling call for *W Magazine*. We'd joke that the first thing asked for on our application was a headshot. Even the cooks who worked the open kitchen were smokin'.

"How much do you make doing this?"

Damon smiled again. "That's for me to know and you to find out."

Sitting in the back of that limo, a full month's rent and enough blow to see me through the week in my pocket, I began to wonder.

"They invited us back tonight," Damon said. "You up for it?"

I had that night off, and nothing pressing the next day. Life of the struggling actor. I could make the time, if I wanted to.

"Thanks," I said. "I think I'm gonna stay in. Catch up on some sleep."

Damon smiled, nodding toward the bindle in my hand. "Yeah, sure you will."

He was right.

I started in on the coke shortly after I'd made myself some dinner, and I'd gone through it all before dawn. I had to sleep most of the next day to pull it together for work that night, and I was a sloppy mess the whole time, but the couple bumps Damon gave me in the walk-in cooler helped me power through to closing. Then we met up with the Texas Roses again, who had decided to extend their stay through the weekend.

The next day I was another five hundred dollars richer, with a new gram of coke burning a hole in my pocket. And I still couldn't tell you their names with a gun to my head.

## CHAPTER

# 6

**NOW**

"WHEN'D YOU GET OUT?"

There was that question again, but this time, I expected it.

Still, Angela had asked it so directly that I hesitated, feeling any answer I gave might be wrong. But I'd better say something before she hung up on me.

"Day before yesterday."

I'd spent Saturday night in my room with takeout Chinese, uneasy about the crowds outside. The soundscape from the boulevard brought all manner of noise. People yelling as much as they laughed, car horns and music blasting past the building. The nightlife downtown sure wasn't the deserted, dangerous city center it used to be. I'd tried to drown it out with the small flatscreen TV mounted on the wall, but that proved fruitless, and watching the shows coming through it was like learning a foreign language. They all seemed to follow supposedly "real people" around their everyday life, and then they'd sit for an interview and talk about what they just did, as if it was really important or dramatic. I didn't get the appeal. I thought the shows and the people in them were just plain boring. I settled on a channel broadcasting black and white reruns from the 1950s and '60s, with commercials that sold life insurance and suppositories. I finally drifted off sometime after midnight.

When I woke Sunday morning, I decided that Angela, my ex-girlfriend, would be the first call on my new cell phone. I'd bought it the afternoon before at one of the ramshackle storefronts on Los Angeles Street, the same area where that scary music video shoot took place all those years ago. I was amazed to see these shops were still in business. I knew that the big brand to have was Apple, or maybe Samsung, but the Asian man behind the counter handed me something called a Xiaomi (which he had to pronounce several times for me). An older model, it only set me back a hundred bucks, and it came with prepaid minutes, voicemail, text, and after a short tutorial from the owner, GPS to help me get around. It was similar to the phones the more powerful gangs managed to smuggle into prison. Those would sometimes be dropped inside the walls by drone.

Hoping nine thirty wasn't too early, I dialed a number from the dingy, dogeared phonebook I found in my room. As it rang, a part of me hoped it wasn't hers, and if it was, that it would go to voicemail. A direct conversation with Angela made me fucking nervous. For years I could ignore the need to have this talk, but now it was a reality, part of my . . . what did Rhett the Barber call it? . . . Mission Statement.

When I'd first gone to prison, Angela had tried to keep in touch, not willing to let our love affair simply drop away, but I told her to stop writing. And to never visit. Can't say she was thrilled about that, but she didn't fight me on it, either.

"Why are you calling me now?" she demanded. I'd expected this—some tension, frustration. Anger. She'd always had a dulcet voice that could calm my worst nerves, but now there was a slight rasp in it that made her sound older. Tired.

"I wanted to see how you were doing," I replied.

"I'm fine," she said, curt, the gravel in her voice more apparent.

There was a long silence. Then the guilt I'd predicted whenever I imagined this moment began to roll through me like a wave. But this was my chance to man up and make amends. I'd never been sure of what I would say if this moment came, but I knew I had to say something if this call wasn't going to end in the next few seconds. So, I said the first words that came to mind.

"I'm sorry, Angela. I really am. I was just so ashamed of everything I did, how badly I'd hurt everyone, I thought it was better if you moved on."

There was another pause, and I thought she was about to hang up on me, then I heard something. I thought it sounded wet, like she was fighting back tears.

"I never thought I'd hear from you again," she said. "I didn't expect that to hit me so hard."

"Sorry," I said again. She didn't respond, so I pressed on. "I guess that's all I really wanted to say. I guess I didn't want to say it from up there, you know? I don't know why. Some stupid reason I forgot a long time ago."

I heard her sigh. "I guess I appreciate it," she said finally. Then her tone shifted. "How'd you get my number?"

"It's in the book," I said. "I was surprised to see it. I thought you'd be unlisted."

"This is my landline, nobody ever called me on it. Except maybe my mother."

"Wow, your mom. How's she doing?"

"She died ten years ago, Jake."

"Right." This was going swimmingly. "I'm sorry to hear that."

"I'm over it." Now her words were rushed. "I only have a land line because it's cheaper to get internet with it. Nobody uses phone books anymore." Then she stopped herself. "I think I'm a little nervous."

"You and me both." I mustered what gumption I had left. "Can I see you?"

She took in a long breath and let it out. "I don't know," she said.

"Oh shit," I said. "You're married. Oh man, I should've asked. I'm sorr—"

"I'm not married!" she said, stopping my lame attempt at contrition. "I just don't know if I want to see you."

"I still should've asked. Bad enough to call out of the blue like this."

"I have a boyfriend."

"Oh. Well, maybe he wouldn't like you hanging around with an ex-con."

"He's not the boss of me. And he doesn't care about that, trust me." I wondered why she would add that last part, but before I could ask she said, "I'll think about it. That's the best I can do."

"Let me give you my number," I said, thinking I sounded too eager.

"I have your number."

"You do?"

"It came up on the caller ID, Jake."

"Oh . . . right." Caller ID. The feature that made it okay to not answer a call from someone you didn't want to talk to.

"Just let me think about it," she said.

# CHAPTER

# 7

At 9:00 AM the next morning, Monday, I was across from my parole agent. He was a tough former cop named Sanchez, who'd decided to spend his sunset years steering parolees and ex-cons toward the rest of their lives. He didn't seem the type to sit at home watching golf. Sanchez must have also known the odds are tough, given that the recidivism rate hovered around forty percent. Maybe this was all that was available to him once he'd taken his pension. This, or moving old case files around the basement of some random precinct.

"You know you come see me here once a month," Sanchez asked.

I was reading the form he'd handed me, an acknowledgment that I had reported to him in person, and agreed to return every month for at least a year, or until the state deemed it was no longer necessary. I looked up at him. "Yeah, I know," I replied.

"Good," Sanchez said, with time-worn familiarity. "This is yours." He handed me an envelope. "The check from your savings account, plus the state funds to help you get started. Twenty-four hundred dollars. That's on top of what you made in your prison job."

I opened the envelope and found two checks, both issued by the state of California, made out to me. Together they totaled $12,672. As California prisons go, it was a pretty good payday. The most you can make a day is two bucks. That shakes out to around twenty-five cents an hour for an eight-hour shift. Over time, and if you keep doing the job, it adds up. Sort of.

"You managed your money pretty well. Most guys come out with next to nothing," Sanchez said.

"This'll help a lot," I said. "Hope it lasts long enough."

"You got any people here? In LA, I mean."

I thought of Carla, the waitress. She seemed like "people." And maybe Angela, though I wasn't holding my breath. "A couple," I said.

"Take this." He slid a few sheets of stapled papers across his desk to me. "That's the jobs list. Any idea what kind of work you want?" When I didn't answer, Sanchez said, "I ask because a lotta guys don't like it out here. Look for ways to go back."

"Not me," I said. "I liked working in the library, so maybe someplace with books." I put the form down on Sanchez's desk, signed it.

"Not the answer I usually get, but if somebody needs boxes of books moved around, you sure have the build for it. You say you got a room at a hostel?"

"Yeah, for now. But I kind of like it around here. Might stay in the area."

"If you keep your nose clean, you'll be all right," the old cop said. "When you move, and if and when you get a job, you let me know."

I nodded.

Something about Sanchez seemed familiar. He was the hard ass I'd expected him to be, but he seemed all right, as if he truly wanted to help people like me find a way to make sense of the world on the outside. My eyes drifted to a display case mounted on the wall behind his desk. It held commendations awarded over the course of his career, ribbons and bars for distinguished acts. Detective Service. Life Saving Medal. Police Star. Police Medal. The guy had seen some real shit.

Sanchez picked up the signed document and inspected it. After a moment he said, "Why're you still here, Ferguson?"

"Excuse me?"

"Most guys can't wait to get outta this office. It's like you don't want to leave."

"So, we're done?"

"Yeah, for a month, anyway. Now get the fuck out."

I headed for the door.

"Aren't you forgetting something?" I turned, no idea what the old cop was referring to. Sanchez leaned forward, picked up the stapled sheets from his desk. "The jobs list. In case the library isn't hiring."

I folded it and slipped it into my inside jacket pocket.

"And Ferguson," Sanchez called to me before I cleared the doorway. "When you apply for a job, give them my number. I'll do what I can."

"Thanks," I said, grateful for the offer. I had to wonder if Detective Sanchez was this helpful with every ex-con. The feeling that I knew him from somewhere kept gnawing at me.

The building was a Gothic turn-of-the-last-century number, and the tiny elevator had never been replaced with a larger, contemporary car. On the way up, I'd stood behind three other people, and had to slither out at my floor, like a snake through reeds. It came too close to the naked, defenseless feeling you get when trying to wind your way through a crowd in the prison yard. It's just too damn easy for someone to knife you and never be seen by the guards. I couldn't face that sensation again, so I took the stairs down the three flights to the ground floor. But being able to make a simple choice like that made me feel like I was beginning to settle into my freedom.

I was intending to visit The Last Book Store, maybe fill out a job application, when my new phone buzzed in my pocket. I pulled it out as I stepped through the revolving door onto Spring Street. It was a 323 area code with a number I didn't recognize, but then I'd only saved three so far. Angela's, Sanchez's, and Carla's.

I walked as I answered. "Hello?" I said, fighting back an urge to sneeze in the intense sunlight.

"Hey, I'm looking for Jake." It was a man's voice. He sounded younger than me. By a lot.

"Who is this?"

"Eric," said the man. "I'm Angela's boyfriend."

I stopped short, and a man behind me cursed under his breath. Apparently, my sudden halt had nearly caused a collision. The man hurried around me.

"OK," I said. I felt myself girding for a confrontation.

"Angie gave me your number."

"She said she had a boyfriend," I said, pressing my index finger to the base of my nose.

"Sorry to call without any warning," said Eric. The man sounded like he expected confusion on my end.

"Hold on." Unable to hold it back any longer, I pushed the phone to my chest to cover the mic, and sneezed. I sniffed a couple times, then lifted the phone again. "OK."

"Bless you," said Eric.

"Yeah, thanks, so . . . what's this about?" One thing I did not need was some kind of jealous altercation or love triangle.

"Sorry for the cloak and dagger," he said. "But she wants to see you."

"Angela?"

"Of course, Angela," he said with a laugh. "Who else?"

"Why doesn't she call me herself?"

"What man can decipher the dark recesses of a woman's mind?" I didn't respond. I heard him clear his throat. "Because she asked me to. Actually," he corrected himself, "I offered."

"Why?"

"I think she feels bad. A little embarrassed. Here you were, trying to say you're sorry, and she shut you down."

"Something like that." I remembered the guilt that hit me when I'd spoken to her.

"We're going to the beach this weekend. You wanna come along?"

I paused. LA has been touted as one of the friendliest places on Earth, but never, and I mean *never*, could I recall a complete stranger inviting me to a social occasion with his girlfriend, who also happened to be *my* ex-girlfriend. "Yeah . . . I don't know about that."

"C'mon, just for a while. I gotta see who my competition is." He laughed again. If prison teaches you anything, it's how to protect yourself from something you might otherwise not see coming, and this conversation was definitely raising those hackles. But the guy seemed friendly enough, and he was offering me a chance for a face-to-face with Angela. A saying my departed father often used came to mind. *Don't look a gift horse in the mouth.*

"OK," I said. "Sounds good."

"Great!" said Eric, with a hint of triumph. "You need a ride? I can send somebody to pick you up."

"No, thanks. I'll figure it out."

"All right! We'll text you everything later."

"That'll work."

"We like to get there early to beat the crowd," Eric said, and hung up.

I saved Eric's number in my phone with a few clicks (I was picking up this tech thing pretty fast) and dropped it into my pocket.

I stood stock still, humanity bustling around me, and marveled at how radically life can change in less than seventy-two hours.

# CHAPTER

# 8

"THE ONLY WAY out is through." Anthony, whom I'd met early on in my incarceration, told me that. Anthony had been in prison for decades. Double murder. I met him on my first job which was to assist him in the prison library. I came to think of him as my real-life "Brooks Hatlen" because he encouraged me to read *Rita Hayworth and Shawshank Redemption* that same day. He reminded me of the older inmate who schools Andy Dufresne in the ways of prison. I always remembered what he said, and I was holding onto that advice, especially now.

The ensuing week consisted of mostly unremarkable—and disappointing—job applications. All were unsuccessful. I'd been warned what to expect by the counselors before my release. To be fair, I didn't feel too much discrimination about my time inside. Jobs were just plain scarce. All the interviewers seemed satisfied that I could give them a phone number to reach me, though my lack of an email address was perplexing to some.

One midweek afternoon, I almost came to blows in a crosswalk with an aggressive homeless man. The guy shadowed me for nearly a block, accusing me of conspiring with the government to kidnap him. Spittle shot from his lips with each condemnation, and his eyes were ringed with dueling spiderwebs of deep wrinkles that the layers of grime hadn't completely settled into. His fists flailed wildly in my direction, but never connected. I kept glancing over my shoulder until I was safely away from the tortured soul. There were plenty of broken psyches in prison, and I'd learned the best tactic was to steer clear.

There were good surprises, too. Especially The Last Book Store. That was my first stab at a job, and I understood why no positions were open once I had a chance to wander the cavernous space. I spent a couple of hours getting lost in the maze of free-standing shelves bulging with new and used books of every kind. I walked through the "book tunnel"—an actual passage erected by the pressure of thousands of books balanced against each other—several times, imagining what would happen if I pulled a single book out, if it would come crashing down like a house of cards. Unbelievable that a precocious child hadn't done it already. I left the store with a bag of used paperbacks. Some classics, some Elmore Leonard that I hadn't gotten to, and some true crime. *Why the hell not? It's a free country.*

Then I made my way to the LA Public Library, a huge Art Deco repository of reading built in the mid-1920s. I'd read somewhere that Charles Bukowski, long before his own work was discovered, would linger inside for days on end, discovering and devouring free books. And although it had been decades since I'd seen it, I recognized that block from the big shootout in the movie *Heat*.

The next day, my job search took me all the way to the old Central Plaza in Chinatown, a hot two-mile walk north of my hostel. It was a good spot to find some shade and have a cool drink.

But as I neared the plaza, I noticed the sidewalks had been commandeered by the telltale presence of Honeywagons, the big white trailers used by production companies to transport filmmaking gear, wardrobe stock, hair and makeup, and mobile dressing rooms. A movie or TV show was shooting here today.

As I turned into the plaza I was stunned to see an old classmate: Winston Greene. He was walking briskly in the center of a small group, who seemed to be both guiding him, and running interference. His eyes met mine as he passed but I didn't sense any recognition on his part. I was so taken aback by the sight of the one genuine movie star that had emerged from our weekly acting workshop, that I lost any ability to utter a greeting. By the time I'd gathered my senses, he'd been ushered into a waiting van at the curb. *So much for that.*

I continued on in search of cool refreshment when I heard a voice behind me.

"Jake Ferguson?"

I turned around. Winston was standing right behind me.

"Jesus, it is you!" he said. "Christ in a teacup, how long has it been?" He extended his hand, and I shook it.

"Hi, Winston," I managed to get out. "How you doing?" A few of the handlers that had rushed by a moment earlier were with him, waiting patiently for the star to take a moment with his past.

"I'm fine, thanks," Greene said. "Wow, it's gotta be twenty years, at least."

*Twenty-five.* "I'm surprised you remember me," I said.

"You kidding? You were our Clint Eastwood." He shook his head. "All the girls had such a thing for you!" He laughed, then his smile faded. "I remember what happened. I'm glad to see you're still around."

"Thanks," I said. "I'm doing OK. Just looking for a job." I left it there as I did not want to get into the struggles of ex-cons on a job hunt.

"You still acting?"

I laughed. "Hardly. I left that behind when I went away."

Greene nodded. He seemed to understand something about that answer that others wouldn't.

"Win?" One of the handlers, a young woman holding a clipboard, set her hand gently on Winston's sleeve. "I'm sorry. They're waiting for us at the next location."

"Coming," he said to her with a nod, then turned back to me. "Company move. We were shooting here this morning, now we're going to Dodger Stadium. Probably be there most of the night." Then an idea struck him. "Hey, you want to come along? There's always some job that needs to get done."

I shook my head. "I appreciate that, but . . . no. Thanks, though."

"OK." He stuck out his hand again. "It's good to see you, Jake."

And then, he vanished as soon as he'd appeared. Now, *there* was a memory I'd never expected to hit me again.

Everyone in that class had thought Winston Greene was the gifted child destined to break out. And, boy, had he ever. I'd also read that he'd had some trouble of his own not long ago. Good to see him on his feet, whatever it was.

The darker elements of my previous life could also arrive unexpectedly. While indulging in a lunch at Phillipe's, a casual and noisy pre-Prohibition sandwich stop, I felt a tap on my shoulder. I looked up from my roast beef on sourdough with a side of macaroni salad to find myself face to face with Pierre Gouache, aka The Ghost. Pierre left Folsom not long ahead of me. I was surprised to see him in LA. He'd told me once that his dream was to chase waves on the other side of the world. The sight of him in this rowdy, very American eatery was incongruous, to say the least, but his was one of the few faces from prison I would classify as "friendly." Though Pierre couldn't help but bring bad memories with him, I was strangely happy to see him.

Pierre had been in my cell block for about a year, doing time for the sale of illegal firearms. He was a French-Canadian with a Gallic accent to boot, who'd discovered surfing and then spent his life chasing waves. Like a lot of surf bums, he'd financed his lifestyle with anything but a normal job. I knew Pierre as one of the nonviolent inmates. He was also on the small side, so I understood why, due to my formidable size, he'd sought out my friendship. Being close with someone who could take care of himself was a message to the predators: You mess with one, you mess with both. He'd made sure I knew how grateful he was for allowing him to stand in my protective shadow, but I advised Pierre the best way to avoid trouble is to do as I do and keep your head down. We'd become friendly, but not too close.

I'd even ordered some reading materials he was interested in. Travel guides to the South Seas, things like that.

Pierre had gotten the nickname The Ghost by procuring what no one else on the outside seemed to be able to find: high velocity, fully-automatic, and very exotic, weaponry. Unlike the illegal firearms assembled from kits, which therefore carried no history or serial numbers, Pierre's "ghost guns" had a different source. His were custom-made, often modified from legal firearms, but many were flat out murder machines. Guns intended to kill as many people as possible, as fast as possible. Ordered by customers who wanted to wipe out their competition, then brag about the weapons they'd used, often posing with them online.

"It's a welcome surprise to find you here, mon ami," said Pierre, taking the seat across from me. "I would have thought you would seek new horizons after our previous home."

"I notice you stayed, too," I replied.

"Ah, yes. I stayed for the ocean. And LA is a good place to build for the future."

"I hope so," I said with a shrug. "Not sure where I'll end up yet."

"Just not where we met, I hope."

"Couldn't agree more," I said, the memories of my time inside flooding back.

"Have you found employment?"

"Not yet, but I'm hopeful."

"I wish you luck," said Pierre. "Now, I must meet a man about some inventory, see if it is adequate for my current client."

I suppose I should've expected that Pierre would revert to his old ways. It's not like aging surfers who never worked a nine-to-five in their preprison life would somehow develop any marketable skills. Still, it disappointed me. Pierre's old clients had included drug barons, gang lords, basically anyone willing to pay for something deadly and glamorous. I had to assume his current customers were no different. And despite his own aversion to violence, Pierre had to know what his "inventory" would be used for.

"Do you need work?" he asked me, rising from the table. "I may have some simple tasks that could help you bridge the gap."

"Keep your friends close, but your enemies closer," a man once said in a movie. Pierre was neither, really, just someone I didn't have a beef with. Or him with me. Best to keep it that way.

"No, thanks," I said. My deepest desire right then was make good on the outside, to redeem myself. He added that if I ever did need anything, a job, a problem to disappear, anything at all, The Ghost would be happy to help, for old time's sake. He produced a business card, scribbled something on the back, and handed it to me.

"I am living nearby. Call me. We'll have a drink."

After he left, I read the card. *Pierre G. Purveyor of the Possible.* I slipped it into my wallet, and promptly forgot about it.

* * *

Among the brighter spots of my life lately was seeing Carla. Since she worked the breakfast and lunch shifts, I timed my visits for when she'd be there. She would always greet me with a warm smile, and by the end of that first week she'd added a quick hug whenever I came in. Sure, the food was good, but the real draw soon became the press of her breasts against me. I noticed she'd augmented her usual minimal eye makeup with some blush and a subtle lipstick. She'd even started adding perfume to her daily style, a crisp, floral scent that wasn't too heavy or sweet. The anticipation of seeing her bordered on craving, and I began to have fantasies about her, the kind that used to keep me company during my years away. But these imaginings felt like one of those real world choices that I didn't know what the fuck to do with yet. Baby steps.

I couldn't quite gauge her reaction when, at my lunch visit that Friday, she invited me to join her and some friends the next night for dinner nearby. When I told her I was meeting my ex-girlfriend earlier that day and didn't know when I would be back, her face seemed to scrunch slightly, which I took as disappointment. I wasn't ready for anything that resembled a date, but that look of hers haunted me. I realized later I'd neglected to mention I would also be meeting Angela's current boyfriend.

Time in prison tends to deprive you of the people skills you'd learned on the outside, replacing them with the language of the yard. It's a very different vocabulary, and often silent. I resolved to be more open with Carla in the future. Lesson learned.

Aside from the job hunt, I also had a chance to better learn my phone's GPS. I was amazed to see how far the public rail system had progressed. It had barely made a dent when I'd gone away, covering maybe a couple square miles from the city center. Now, you could ride the Metro Line all the way from downtown to Santa Monica, just blocks from where I would meet Angela. The city was returning to the LA of old, when the distinctive Red Cars were part of what was considered the best public transportation system in the world. LA might yet again be called the City of the Future.

I also set up a bank account where I deposited my checks, and received my first-ever prepaid debit card. I figured five hundred dollars was safe to put on it for now.

I was beginning to feel like a full-fledged citizen.

# CHAPTER

# 9

ON THE MORNING of my second Saturday of freedom, I descended into the 7th Street Metro Station and boarded the Expo Line. I was headed to Santa Monica beach, where I would find Angela and, maybe, redemption. The counselors had advised me that *patience* should be at the forefront of any newly freed inmate's aspirations. Considering what hopes I had to gain from seeing Angela again, I also didn't want to demolish them before I even got started. *One step at a time, Jake. See how it goes. Breathe.*

By the time the train emerged from below ground to the overland segment of the ride, the morning marine layer of fog had mostly burned off, enough to view the expanse on both sides of the tracks. I hadn't had occasion to tour any of downtown LA's shiny new skyscrapers yet, so this was my first elevated view of the LA Basin. Through the broken patches of gray mist, the city spread as far as I could see.

In the distance, the iconic landmarks that dotted the Hollywood Hills—Griffith Observatory, the Hollywood Sign—were perched above the hillside mansions, like sentinels observing the LA Basin, where the common folk dwelled. I'd once called Beachwood Canyon home. I'd emerge from my apartment in the afternoon, groggy after a hard night, to find groups of tourists posing for photos in the middle of the street. They were always trying to get the sign in the background, while they dodged the delivery trucks that raced down the hill.

To the south, among the carpet of single-story houses, oil rigs dotted the low hills, still siphoning crude from the ground. I always thought they looked like dinosaurs feeding in slow motion. We crossed over La Brea Avenue, where its six lanes snaked through those same hills. I used to take that route to LAX airport to pick people up, either a friend or, later on, a client.

The train crossed the 405 Freeway, the official demarcation into West Los Angeles. The freeway and cemetery were the kind of landmarks Angelinos used to gauge how much farther you had to drive. On the 405 in rush hour? It's a good hour to cross town, even when it isn't a parking lot of stalled traffic. Cutting around the cemetery? Watch that left onto Wilshire, or you could still be there on your next birthday. Countless trips of feeling yourself grow older behind the wheel, with nothing to do but watch the ass end of the car in front of you, as you all move at a snail's pace.

After so many years away, I didn't expect the train ride to feel so liberating from this city's tether to the automobile. But I also didn't expect the crush of memories I'd tried so hard to forget to come careening back to my mind.

The slog of endless drives through what seemed like twenty-four-hour traffic jams, just to make it on time to another frustrating, discouraging casting session in some dreary office.

Sitting in a room with sixteen other guys who look so similar we could be each other's body doubles. The competition trying their level best to play mind games on you. Your hopes and dreams being chipped away a little more each day.

# CHAPTER

# 10

## THEN

**1999, nine months before the robbery.**

"THAT'S A FIRST-WORLD problem," was the reply I would hear most often whenever I vented to outsiders about my bad experiences in Hollywood. But what they didn't realize is how grueling it is to maintain the drive that compels you to take the risk of the Hollywood Dream in the first place. It's a punishing daily grind of convincing yourself that you might, *might*, have a place here, that one day you could be invited in, and all the work and hope you put into it will pay off. But the disappointments and humiliations you endure along the way can knock you so far back down the ladder that you can no longer make the climb. What's that saying, "One step forward, two steps back"? If they come hard and fast, it's more like one step forward, six steps back.

I met my agent, Harold, a couple of years earlier. He had seen me in one of my acting coach's regular "Industry only" showcases, performing a two-person scene with a young woman from class. Harold invited me to meet with him and his sister, who was also his secretary (her name escapes me now) at his tiny Beverly Hills office. He was a kind, older gay man and, despite his alcoholism, worked very hard for his clients. "I don't give up easy," he assured me. I signed the contract right there.

He sent me on some meetings and was encouraged when the feedback was positive, that I had a young "Eastwood" quality but with an emotional depth unusual for guys my size. To Harold, it was all about matching the role to the actor, and in the beginning that always takes some trial and error. I became concerned and frustrated because I wasn't landing the jobs, but Harold was unperturbed. "It's like making a bank deposit," he would say. "Eventually, the interest grows and it pays off."

Harold arranged for me to go to the offices of Corronade Films on Wilshire Boulevard in Beverly Hills, a successful independent company that mostly specialized in B-grade action movies. The studio had been taken over by a pair of Israeli brothers, who kept up the profitable exploitation output, but had also struck gold with some auteur films they'd acquired at high-end film festivals like Cannes and Sundance.

I was to audition for one of the leads in what you'd generously call an "ensemble piece," but was really a comedic coming-of-age story with tits. "You have to start somewhere," Harold said. If I got it, I would be the gentle giant who is secretly in love with the quiet homely girl no one pays any attention to. The reading was for a woman director, which was unusual for that time.

Like the company bosses, she was also Israeli, a tall, intelligent, regal woman with a long mane of auburn hair. I thought she was very attractive, which was also unusual; a good looking director. Usually, it was some nerdy guy with glasses and a beard trying to look like Steven Spielberg. On first glance, this movie seemed beneath a refined, worldly person like her, but who knows, maybe she had an established career somewhere else and was looking to break into the US market.

It was late morning, I was well-rested, I knew my lines, and I was ready. The office suite looked cheaply furnished, temporary. I guess they put their money into the movies instead of the furniture, and the walls were completely covered with oversized posters of their films. Nerves are always a problem at auditions and could even be paralyzing if you let them, so on my way into the casting office, I paused outside the door to take a deep breath and center myself, a pro tip you learn in class. Then I went in to meet the aforementioned director, and the woman running the session, the casting director, who would be reading the other roles with me.

Since they need to be up to speed on what's hot and who's next, casting directors usually have a sense of the contemporary about them. But to me, this woman embodied a frumpy, midwestern housewife. She wore polyester, had a boy's haircut, and these horn-rimmed glasses she was constantly pushing back up the bridge of her nose. We'll call her Ms. Frumpy Glasses.

I took a spot near the wall over bright orange tape that had been crisscrossed in the shape of a large X on the worn carpeting. in the shape of a large X. Once I was set, Ms. Frumpy Glasses reached up to a video camera mounted on a tripod and pressed Record. This footage would be used later to review all the candidates.

I began my audition. "Have you ever thought about contact lenses?"

"Why would I do that?" Ms. Frumpy Glasses replied, her eyes fixed on the paper, reading her lines with all the passion of someone checking ingredients off a shopping list. You get used to that, so that wasn't the problem. That was yet to come.

"I have a confession to make," I said, summoning as much emotion as possible, but also trying my best to hide it, as I thought the character would.

"What do you mean?" came Ms. Frumpy Glasses's dead reply.

"I wonder what you'd look like without your glasses. I bet you'd be even prettier."

"No one thinks I'm pretty."

I took a dramatic pause for effect. "I do."

I could feel the director watching me intently. This went on for another few minutes, through three different scenes, and Ms. Frumpy Glasses never took her eyes off the page. But I'd done my homework. I was prepared, and had forged ahead, never letting her disinterest sway me from giving the best audition I could. That could be what the director responded to, but I'll never know.

Looking back now, not knowing her or her story, Ms. Frumpy Glasses may have been affected by the material, and not in a good way.

After my miniperformance, the director and I chatted, mostly small talk. Where you from? You have any hobbies? That kind of thing. I learned that she had been a captain in the Israeli Defense Forces. In other words, this languid, confident, soft-spoken woman could kick my ass and the ass of everyone I knew. I was impressed, and it probably showed, but I didn't care. I found her very easy to talk to, which was another unusual condition of these meetings. Most of the time you're ushered in and out so fast you never have time to interact at all.

Then she really surprised me. "That was an excellent audition, Jake. I think you're very right for this role."

"Thank you." I said, "I don't know why, but I feel close to this guy," which was true. Sometimes you feel a mysterious bond with the character you're playing.

It was then that Ms. Frumpy Glasses said, "You know, we have other prospects coming in later."

It should be said the accepted rule was that your audition time was *your* five minutes. Discussions on who was right or wrong for a character would be had *after* the actor had left, typically in a meeting with the producers and screenwriter. Ms. Frumpy Glasses's behavior was considered not only disrespectful, but unprofessional. (Besides, where I come from you just didn't talk about people right in front of them as if they weren't there.)

"I know," said the director, doing her best to steer the conversation off the subject, at least until I was out of the room. "Jake, do you have a demo reel? I'd like to show it to the producers with your audition."

"Yeah," I said, "but I can't say the quality's great." Digital video was just becoming widely available, and since I didn't yet have any significant gigs to pull from, my agent had convinced me to get together with some friends and shoot scenes on our own. That way he would have *something* to show. "I'll ask my agent's office to messenger one. Or I'll just go over and get it myself and dro—"

"I don't think we need that," Ms. Frumpy Glasses interjected. She pushed those glasses back up her nose, pursed her lips, and looked up at the director. "There are more appropriate choices coming in soon."

If she had looked my way, she would've seen daggers forming in my eyes, but she was avoiding eye contact with me. I wanted to scream, "*It's time for you to shut the fuck up! The person in charge is sitting right next to you, and she is telling you what she wants, and that's* me!" But all I could do was sit quietly.

The director, her patience wearing thin, finally told the casting director to zip it. "We can discuss it later. Right now, I am talking to Jake."

"Fine," said Ms. Frumpy Glasses, pushing her spectacles up her nose one last time before crossing her arms in defiance. "We'll talk about it later."

The director looked at me apologetically. "Thank you for coming in, Jake. I'm sure your reel is fine. Please get that to me by the end of the day, if at all possible. Your audition really was excellent." She was sincerely apologetic. And I can still see the look of mortification on her face.

And with that I stood, shook her hand, and said goodbye. With no contrition coming from Ms. Frumpy Glasses, I didn't bother shaking hers. Her forearms seemed to be glued across her chest, anyway.

I walked to my car feeling dejected, just the opposite of what I should've felt after doing such a good job. But as I trudged to my parking place, only to find a ticket tucked under the wiper blade, I knew in my gut the role would go to someone else.

In the end, Ms. Frumpy Glasses must've had some pull. Maybe she was a relative of a producer or the company's owners—otherwise, her behavior never would have been tolerated. And I never heard of that director making anything else in the US again. I hope she's a big deal somewhere out there.

Not long after that blow, Harold called, this time for me to drive almost an hour north to Santa Clarita. A company up there was producing a low budget Vietnam war movie to be shot in the Philippines.

This was when actors were still given paper sides to read from, and if they weren't willing to fax or email them for you to print out, and some were not, you had to learn them on the spot. If you were a star, you'd get the entire script, but for everyone else, and until they offered you the job, all you had to go on was your audition pages. I took the sides back to my car and worked feverishly on them in what little time I had. It was a five or six page scene about a platoon of soldiers arguing over what to do about a young female POW. One of them, the "villain" soldier, had dragged her away during a firefight intending to rape her. My character was making the case that we should let her go, while others wanted to kill her, and still others wanted to rape her and then kill her. To me, I thought it was trying too hard to be a knock-off of the movie *Casualties of*

*War*, and I was the conscience of the group in the guise of an oversized Michael J. Fox.

After digesting the scene, I went back to the office to read for the room full of producers, and a young Australian director. This director had predictably grown his requisite "auteur" beard (the accoutrement for Spielberg wannabes). I almost had to stifle a laugh when I saw he had put on a bush jacket for the casting session, and even had a fucking viewfinder hanging from his neck. He could've just tacked a sign over his head that said, "Movie Director Here."

I started, and as I got going in the scene, I began to feel the virtue of the piece, that the argument I was making as this character was one that I would have made, as well. "You can't just kill her."

"What are you, some kinda gook-lover?" replied the casting director, a young guy that was truly engaged, not anything like Ms. Frumpy Glasses.

"What do you think we're doing here?" I said. "We don't kill civilians."

"She's the enemy, and I say we have us a little R&R before we waste her!"

"We don't kill *prisoners*!" I roared.

I almost couldn't believe it myself. With only ten or fifteen minutes to prepare, I was crushing it. And my height and stature didn't hurt. At the start of the scene, I noticed several of the producers lean in, wanting to get closer to the action in front of them. When I erupted in anger, they jerked back, as if they believed I was about to attack them.

Then I settled into an eerie calm. "And if you try to touch her, you're gonna have to go through me."

The scene was finished. I sat down in an open chair, partly to calm myself, but also to lessen the tension that my size and display of anger had obviously created. The room was dead quiet. I couldn't even hear activity out in the waiting room. Then, to my utter surprise . . . came *applause.*

The lead producer, a friendly and engaging woman, started it, followed by others on either side of her.

"That was terrific!" she said. "And I was going to apologize for the short amount of time you had to prepare."

Everyone laughed, including me, though I think I was more relieved than amused. Her colleagues on the producing side, seven or eight of them, more women than men, nodded and voiced their agreement.

This was rare. Despite the humiliating experience with Ms. Frumpy Glasses not long before this, I was reading well. And so far, there was no opinionated casting director voicing opposition to me right to my face. Instead, he was giving me a thumbs up from behind the camera setup. It was like I felt that previous wound healing in this very room.

*I might have an actual shot at this gig,* I thought.

But then, I noticed the director hadn't moved. He was sitting there like a statue, staring at me. And that's when he, in his peculiar Aussie brogue, and a snide, superior tone, decided this was the perfect time to berate me in front of everyone.

"You did this all wrong," he said.

The room hushed. I could see jaws drop open, and heads swivel toward him.

"You see," he continued, "there's absolutely no way a *soldier* would act like *that* in the middle of the jungle in the middle of the night, unless he *wanted* to get killed!" Somehow, he delivered all that with a smirk on his face. He was enjoying this.

When I say it took everything in me to keep my cool, I mean it took *everything*. I was still on the adrenaline rush of doing an emotional zero-to-sixty and back again. I couldn't believe this was happening. I wanted to rip this asshole's head right off his neck. But instead, I thought of my agent, Harold, and how disappointed he would be if I was anything less than professional. I took a deep breath.

"Oh, thank you," I said. "I didn't have that information in the material."

That was true. None of that background, that the platoon was hiding in the jungle under threat of discovery by the enemy, was in the sides or the character breakdown that had been given to me when I arrived. And of course, he knew that. There was something else going on.

There was some uncomfortable shifting in seats, and I sensed a rising embarrassment in the producers, one that gave me the impression they'd been dealing with displays like this for some time. They were mostly young-to-middle aged women and, given the uber-male condescension dripping from this arrogant asshole, I felt a bit sorry for them.

The nice lead producer chimed in. "How do you feel about doing the scene again, Jake?"

I felt this must be one of those times when you just have to keep going and try not to think about the people who want to undermine you. It could make all the difference. And besides, this woman was doing whatever she could to give me the chance to change the director's mind.

"Sure," I said.

I did the reading again, taking the director's "note" into consideration. Feeling all the rage and protectiveness, but this time while crouching on the floor, as if we were "in the jungle, in the middle of the night." I played it all without raising my voice so the enemy wouldn't, you know, hear us. Jesus. But by now, I was warmed up, and I had something to prove. I adjusted, and I killed it. Again.

All eyes turned to the director. "That was better," he said flatly. "Thank you." Then he picked up some sheets of paper from the coffee table in front of him. There were small squares printed on it. Headshots of young men, with their name and age next to them. I'd seen lists like that before. Even upside down, I could tell they were the other contenders for this same role.

The encouraging producer said, "Thank you, Jake. You'll be hearing from us."

The director's face froze with indignation.

I rose from the chair, said the requisite thank yous and goodbyes as graciously as I could muster, and left the seething tension in the room behind.

A few days later, Harold got a call from the producer herself. She wanted me to know that everyone else in the room wanted me for the role, but that the director was unmoved. The word she used was that he was "adamantine." (I had to look that up.) He had used his contractual leverage as a member of the Directors Guild to hire a friend of his for the part, instead.

"Who happens to be Australian," Harold told me, uncharacteristically letting his own disgust with the situation show.

The producer wanted me to know how truly sorry she was but hoped we would find another opportunity to work together sometime in the future. I thought it was very nice of her to make the call, but after a while you learn a promise like that and a quarter won't even buy you a cup of coffee.

Despite these setbacks, Harold and I pushed on, the pursuit of my Hollywood dreams still the driving force in my daily life. Then things became almost tauntingly cruel.

Harold sent me to read for another independent movie, since that was one of the best ways to break in at that time. These were more accurately described as "direct-to-video" fare. This one would shoot in Poland, of all places. I drove over to the old Venice Beach studio where Roger Corman made a fortune shooting cheesy science fiction rip-offs. I thought it would be cool to see the old man himself, but by then he mostly just rented out the place.

As I recall, the movie was some kind of hybrid mystery/comedy/romance. I had a tough time grasping the concept, but mine was not to reason why, mine was to try to make them laugh. And like the young Clint Eastwood, comedy wasn't really my strong suit.

Once in the office, I took a seat across a desk from three men. The producer and the director (amusingly, they both wore beards and glasses) were seated opposite me flanking a younger man. (He was their production assistant and would do the reading with me.)

I started, as usual, and when we were about halfway through the scene, the assistant delivers the line, "Your ex-wife says you never bought her flowers. Is that true?"

"To be honest," I answered, "I never knew she sold flowers."

The last thing I would expect is for a bad old joke like that one to get a response, but to my astonishment, the two older men chuckled. And then, something happened I'd never seen before.

The director, one hand to his whiskered chin, silently leaned back in his chair, and looked over at the producer. When the other man, equally silent, returned his look, I expected the director to make a face, or shake his head, something that said, "he's not the one." But instead, and ever so slightly, he nodded.

Generally, no one tells you right then that you have the job. And after the Vietnam movie, I never expected it to happen again. But this felt different. I could barely keep it together to finish the scene, but I somehow managed. When I was done, I stood up, shook hands, there were smiles all around, and I left.

"My boy, we did it." Harold's voice floated through the phone like a warm breeze. "You had the luck of the Irish today."

Harold could barely contain his excitement, but I had to hear him say it. "How so?"

"Somebody dropped out. Whoever they'd hired, and I don't know who, left them scrambling. I just happened to be on the phone with casting about something else entirely when they got word. I snuck you in before anybody else."

"Way to think on your feet, Harold!"

"It's what I do, Jake. But you had to deliver. They loved you! And now, you're going to Warsaw to make a movie!"

Harold liked to say, "Hollywood is one of the only places in the world where your life can completely change with a single phone call."

Baby, you ain't kiddin'! A phone call, and timing.

I felt I was *finally* on my way. I'd gotten my passport of couple years earlier, so I was a Go for a trip to Poland. I immediately quit my job at Bonetti's. The staff was happy for me, and I was going to miss them. Damon seemed saddest of all, but . . . life goes on. And Hollywood doesn't send the same invitation twice.

At 9:00 PM on a Tuesday, my bags were packed, a first-class air ticket was in my pocket, and I was waiting for a car to drive me to LAX for a midnight flight to JFK Airport, where I would connect to Warsaw. Angela had come over for an early dinner, some goodbye lovemaking, and to see me off. The car was due to collect me around 8:30. At a little after 8:00, the phone rang.

"Good, I caught you."

"Harold!"

"I got bad news, kid."

My stomach dropped into my ankles. I couldn't respond. Maybe I thought if I didn't say anything, then neither would he, and I would be on that plane at midnight. Kind of like pulling the bed covers over your head during a hurricane, and pretending your house isn't about to blow down.

"I wish I could say it's never happened before," Harold said. The disappointment in his voice was unmistakable.

"I'm not going, am I?" Angela saw the look on my face, and came over to me. She took my arm.

"No. Sorry, kid."

"Why? How can they do this?"

"They lost their principal investor at the eleventh hour. The whole movie's off. Everybody's out of a job."

"Don't they have contracts or something?"

"Probably. But what are they gonna do? Hold a gun to his head?"

For a second, I didn't think that was such a bad idea.

"It's not a total loss," he said. "You booked one of the leads in a movie. I can run with that. And you can keep that airline ticket. Use it any way you want."

Bless Harold for putting a good spin on things, but it's hard to see a silver lining when your lifelong dream, that you've nurtured, and struggled for, and fought to keep alive, just got smashed into a thousand pieces.

"All right, kid, try to have a good night. We're back at it tomorrow. I promise." I heard the line click dead. Harold's voice was replaced with a deafening, sickening, silence.

There was a knock at my apartment door. Angela went and opened it to a man wearing a chauffer's uniform.

"Good evening," he said with a smile. "I'm here to pick up Jake Ferguson?"

Angela informed him that I wouldn't be going to the airport after all.

Only a couple of days had lapsed since turning in my notice, so Bonetti's hadn't replaced me yet. After some serious groveling on my part, they were gracious enough to hire me back. That night Damon and I partied until dawn. I told myself I deserved a little fun after such a letdown.

A couple months after my first real break evaporated, I spent the morning at a major network's Burbank offices for a "callback" (which is a second or third audition, however many it takes) for several executives. They were in final casting for a science fiction miniseries and had yet to find a handsome young man to be the love interest for the ingenue in the story. She was being portrayed by one of the network's stars, who was using her hiatus from her hit sitcom to do this serious role.

"Well, he looks like he could be a handsome alien to me," said one of the seated executives as she looked around the room for agreement.

My thin knowledge of the show told me that it was about what appeared to be a friendly alien visitation of Earth, but the invaders were secretly hostile. The character I was gunning for falls in love with a human girl, and vice-versa, complicating the takeover plan. Someone said the aliens were a metaphor for the Nazis, but the connection eluded me.

My recent professional heartbreaks had made me cautiously optimistic about any potential opportunities. I'd left my discount cell phone in my car, so it wouldn't be a distraction. I got to my car and powered up the phone to find that Harold had left a message to call him immediately. In the time it took me to walk across the parking lot, the network had called to say the job was mine. And that I would be starting the next day.

Cautious optimism be damned. I called Angela at work to give her the news. At the time she was answering phones for a medical supply company, a gig that had all the glamour of a mugshot. She shrieked with joy, and then insisted we have a light celebration that night. She wanted to cook dinner and then help me work on my lines, so I'd be ready for the next day.

But I just couldn't bring myself to leave the guys at Bonetti's in a lurch again. I had the early shift that night, so I'd be off at a reasonable hour, and the next night I had off anyway, so they'd have time to fill my spot, even temporarily. And Harold was told my first day on the show would be minimal, one shot to visually introduce the character. I'd probably spend more time in wardrobe fittings than I would on set. I decided I should report to Bonetti's, announce during my shift that my big break had indeed arrived, and that sadly I wouldn't be back. That afternoon, as I was getting ready to go in and drop the news, Harold called again.

There was someone else I needed to see.

"You mean I have to audition again?" I asked, feeling the all-too familiar walls closing in. "I thought I had the part."

"You do," he assured me. "But their boss couldn't be there today, and he wants to be able to sign off on you." This felt weird. What was I missing now? "They've already started shooting so you have to go to the studio and meet with him and the director."

"But I met the director today."

"Yeah, well, you have to do this, or they'll just go to their second choice."

"OK," I said, resigned. "What time?"

I arrived at the studio on Sunset Boulevard with about an hour and a half before I'd be late for work at Bonetti's. The gate guard had a drive-on pass for me, so I parked and made my way to the soundstage. I checked in and was shown into a Green Room, where an assistant handed me the exact same audition pages I had read that morning.

After a few minutes, another young actor—a blonde, blue-eyed guy I'd seen at the initial audition a few weeks prior—came in and took a seat. I'd seen him around before, but I'd never learned his name. He stared at me from across the room, then focused on his sides. Though I'd been told I had the role, obviously I'd be auditioning against him again.

He was one of those guys who was always trying to convince the casting director to bring him in last for his reading, thinking that way he would be better remembered than the rest of us. It was a ludicrous idea, but apparently one he believed would give him an edge. *Hey, how about just do the damn scene?* It's akin to the guys who would play mind games on their rivals in the waiting room. Comment on your clothes or your haircut, just try to get under your skin. Not much talent, but they made up for it with moxie. They always reminded me of how competitive Hollywood can be. And why I had so few friends.

Finally, someone came to get us, and we were led down a long hall to a waiting area outside an office. The director I had met that morning (glasses, beard) rushed by and into the office without acknowledging anyone and closed the door behind him.

I happened to be on my feet, rather than sitting where the chair can suck the energy right out of you (another audition trick I'd learned early on), when a tall man with a tailored suit and expensive haircut appeared. Someone I didn't know announced, not in so many words, that the boss had arrived, and we would begin soon. The man would have to walk right past me to the office, so I thought I'd try to ingratiate myself out of the gate. As he got to me, I offered my hand to shake.

"Hi, I'm Jake Ferguson."

Without meeting my eyes, or returning my shake, he said, "I know who you are," and continued into the office.

Like that day I met with the Israeli woman director, I felt the sinking feeling of the role slipping away in real time. The guy had already made up his mind, but I had no idea how or, more importantly, *why*. Blondie, who had watched this over the top of his sides, was smirking from his seat. He knew something I didn't.

I was taken in to read first. (Had Blondie made his "see me last" case again?) The director looked up over his glasses and offered a curt, "Hello, Jake." I couldn't tell if he was bugged that he'd been pulled away from his shoot, but there was something other than this meeting on his mind.

I did the audition the same way I had that morning. Mystery Exec sat and watched with all the expressiveness of a Sphinx. It was as if he was more interested in reading the credits on the movie posters on the wall behind me. The director then asked me to wait outside for a few minutes. I left and Blondie went in for his turn.

After what seemed like a very short amount of time for an audition, the director came out and shut the door, leaving Blondie and Mystery Exec inside. I must've looked as dejected as I felt, because the first thing out of his mouth was an apology.

"Sorry, Jake. The actress in this couple is dark, same coloring as you, and I need the visual contrast so I'm going to have to go with the other guy." I knew that was bullshit, because the lead actress was famously blonde and blue-eyed. But that was not something I was going to bother arguing. It no longer mattered. I'd lost the role.

And with that, like a puff of smoke, another big break floated away.

A few days later, Harold explained that I had been caught up in a corporate power play. Because Mystery Exec hadn't been included in the decision to cast me, he felt he needed to enforce his authority. Never mind that in the process he was smashing someone's dream opportunity (after I had already earned it, fair and square). He took the role away from me and gave it to Blondie only to make a point. It had all the subtlety of a cannon shot, but with me as the fodder.

The miniseries was heavily promoted, but I couldn't bring myself to watch. I did catch some of a rerun months later and saw that the blonde actress performed her role under a brunette wig and wore dark contact lenses. I'm sure the official story was that she wanted to stretch her acting skills beyond her comedic image. But I wondered if Mystery Exec had forced the look on her, just to affirm that he, and nobody else, was in charge.

Blondie's performance was just plain bad. Stiff and wooden, he was what we called a "post." I never saw him in anything else again (which still makes me smile; I'm not above a little schadenfreude). So, in the process of making sure no one ever made a decision without him again, Mystery Exec had effectively ended not one, but two careers.

Angela would still be at her own job, so I phoned her from the car before I left the studio lot.

"Oh, honey," she'd said. "Why would they do this?"

"Because they can, I guess."

"I'm so sorry, Jake." She went into nurturing mode. "OK, I'm going to come over when I get outta here. I'll fix you something nice, and we'll—"

"I gotta go to work, Angela," I said, cutting her off. "You may as well go home. Nothing to celebrate, anyway."

"Um, OK," she said, her voice trailing off with the rejection. "If that's what you want . . ."

I could tell she was hurt. She was trying to be there for me, to be the shoulder where I could lay my head. But what she didn't know, and what I didn't realize yet, was that the walls inside me were already being built. The emotional body blows were leaving deep scars. The kind you can't see.

"This morning, I get my break," I said. "Tonight, I'm a fucking bartender."

"Jake," she said, as if she thought her words would save some part of me that she knew was slipping away from both of us. "I lov—"

I hung up. I just couldn't hear it. It was a small, defiant, self-immolating act that became another regret in a long list of them. Even if she really meant it, I wouldn't let myself believe it. The walls were already too high.

I drove to Bonetti's, but I didn't tell anyone of that day's epic ups and downs, the elation shattered by humiliation. I spent my tips that night on a gram of blow and stayed up alone until dawn, licking my wounded ego. I was so angered when the coke ran out, and the sun intruded on my self-pity party, that I put my fist through a wall. I hung a picture over it so the landlord wouldn't notice.

I'll spare you the details of my very last audition and just give you a quick rundown.

It was for a middle-aged male casting director who told me he couldn't wait to schedule my callback for the producers of the TV pilot he was casting. It was based on a role-playing game kids were into then, something to do with dragons. I don't know if it ever went forward to series or not. Most of them didn't.

He was patting me on the back as he walked me to the door when he grabbed me by the elbow, looked me in the eye and said, "You're beautiful." Then he grabbed my crotch, and pressed himself hard against me. If I concentrate, I can still smell his cologne, which reminded me of the sweet jasmine that grew outside my apartment building, mixed with old sweat. I don't know what I did that made him think I was open to that, but I responded by pushing my forearm into his neck and shoving him hard against the wall. I could still hear him coughing to catch his breath as I marched through the outer office past his confused secretary. The callback never came.

Not long after that, I lost Harold. He was my first and only agent. Not because he lost faith in me and dropped me as a client. No, the mean streets of LA got him. He was driving home after a night of carousing in West Hollywood, and had stopped for a red light on La Cienega Boulevard when he was carjacked. His blood alcohol level was high enough that he probably never saw them coming, but whoever it was dragged Harold out of his Mercedes 450SL, threw him face down on the blacktop, and pumped two bullets into the back of his balding, sixty-year-old head. They sped off in his car and, as far as I know, were never caught.

That man was a like a surrogate father to me, much like Anthony had been in prison. Harold did his best to help me create a future that, in the end, I only dreamt of. Supportive, energetic, and always positive, he'd lived alone all his adult life, pouring his energies into his clients, whom he loved like his own children. When they succeeded, he celebrated as if he were on the precipice of stardom himself. And I howled like a baby when his sister called to tell me he was dead.

That was it for me. I'd hit the wall. Not everyone does, but I did. I'd devoted . . . scratch that . . . I'd *sacrificed* five long years, to classes, showcases, auditions, to scratching, scrambling, and struggling. I'd experienced electrifying triumphs that had been snatched away to become paralyzing defeats.

Something inside of me broke. And I was barely twenty-five years old.

I searched for something I must be doing wrong. Was I putting people off or not doing what was expected of me? Along with the countless other futile endeavors, I examined the most recent experiences that should have borne fruit; the Israeli director/Army captain, the Vietnam movie, the Poland movie, the miniseries, the molesting casting director (there were plenty more like him, but I won't waste your time). I couldn't recall anything that would reveal willful self-destructiveness on my part. I always planned ahead; didn't party hard the night before, got some exercise to loosen up before meetings, so I could show up as prepared and flexible as possible. I wondered if there was some part of me that couldn't accept that when it came to real, tangible, successes, there was absolutely nothing under my own control.

In truth, I wish it was that simple, that I gave up because I had no (as they say today) agency. It went much deeper than that. The day Harold died, my dream died with him. I gave up on myself.

And it wasn't easy, as nice a guy as he was, watching Winston Greene's career take off. It is possible to feel two things at once: to be happy for someone on the one hand, while hoping they fail in order to make room for you on the other. I can't tell you how surreal it was to have some of his movies be the Saturday night entertainment in Folsom. (I always kept that tidbit to myself.)

I decided I should stay at Bonetti's until I figured out what to do next. The money was decent, and Damon or one of the other guys provided easy access to my increasing indulgence in substances. I may as well get in some partying while I figured out what to do with the rest of my life. I told myself it softened the blow, but deep down I knew all I was really doing was trying to kill how I felt about myself. I was a fraud. A loser.

I still have trouble grasping how strong the dream is that draws you here. It runs soul deep, and is with you day in and day out. When that dream gets chipped away, bit by bit, piece by piece, it's like your very essence is being sliced away, as if someone is shaving off your skin in torturous fragments. So much of what drives you is taken on faith, and after a while you feel there's not enough faith left to keep you going. That's how it was for me, anyway.

So maybe acting wasn't my thing. "Hollywood" sure wasn't. I must've been misguided to believe otherwise.

Then Damon came up with his great idea. That was another delusion. I convinced myself that taking money to fuck older women was somehow taking back some of what Hollywood had taken from me. What a joke.

I didn't even bother to look for another agent. Truth is, some can hack it, but most can't. It feels like defeat, plain and simple. It's how you respond to that defeat that counts. I did not respond well.

# CHAPTER 11

## NOW

I DISEMBARKED THE TRAIN at the gleaming new Santa Monica station, the last stop. A combination of vague memory and my new GPS guided me to the ocean. I was happy to see the Santa Monica Pier still standing at the end of Route 66. It'd never hit me before, but I realized that meant two great American landmarks for the price of one.

Pacific Park was still on the pier, with its over-water fairground, including the small roller coaster. So was the 1916 Hippodrome that housed the Carousel (that had doubled for Paul Newman's East Coast carnival job in *The Sting*). I wondered if the carousel was still operating, with its vintage hand-carved horses, lit by over one thousand lights. And there was the big restaurant perched at the very end, which was always a middling seafood joint, but with a million-dollar view. At least you knew what you were paying for.

From where I stood several hundred yards away, the pier almost looked like a day-glow toy skyline someone had built for their kids. I once brought Angela to this park, where we ate junk food, wasted quarters in the arcade, and took our turn side-by-side on that carousel. A perfect night when love was the only thing that mattered.

The train had gotten me here sooner than expected, a good half hour, so I crossed the parking lot south of the pier to Ocean Front Walk, the bike and pedestrian path that demarcated the parking lots from the sand. I stopped at the edge and closed my eyes, and the peculiar sounds of the beach filled my ears. It was so different from downtown. Gulls and pigeons cooed overhead. It wasn't even 10:00 AM, and excited children spilled out of their parents' cars. Amid the shouts and laughter of their youngsters, adults and hauled blankets, coolers, and umbrellas to choice spots on the sand.

The rhythmic hiss of waves turning was a constant balm for those lucky enough to live here. I never had, but I'd sometimes stay over with one of my "benefactors" during my darkest years. Justine (she'd never offered her last name) was about thirty years older than me, a handsome bleached blonde former beach bunny who had gotten the ocean-view condo in the divorce. It was close enough to the waves for the sound to lull me to sleep after I'd serviced her. She was one of the rare few who liked me to stay over, even got a kick out of making us breakfast in the morning. But by that time, all I wanted was to pack my nose with blow as soon as I woke. Sometimes, she would pay for another round of sex before we both showered and headed into our respective days.

Jesus, the sordid memories this simple trip across town was stirring up. I bounced my palm off my temple, trying to knock the images from my head.

Besides the hunt for work and an apartment, I'd spent the week augmenting my wardrobe from some of downtown's many discount outlet shops. And I'd come to accept I might have to stay at the hostel until I can land gainful employment. The landlords I'd spoken to had been unwilling to rent to an unemployed ex-con (but at least they had the good taste to cite my lack of employment as an excuse). I considered offering a few months' rent in advance, but if I didn't land a job, I'd be on the hook for more but with my savings gone. Better to keep the cash handy and stay at the hostel. I was getting used to it there, anyway.

And Sweet Carla, as I'd come to call her, offered to ask around and even found a spare bedroom I could rent with a couple roommates. But if there was anything I didn't want right now, it was having to share my living space. Somehow, the hostel felt more private. And despite the flirty vibes I'd been getting from her since we'd met, it still surprised me when she suggested I could stay with her if I needed to leave the hostel. God, she was a sweet one. Sexy as all hell too, but I wasn't ready to go there. If the joint teaches you anything, it's how to think about what you really want. And I wanted, I *needed*, to make my own way.

The marine haze had cleared, leaving the sky cloudless, and carnival noise floated across the sand from the pier. The cool breeze felt good on my face.

I was to meet Angela and her boyfriend at Beach Park 1, an easy stroll south. From the edge of the path, I looked across the wide beach to the water. That cerulean blue had always captivated me, as it does everyone, but seeing it now was like seeing it for the first time. And, in a way, I was.

I started to cross the bike lane to the pedestrian path on the ocean side when a bicyclist who must have been training for the Tour de France came screaming by, dinging his handlebar bell incessantly, an auditory warning for anyone ahead of him to *get the fuck outta his way!*

I let him pass, and then stepped across, keeping my eyes open for other riders coming from both directions. What twisted logic directed the city planners to put the walking lane on the far side, forcing people to negotiate through oncoming cyclists? And if that was the most penetrating question I asked myself today, then it should be a pretty good one.

I decided to use the extra minutes to walk down to the shoreline. It had been a quarter century since I'd seen any natural body of water, let alone the largest and deepest in the world. I stopped at the edge of the wave line, that clear demarcation that tells you how far you can go before your shoes get soaked. *Like riding a bicycle.* The surf was small that Saturday morning, making just enough sound to drown out the rising cacophony of the weekend beach life behind me. I shut my eyes and took in a deep breath. As I listened to the undulating waves turning over on the sand, the salty, frothy loam filled my nose. It smelled both musty and new at the same time, and I gave myself over to the ocean's mysterious effect. I felt my pulse quicken.

Pierre would say that ocean waves are caused by energy, and that when you catch a wave, that energy infuses your body, causing a rush that courses through you, going even deeper than the excitement of riding the wave itself. He also said it's that rush that surfers get hooked on. *If only I'd taken up surfing instead of drugs.* I don't know if it was energy, or nostalgia, or just the sense of freedom of being able to stand at the ocean's edge, but I felt water gather behind my eyelids. So much that I had to open them to release it and let it stream down my cheeks. Once my vision cleared, I could see raised lines running across the water in the distance. A set of larger waves was on their way into shore. It was hypnotic. I just wanted to stare, transfixed, at the ocean all day long. But I had somewhere to be.

I must have been gawking at the ocean for a while, because Angela and her boyfriend managed to beat me there. At this hour, the area hadn't yet been overrun by revelers, and I found myself focusing on a portable blue half-dome shelter that shaded a large, bright, multicolored towel spread over the grass. Adjacent to that was a concrete picnic table on which was a two-tone cooler and a wicker picnic basket anchoring a red and white checkered plastic table cloth.

A woman wearing shorts, sandals, and a light coverup over a bathing suit top was standing next to the table, looking intently at her phone. After all this time, her profile was unmistakable. And if I wasn't mistaken, my heart forgot a beat.

Angela.

Tall and slim, though thinner than I remembered. Under the baseball cap that shaded her face, she wore her dirty blonde hair long and slicked back over her ears.

I remembered that she liked the ocean well enough; it was sand she wasn't fond of. I guessed that was why they'd decided on the grassy knoll beyond the beach.

I kept my distance, hoping to observe her for a moment without being noticed. She'd stopped straightening her loose natural curls. Held in place by the cap, her hair flowed down her back, the soft strands clung to her shirt.

Second thoughts flooded in. *What am I doing?* I looked around for a place to hide before she spotted me. I needed to gather my thoughts. And some nerve. I turned and the sun hit me square in the face . . . and I sneezed. Hard. "Fuck!" I said, under my breath, and looked over at her just in time to see her do a double-take in my direction.

She stared at me, her lips parted. The hand holding the phone slowly lowered to her side.

No turning back now. I mustered a shy wave. "Hello!" I called, and walked over.

"You made it," she said as I arrived. Then she looked to someone behind me. "Eric. He's here." It's not like I expected a hug and a kiss, but her tone was flat.

A fit and strikingly handsome young man in board shorts and a loose T-shirt had been crouching unseen behind the shelter, pushing the last grounding stake into the dirt. He rose, strode to us, and stuck out his hand.

"How you doin'? I'm Eric."

"Yeah, I figured." I said, meeting his hand with mine. "Jake."

Eric nodded, and I returned a friendly smile. "Have any trouble getting here?"

I glanced at Angela, who had turned away, back to whatever she was doing on her phone. "Uh, no," I said. "Easier than I thought. I may never take anything but the train again."

"I'd hold off on that until you see where it *doesn't* take you," Eric said. He opened the cooler on the table. "Like a drink? Sorry, but alcohol's not legal on the beach."

"Fine with me," I said. Booze hadn't been a part of my life in decades. The withdrawals I'd endured after my arrest fueled a decision that when I left this world, I'd like to take a functioning liver with me. I never even tried the corrosive home brews in Folsom. "You wouldn't have a ginger ale, would you?"

"As a matter of fact, we do," he said, reaching into the ice. "Anj? You want something?"

"No thanks," she answered without lifting her head from the phone screen. Her tone was still tortilla-like.

"Go ahead and have a seat," he said to me, then turned to Angela. "Anj, can you help me with this damn thing?"

"Anything I can do?" I said, trying to be useful.

"No," Angela answered, as she moved to help Eric.

Sensing some tension, I moved to the opposite side of the table and sat on the concrete bench. Watching them whisper to each other as they pretended to secure the shelter, I felt out of place, like a third wheel without any hope of finding an axle to call home. I looked out at the water, hoping that gave them the privacy Eric was obviously seeking.

I looked at the sweating soda can, taking note of the changes in packaging since I'd last seen one. It looked brighter, "greener," than I remembered. I popped the top and took a long pull, raising my face to the bright sun. The sweet, effervescent liquid made for a satisfying gulp, then I felt another sneeze begin to launch. I quickly dropped my look to the ground, saving myself from shooting a mouthful of soda through my nostrils.

The beach crowd had thickened considerably just in the thirty or forty minutes since I'd arrived from the train. Families and couples had staked out spots fairly close to us. The ocean breeze whipped the hanging edges of the plastic table cloth. The red and white checks looked festive set against the green, white and blue environment. Over the beach sounds I could make out some of Eric's and Angela's exchange.

"Well, he's here now . . ."

"I thought I was ready . . ."

"Just talk to him . . ."

"Fine!"

I was raising the can for another drink when Angela brushed by.

"Let's take a walk," she announced as she passed me. I looked back to Eric, who was watching the action unfold. Angela stopped. "You coming?"

I was so surprised, I hesitated, and could see her losing her nerve in the space of time it took me to answer. "Yes!"

I set down the can and caught up to her as she headed across the lawn toward the volleyball courts. I matched her pace, which was faster than a normal stroll at the beach. I knew I should be the one to get this ball rolling, but as many times as I'd imagined this encounter, I was at a loss as to how. So I figured I'd just take a shot at honest, abject ignorance.

"I don't really know where to start," I said.

"You and me both," Angela replied without looking at me. We were each avoiding eye contact with the other. She wasn't going to make this easy, and in my mind, she shouldn't have to. "Can we sit down for a minute? Just . . . talk?"

She took a few more steps, then turned back. The look in her eyes betrayed the argument she was having with herself: *Why should I listen to this guy? Because you want to hear him say it.* After a beat, she crossed to an empty bench and sat down on one end. I settled on the other.

"Thanks," I said.

"Wasn't my idea."

I needed to choose my words carefully, deliberately. If I didn't, they could have the same destructive effect as my being shipped off to prison all those years ago. I didn't think I could erase that history, but I also didn't want this to become emotional chum in the water, and give her something to feed her lingering anger. I focused on trying to keep things on an even keel. "I'm just glad to see you. To tell you how sorry I am."

"For?"

"Everything." I raised my hands in surrender. "For leaving. For shutting you out. For what I did that put me there. For what I let myself become, and why I did it." She was staring at me. I dropped my hands to my knees. "It's kind of a litany, isn't it?"

"Huh," she said, doing another double take. "Never expected to hear you use a word like 'litany.'" She looked at the volleyball courts. The games were in full, raucous swing. "Were you ever afraid in there?"

I'd expected people to be curious about my time inside, but the question still caught me off guard. "Oh, yeah. Especially when you first get there. You're scared pretty much all the time."

"So how did you cope?"

Her use of "cope" was unexpected. That's a word with *consideration* behind it. She'd wondered about me before now. "You make sure you don't owe anybody. If you don't get high or gamble, you won't need to borrow money. As a white guy, I was expected to do some errands for the Brand, but that was it."

"The Brand?"

"Aryan Brotherhood. Everyone's associated by their race, and they all have their own gangs. You don't have to join one, but you're still expected to do some jobs for them. I delivered some messages, but that's all."

"You had to hurt somebody?" She looked like she didn't want to know the answer.

People have such strong ideas about prison, mostly taken from the movies. I did, too, when I first went in. I still remember that early fear, as tangible as this sunny day. It must've read on my face, because now she looked like she thought I was crazy. "No," I said quickly. "I *literally* delivered some messages. A piece of paper, or told one guy what another guy said to tell him. I only had to do it a few times. It's not like I agreed with what they stood for, but that's not the point. They went their way, I went mine. Live and let live, kind of thing." I looked at her. "Respect is a big deal. Little things can make someone feel like you've disrespected them, and then you'd have a problem."

"Sounds complicated," she said.

I nodded. "It can be. It's a different world, but I made a friend early on. Anthony. He ran the library, and I started hanging around there. It was about the quietest place to be, and probably the safest anywhere outside your own cell. He showed me how to get along."

"What does that mean?" There was a nervousness behind her questions, like she was wary of my answers.

"Anthony taught me that in prison a book is a means of survival. You could go all the way to Fiji, or to outer space, or even travel through time, without ever going over the wall. It was a way to . . . *endure* it. And learn a few things you didn't know."

"Why was he there? Anthony."

"Killed his wife and her lover. He caught them somewhere, and he said he just went crazy with rage. Irony is, he was a college graduate. An actuary, if you can believe it, and that was the only time in his life he ever broke the law. Said he'd never even raised his voice at his wife. When I met him, he said, 'Just think of me as Brooks Hatlen.'"

"Who's that?" she asked.

I chuckled. "That's what I said." Angela was starting to look a little impatient. "He's a character in a short story. He said to me, 'Don't you read Stephen King? *Rita Hayworth and Shawshank Redemption*. One of his best!' I read it that day."

"I think I saw the movie."

"James Whitmore played that part."

She nodded slightly as if she remembered him, but I could tell she didn't.

"Wasn't it dangerous, though?"

I could see her back had stiffened, and she was pressing her palms flat into the bench. I'd wager that, like most, she'd had a picture in her mind of what my time inside had been like all these years. I can't say that prison life isn't dangerous, even nightmarish, but there are small favors of humanity that can make it bearable. Survivable. And now she had to negotiate that mental picture with the truth. I couldn't help but wonder if she'd ever wanted me to suffer for the pain I'd caused.

I don't know why, but I thought now might be a good moment to inject some humor into this exchange. "Don't you mean, how did a handsome stud like me get along?" She stared at me, aghast. Guess my timing ain't that great, after all. "Sorry. Being six four and two hundred twenty pounds didn't hurt. The movies can make it seem like it's just one big riot all the time, everyone trying to kill each other over a scrap of food."

"But the gangs, and . . . what do they call them? Punks? What about all that?"

"There is that, but . . ." I looked to the sky for help. "It's hard to explain. It's like a whole culture in there. It's like that, but it's *not* like that. If you mind your own business, people pretty much leave you alone."

"So, you never had any fights or anything?"

"Once, yeah," I said, not relishing the memory. "Like I said, respect is a big deal. To this day I don't know why, but this guy thought I'd disrespected him somehow. He came at me in the yard with a spoon he'd sharpened into a kind of knife. I was spending a lot of time lifting weights, like a lotta guys do. I just happened to see him before he got to me, and I punched him. I thought I killed him. Thank God, I just knocked him out. When he didn't get up, everybody just moved on, and nobody ever bothered me again. The guards didn't do anything, I don't know if they even saw it." I sighed. "I guess I didn't know my own strength."

She looked at the ground, as if she was searching for something there. "This doesn't make it any easier. I thought you never wrote because it was so hard in there. Except for that one thing, you make it sound like all you did was hang out and read."

And here came that wave of guilt, like the waves I could hear picking at the shoreline, starting to hit the sand with a *whump*. "That's fair," I said. "I think I told myself for so long that it would be better if I didn't reach out, that it just became a truth for me." I shook my head. "It's one of the ways you deal with it. You pretend the world out here doesn't exist."

"So, I didn't *exist* to you?" Now she sounded incredulous.

"No, it's . . . of course you did. I just couldn't acknowledge it, or I would've done something stupid, like hurt myself. I don't say that to get sympathy, but that's what you do, or it just eats you up." Now I started looked for something on the ground. I found it: Shame. "The irony is, it still does."

Angela rubbed her palms together, maybe to wipe off the dust from the bench, but it felt more like a nervous habit. "So, it was really for you, then. Not anyone else's benefit."

I let out a heavy sigh. "In a way, I guess it was," I admitted. "That's what Anthony taught me. It seemed to work for him, so that's what I did." The words sounded stupid coming out of my mouth. "I really am sorry."

She answered with an almost imperceptible nod. "What happened to him?"

"Anthony?"

"Yeah."

"Oh, he died in the infirmary. Cancer."

"Did he have anyone?"

"I think anyone he had wrote him off when he did what he did. Just another forgotten inmate in the California Penal System. He's buried up there."

She looked like she was thinking about something. "Never expected you to use a word like 'irony,' either." There was something cynical, but playful, behind her remark. I felt a sense of relief, like things were beginning to turn.

"That's the thing about libraries." I ventured a small grin. "Nothing to do but read."

Angela took a deep breath, looked across the courts. I couldn't tell if it meant she had acquiesced to something, or made a decision about it.

I ventured a bit further. "What do you do now?"

"I work at a radio station."

"Oh, finally made it in showbiz."

"If only," she said, then she let out a small laugh, though it was absent of humor. "It's one of the last of the independents. I'm in Business Affairs, which is just a fancy way to say 'bean counter.' The way radio's going, there may be no business to have an affair with soon." She shook a worried look from her face. "And I never wanted to make it in showbiz. That was you."

"You saw how well that went."

"I thought I would die when you went away."

I looked at her. "And I thought this talk would take *away* some of the guilt."

"Was there anything I could've done? I felt like if I'd tried harder . . ."

"No, Angela," I said. "There wasn't. What I did, I did all by myself. There's no one to blame but me. Please know that."

She held my look for a few moments, then turned to face the ocean, as if she was letting my words sink in.

Having felt like I'd made some headway, I thought now might be a good time to change the subject. "So . . . Eric."

She turned back to me. A slight smirk had appeared on her face. "What about him?"

"Seems to be quite an age difference."

Her eyebrow raised into an arch. "Remind you of your old line of work?"

"I didn't want to say anything, but . . . yeah."

"So I remind you of your *clientele*?" The edge in her voice was coming back.

"No!" I protested. "I just couldn't help but notice, that's all."

"It's not the same, despite how it looks," she said. "He's not complicated. I hate complicated."

I shrugged. "Whatever works."

# CHAPTER

# 12

BY THE TIME we'd returned, Eric, now shirtless, had laid out plastic containers of food across the tablecloth. My unfinished can of ginger ale had disappeared.

"I decided it's lunchtime," he said.

"I guess so," said Angela. She wrapped her arms around Eric's slim waist. With his tan and bricked abs, the guy looked like a bronzed surfer. Or the star of a '90s-era primetime soap. When I first arrived in LA, TV was still all about those good-looking young people. It was part of what made us wannabes think we had a chance. "Beautiful people doing stupid things badly," we used to joke in class. Of course, had any of us gotten one of those gigs we would've held onto it for dear life.

"How 'bout you, Jake?" Eric asked. "There's plenty."

I waited, expecting some resistance from Angela, but when none came, I said, "I could eat."

Eric clapped his hands together. "Great!"

Angela and Eric each took a seat on one side, and I settled across from them, and we passed around cold fried chicken, poached salmon, pasta salad, and coleslaw.

"So, you just got out of prison," Eric said, as he scooped out some slaw, as if reminding me where I'd left off in telling a story. Angela's boyfriend apparently didn't believe in working up to a subject.

"Eric!" Angela said. "Manners."

"What?" he said. "It's not like it's some big secret."

"It's OK," I said to Angela. "Yes," I said to Eric. "End of last week."

"And you came right back here?" Eric pressed.

"Not really my choice," I said. "It's called County of Last Legal Residence. Means you have to return to the jurisdiction you were convicted in."

"You have a parole officer or something?"

"He doesn't need a parole officer," said Angela. "He paid his debt." She passed me a container. "Pasta?"

"Thanks." I took the container, surprised by Angela's graceful attempt at a rescue. But since I was on this mission-of-honesty, I felt I should clarify what apparently neither of them knew. "They're called parole 'agents' now, and I do have one. I have to see him every month." They both looked at me, Angela more surprised than he was. "Hardly anybody serves a full sentence anymore, it's just too crowded." I scooped out a serving, then handed it to Eric. The young man did seem genuinely interested in me, but the questions were still a bit unnerving.

"Sorry," he said. "My curiosity can get the best of me. So, you robbed a bank?"

"Eric," Angela chided, despite the laugh that escaped her. "Can we save the third degree?"

I held up my hand. "Really. It's OK," I said, and turned to Angela. "But thanks." I looked back to Eric. "They told us to expect people to be curious. No, it wasn't a bank. Me and a couple friends thought it was a good idea to rob a street gang of their illegal drug proceeds. Didn't go quite like we thought it would."

"How do you handle it?" he asked. "I mean, all that time."

I had to take a moment to answer. "You remind yourself . . . you're the only reason you're there," I said. "I knew going in I got what I deserved."

Eric nodded thoughtfully, then forked a bite of coleslaw.

* * *

"Angela said you were looking for a job."

After a couple of hours, I'd decided this pasty ex-con had gotten enough sun for one day, and announced it was time to catch my train. Eric offered to tag along, saying there was something he wanted to run by me.

"Yep," I answered as we crossed the parking lot toward the hill that would lead to the Metro station.

"How's that going?"

"Not too well, if I'm being honest. What they say about ex-cons getting work is true." I shrugged. "I'll keep at it."

"How do you feel about driving?" Eric said. "For a job, I mean."

I stopped, and waited for him to elaborate.

"I need a driver," he said. "I go place to place all day long just putting out fires, *and* I'm on the phone the whole damn time."

"What do you do?"

He shrugged. "I own nightclubs. Me and some friends. And I have an interest in a few restaurants. Basically, hospitality stuff." He cocked his head in the direction of the picnic site. "Angie's been bugging me to get one. Says I'm gonna kill somebody if I don't."

I looked away.

"Oh, shit. Sorry, man, that didn't come out ri—"

"Don't you need a chauffeur's license for that?" I said, cutting him off.

He thought for a moment. "I don't think so. It's just a town car. Garden variety sedan. You'd be doing other things for me, too. Errands, stuff like that. Technically, you'd just be an employee of the company."

"The . . . nightclub company," I said.

He nodded. "It's busy work, but it's fun. You could learn a lot if you're interested. And driving me would make the citizens of LA a lot safer."

I leveled my eyes. "Why are you doing this?"

He smiled. "I was wondering when you'd get to that."

"Most guys don't go around offering jobs to their old lady's ex-con former boyfriends."

"'Old lady.' Haven't heard that one in a while." Then he said, "Angie has a soft spot for you, even if she can't admit it. I think she'd like to help but that place she works is laying people off practically every week. Those stations are dropping like flies." He smiled. "Call it my good deed for the month."

"How would she feel about it?" To be honest, I wasn't sure how *I* felt about it, but beggars can't be choosers. Especially ex-cons who can't get a foot in the door.

"You'd be working for me, not her. The pay isn't great, but I'll make sure you can live on it." I ran my fingers through my hair. "Think about it a few da—"

"I'll take it," I said.

Eric, his mouth still open to an "a" sound, stuck out his hand. "I don't suppose you still have a driver's license?"

"You know," I said, shaking his hand. "I let it lapse."

# CHAPTER

# 13

Having not had a driver's license in two decades, or driven a car for even longer than that, I needed to rectify the situation if I was going to do this job. Since my license was technically being reactivated, rather than issued for the first time, the state assumed that I already had the basics of how to operate a vehicle, and I wasn't required to do a behind-the-wheel road test.

I stood for a photo a few feet in front of what looked like a gadget from a James Bond movie, and my face appeared on a screen next to the operator. With my new haircut and beard stubble, I almost didn't recognize myself. In a few weeks I would have my permanent license. In the interim, temporary printed documents were folded neatly in my breast pocket.

Angela had suggested I take a driving refresher course, but I'm of the belief that, like many other activities I hadn't performed in a while, driving a car is like riding a bike: once you do it you never forget.

I let Eric know I was now street legal, and then made a call to Sanchez, my parole agent, to inform him I was now gainfully employed. He expressed his pleasure at my securing work and wished me luck, before reminding me that I was still required to report to him in person soon. Two days later, I was summoned to Eric's office.

Hollywood Boulevard had changed. A lot.

When I first came to LA, I settled into an apartment just a few blocks from the famous Chinese Theatre. What I could afford back in those salad days was a one-room studio on the third floor of a four-story building. My "view" was of my next-door neighbor's living room. But it was mine, and I loved it.

Back then, many of the two- and three-story Art Deco buildings were crumbling. The fine haberdashers and jewelers of old, with doormen and security buzzers, had been replaced by open storefronts where cheap T-shirts and tacky tchotchkes were sold. And of the old stalwarts, only Musso & Frank Grill and the Chinese Theatre remained.

The boulevard had undergone a total makeover since my early days. Eric's "office" was in a new hotel and private club on Vine Street just off Hollywood Boulevard called the Astoria. I entered the lobby, noting how the black walls instantly absorbed the daylight's gleam, easing the painful squint in my eyes. The front desk, dwarfed above by a huge chandelier made of what looked like long rectangular crystal rods, was manned by a handsome young couple in dark uniforms. They directed me to the elevator, which took me up six flights to the roof.

I had heard about the rooftop lounge phenomenon, but I'd never had the pleasure. The first thing I saw when I stepped off the lift was a long, large covered bar, the stools surrounding it already occupied by several drinkers at 11:00 AM. There was a huge LED screen mounted on a brick wall, with long couches arranged before it. Several saguaro cacti stood tall in large planters, their boughs wrapped in tiny white lights that must look beautiful at night. It really was a different world up here.

Beyond the bar, I spotted Eric with several other young men, all seated or standing among thickly padded Adirondack-style chairs and sofas. Eric was dressed in what I learned is his typical daytime uniform of faded jeans, sneakers, and a rock-n-roll T-shirt, but everyone else wore a black suit and open collared white shirt. A few of the men had their jackets off, their sleeves rolled to the elbow. They had all taken refuge under a collection of large umbrellas to escape the late morning sun.

The sunlight was intense up here. The glare hit me in the face, so I dropped my head and put a finger to my nose to head off any potential sneeze. Eric, speaking animatedly with a phone to his ear, saw me coming and snapped his fingers to get someone's attention. A few of the heads turned in my direction. In the short walk across the roof, I could already feel my shirt getting wet under the arms and down my back.

One of the group, a burly, overweight man with a thick dark mustache, rose to meet me. He was shorter than me, but wider in the shoulders, and his well-fed gut sagged through his open jacket, hiding his belt buckle.

"Name's Rudy," the man said to me. He had a slight accent I couldn't place. LA is like a thousand different countries.

"Jake," I replied, extending my hand.

"I don't shake." I would describe Rudy's greeting attitude as "curt." Not what I would call a good first impression. I let it roll, and dropped my hand.

There were half-eaten trays of canapés and charcuterie spread across the low tables. Open bottles of mineral water and sodas were ready to refill ice-condensed glasses. I looked at Eric, who pointed at Rudy, then gave a thumbs up and went back to his phone call.

I quickly scanned the faces staring up at me. Most were obscured by dark sunglasses, and my nod of general greeting was not returned. There was nothing about these guys that said "up-and-coming-businessmen" to me. The hairs on my neck sent me a signal, like a red flag going up a flagpole. These guys felt like the type my parole agent would warn me to stay away from. But I'd served out my sentence, so I was free to take whatever job was offered. I also had a fast-diminishing checking account. So, in this new world of choices, I had a choice . . . but I didn't have much choice.

"C'mon," said Rudy, as he passed me on his way to the elevator. We stepped into the car, and Rudy pressed five, two floors down. When the door opened, I followed him the length of the hallway to an open door, which led into a two-room corner suite.

Inside was a sofa and armchairs aimed toward a flatscreen on the wall, and a desk that, judging by its mismatched style, had been placed where perhaps a bed used to be. The door to the bedroom was closed. There were a couple of cheap metal file cabinets lined against the wall behind it, alongside some rows of Bankers Boxes, each stacked four or five high. They must have been stuffed full of documents, because they leaned unevenly against each other. They looked like one heavy breath would tip them over. Beyond the windows was a spectacular view of the LA Basin. A young man in the shirt and slacks uniform was seated behind the desk talking quietly into a landline telephone.

The door to the bedroom opened, and another young man with mussed hair emerged escorting a young woman dressed in a tight, shiny blue minidress. Her enhanced breasts threatened to spill out the front, as she stumbled in her high black fuck-me pumps as the man guided her gently by the elbow. *This is how porn stars dress to go out for the night.* She looked at me as they passed.

"Hi," she said with a day-drinker's giggle, the scent of whiskey competing with her sweet perfume. I returned a nod, and the man guided her through the open front door. I could hear that giggle all the way to the elevator.

Rudy went to the man behind the desk, who produced a key fob from a drawer and handed it to Rudy. Rudy turned back to the door with barely a blip in his pace. "Let's go," he said, and the Rudy-and-Jake parade commenced again back down the hall.

As we waited for another elevator car, I asked, "So, you guys use a hotel room for an office?"

"Yeah," said Rudy. By his tone, the only thing missing from his answer was "you fucking idiot."

When we reached the subterranean garage, Rudy led me to a sleek black sedan. It had the glossy look of having just been waxed.

"You can use it for personal business, but keep track of the mileage," Rudy said. He used the key fob to unlock the doors, then handed it to me. He went to the passenger side. "Your building charges for parking, but the company'll reimburse you."

"You know where I live?"

"Yeah," said Rudy, with that "fucking idiot" bent again. "Get in."

I got behind the wheel and, after a quick primer from Rudy, drove the two of us around Hollywood until I felt comfortable. (My theory on forgetfulness turned out to be right.)

"What's the name of this company, anyway?" I asked, pulling up to the club.

"Fly-By-Night Enterprises," he said, his tone suddenly affable. I chuckled. "But that might change," Rudy added.

My guard went up and down like a periscope at the rapid shifts in Rudy's demeanor, but I forged ahead. I wanted to keep things on the right foot. "Why's that?" I asked, making sure to sound polite.

"Cause Eric wants to. That's why."

In the span of fifteen minutes, Rudy had gone from brusque to impatient to cordial to irritated. A mercurial personality. Hard to anticipate.

"OK. Just want to know what to say if somebody asks where I work."

Rudy looked at me, something simmering behind his unnervingly dark eyes. "You got a PA?"

"PA" is convict-speak for Parole Agent, and now his attitude was beginning to make sense. Rudy had done time. Behind the walls were men you just steered clear of, because you never knew what would set them off. An inability to rein in their reactions is often what landed them in prison to begin with. Rudy appeared to have the earmarks of an impulse control problem.

"Yes," I said evenly. "I have a parole agent. I'll see him again in a couple weeks down by where I live. I already told him about this job." I monitored how long it took Rudy to absorb that, and then settle back into normalcy. Not too long. But why did Eric have this live wire on the payroll? "You need a ride somewhere?" I asked.

"No," Rudy said. He handed me a business card. "Eric's home address is on the back. Somethin' else." He pulled an iPhone from his inside pocket. "Company phone. You use this for all company business. We only call you on that so keep it with you. You start tomorrow morning. Nine o'clock. Don't be late."

With that, Rudy climbed out of the car, closing the door a little harder than necessary. Instead of going back into the hotel, he jaywalked across Vine, then got into another dark sedan that I hadn't noticed. The windows were so tinted I couldn't see the driver. The car pulled away and disappeared into city traffic.

I inspected the iPhone. I wondered if it was too late to return the Xiaomi. *Fuck it, it's paid for. I'll keep it, just in case.* I checked the glove compartment, finding nothing more interesting than an owner's manual. Then I opened the center console. Empty. I tapped the screen above the radio controls, and it illuminated with a pleasant cool glow.

"OK darlin'," I said to no one but the car. "Let's see how you do outside the neighborhood."

# CHAPTER

# 14

WHEN ERIC SAID he spent his days going from one end of town to the other, the dude wasn't kidding. Over the past six, now going on seven weeks, we'd visited every corner of LA County, made a couple of trips to Anaheim, and even ventured once as far east as Palm Springs. It was like the kid had a piece of too many businesses to count.

But Eric had kept his word. I had a job. He'd even signed a statement confirming I was employed full-time, which, along with my slightly increasing bank account, was enough for a landlord to rent me a furnished studio apartment downtown, secured parking included. With a job and a place of my own, in all practical terms, I was on my feet.

At my next meeting with Sanchez, he informed me that employment didn't absolve me of our obligatory monthly get-togethers, and it was my responsibility to report any conflicts to him sooner than later, so we could reschedule in a timely fashion.

On my way out of that meeting, he asked, "You got anything else you want to tell me?"

"Like what?"

"How's it being back in LA? Any old memories bothering you?"

I thought that was weird, but when your PA asks you a question, you're expected to answer.

"All kinds of 'em," I said. "But I'm handling it."

He stared at me for a moment, his ruddy face like stone. "Well, you let me know if anything comes up you want to talk about," he said, and went back to his paperwork.

My mornings now consisted of rising around six, working out in the basement gym, and heading out to pick up Eric. If I woke early enough, I'd swing by and see Carla, have her bring some dish I hadn't sampled yet (though I was running out of those), and see if my flirtation skills were improving. It seemed they were. On the days she wore a button-up shirt she would lean over the table just enough for me to glimpse her cleavage. I wished I could figure out what to do about it, but taking the next step was a skill I had definitely lost along the way. Though she seemed to be patient with me, I hoped those skills would return before she lost all interest.

Eric's Echo Park home was a restored craftsman just a few blocks north of Sunset that had been updated with solar panels on the roof, and some kind of low emission air conditioning.

I'd pull into the driveway and ensure the car's AC was running to cool down the interior. Eric hadn't requested that, I'd just done it one day, and he decided that's how he wanted the car to feel every time he got in. I would text him when I arrived, and receive a text back for the address that would be our first stop.

When Eric would emerge from the house, he was often already deep into a call by way of the earbuds that seemed permanently plugged into his skull. He always had an expensive-looking natural leather bag that doubled as a briefcase slung over his shoulder. I'd get out and open the rear door for him. He'd nod a greeting and slide into the back seat. Like clockwork.

One time, I saw Angela watching through the front window. She was wearing a man's dress shirt and holding a mug. I waved to her. She waved back, and then disappeared. I hadn't seen or spoken to her since their beach talk, and I was surprised by the pang of jealousy I felt, but shoved it down.

The stops we made over the course of the day tended to be short, around thirty to forty-five minutes, and then off to the next. Eric would go inside some establishment, an eatery or bar, while I waited in the car, the engine idling to keep the AC going.

I'd use that time to check emails on my Xiaomi, of which there weren't many. (Carla had advised that if I use two phones, to keep them separated by business and personal.) I caught up on the news. And I acquainted myself with social media; seemed to me a lot of people had way too much time on their hands. But I also understood how easy it was to fall into that black hole. Once I was startled by Eric's return because I was transfixed by a video of a dog bathing itself in the family shower.

"Sorry," I said. "Didn't see you coming."

"How could you? What with that fucking phone in your face," he'd joked.

I was beginning to see why people said those things were like crack for the eyes. Given my history of addictive behavior, I resolved to limit my time on it.

The clubs were closed during the day, giving Eric and his various partners a chance to hold their meetings in peace. It was like that seven to ten hours a day, depending. At the end of the workday, Eric might want to make a stop at his gym, where he kept a locker with a change of clothes, in case he needed to go straight to one of his clubs afterward. But mostly he would want to shower at home. At that point, it was quitting time for me. Eric would get himself to whichever night spot he was in charge of that evening. I have to say, I was impressed by the man's work ethic, but I also had to wonder when he slept. Maybe he was one of those guys that got by on four hours a night.

Rudy seemed to be Eric's right-hand man. But outside of the occasional text or phone call to inform me of a change of location to meet Eric, I had no interaction with him or the other employees.

Even the solo errands I was sent on were benign and unchallenging, and I'd rarely leave the car. I'd drive somewhere, a club or office building, and someone would bring out a package, or maybe a crate of fresh fruit. I would press the button to open the trunk, the nameless person would put the item in and shut the lid, and I would deliver it where someone else would come out and retrieve it.

I drove. That was it.

My working hours would sometimes stretch into the night. Eric explained that his kind of business had always been driven by a loose collection of investors, most of them legit and aboveboard. But there were some who would use their nightclub investment as cover for whatever money they were trying to hide from someone. Alimony to a soon-to-be-ex-wife, or an attorney's bill that had ballooned to the point of being impossible to pay without taking a second mortgage. As bars and restaurants still took in much of their proceeds in cash, those investors could likewise be quietly repaid in kind.

The mutual benefit was that it would not leave a paper trail. The investor could take the bundles of cash, and still claim the investment hadn't yet paid off. The business could write down their profit, thereby lowering their projected taxes. A simple bending of the rules that many cash-heavy businesses employed that handed the parties a win-win (except, of course, for the ex-wife, the attorney, and the government). Eric never asked me to deliver those envelopes. Only he or a partner would do that.

Some of the revenue came from an even seedier source. One night I drove Eric to an Italian restaurant, a long-established red sauce joint near Beverly Hills. This time, Eric asked me to follow him inside.

It was one of those family-friendly spots you find in every major city. Dark with twinkling lights, Chianti fiasco bottles in straw baskets hanging from the ceiling, and lots of hearty pasta and antipasto. The pleasant hum of Rat Pack standards emanated from invisible speakers. Eric greeted the maître d', a slender man with coiffed hair and a pleasant, classically Neapolitan face.

The man pointed across the sparsely attended dining room to another well-dressed man seated at a table with what looked to me like his family. He could've been the host's older brother.

It reminded me of my own family. My father had owned a casual family restaurant like this. Working there gave me the experience that helped get me hired at Bonetti's back in the day. (Who could have guessed that would lead to such a train wreck?) My sister, Jessica, cut me off entirely when I got into trouble. I guess she felt the pain I'd caused our family deserved total abandonment. Our prior lack of interaction meant that her absence didn't have much effect on me. The hard part was my folks.

I'd written to them a lot from jail, before and during the trial. I'd tried to explain that my failings really had nothing to do with them, that I owned every mistake I'd made, but they just weren't the kind of people to absolve themselves. They'd raised me, and I'd fucked up, so it had to be on them, somehow. Once in Folsom, I let them know that, for my own good, I should probably stop writing, but I left the door open for them to, if they chose. My mother did for a while, but then her letters trailed off, probably because I didn't have it in me to reply back then. I wish I had. Another regret. They both died before the end of my sentence, and I wasn't allowed to attend either of the funerals.

The man rose to greet us when he saw us coming. He shook hands with Eric, sized me up for a moment, then took Eric by the arm and guided the three of us toward the kitchen.

By the time I came through the swinging doors behind them, the man was already pleading with Eric.

"These people just show up," he said, in his slight Italian accent. "Eat what they want, drink the bar dry, and never fucking *pay*! My regulars are scared of them." He indicated the empty dining room we'd just left. "You see!"

"Are they here now?" Eric asked the man.

"They're always here! Tonight they're on the patio."

Eric sighed. "OK. Give me a minute." He cocked his head for me to follow him.

Eric led us back into the dining room and then turned down a hallway toward the rear of the building. I could hear what sounded like the cacophony of a party fading up as we got closer. We came to an outdoor dining area.

The night sky was blocked by a large canvas canopy strung over us. Tall space heaters, unused in this warmer weather, were lined against one of three ivy-covered walls. More fiasco bottles dangled from anywhere they could be hung, including the crisscrossed strings of white lights below the canopy. Any other time this space would be a cozy retreat from the world.

The small bar setup was manned by an attractive, but sullen, young woman. Her complexion suggested she shared a Mediterranean background with the owner. The tables and chairs that, on a normal night, would be filled with diners were shoved outward in a clumsy circle to create a makeshift dance floor. The music was too loud to carry on a simple conversation.

The improvised space was crowded with smarmy, overdressed men in shiny silk suits, with stick pins and bright silk ties. The heavy grease in their hair had run onto their jacket collars, creating dark rings. Most of them carried themselves in a lumbering attempt at what I guess they called dancing. Awkward moves that explained the uneven border the chairs had been kicked into. Terpsichoreans, they weren't.

Over the din, I could hear the crack of a highly polished shoe against wood every time one of these goombahs would bump into a wicker chair leg. Their clothes, though expensive, would've looked better on just about anyone else, but these mooks looked like they'd done their own tailoring. Their ravioli-fed bellies didn't help; their coat buttons strained against the mound of gut that dimpled over their belts.

Their women, on the other hand, were the personification of dainty. Compared to their husbands (or sugar daddies, who knew which) they moved like delicate dolls while protecting their tiny feet from being crushed under the Florsheims and wingtips. They mostly wore patterned sundresses, the bottom halves ballooning under tight belts as their partners twirled them with the music. One couple reminded me of a dense-looking Andre the Giant and a miniature Gina Lollobrigida, with heavy makeup and hair done up like her inspiration's 1950s gravity-defying glory. It was like a West Coast version of *Goodfellas*.

Eric surveyed the room until his eyes landed on a mustachioed guy with curly hair held down with grease, sporting a shiny gold tie under a shinier blue jacket. He was dancing with a half full martini glass in his hand and, between the grease and the sweat, the ring behind his neck was growing with every passing minute. But when he saw Eric, he stopped moving, and his smile disappeared.

Eric turned to me and shouted, "Stay here, but watch my back."

He moved toward the crowd. What the hell was he doing? Standing there alone, I felt a growing alarm that whatever was going on here could go sideways any second. I may be a free man, but I wouldn't be for long if I got involved in some dust-up that got someone hurt.

Greasy Man left his buxom date behind and met Eric halfway. His date, who was dressed in a matching shiny black strapless cocktail dress, raised her hands in a what-the-hell gesture, then headed to the bar, her shoulders drooped in disappointment.

I could only make out bits and pieces, but it sounded to me like Eric was explaining the protocols of restaurant ownership to the guy.

Eric: "You can't expect . . . (unintelligible) . . . no profits coming in!"
Greasy Man: "What do you mean? We're . . . (unintelligible) . . . my investment covers that."
Eric: "Usually an invest . . . (unintelligible) . . . like everybody else."
Greasy Man: "I'm not everybody else!"

Then Eric leaned in to say something directly into Greasy Man's ear. Eric's head was angled so that the man could see over his shoulder, giving him a direct line of sight to me. Eric glanced back at me, then he looked at Greasy Man again, and said something else I couldn't catch. Greasy

Man kept his eyes on me, as if he was figuring the odds of something, and concluded that they didn't favor him.

He turned and went over to his date, picked up her jacket, and held it up for her to put it on. She shook her head, apparently not wanting to do whatever it was he'd told her they were about to. He angrily tossed her jacket onto the paver floor, and then reached over the bar. The music came to a sudden stop, giving rise to audible protests and murmurs. Shuffling feet slowed to a confused standstill, as there was no longer any rhythm to guide their cumbersome movements.

Greasy Man announced, "Party's over!" He looked around at the gaping maws staring back at him, as if they needed instruction on how to exit. "Now!" By this time his girlfriend had picked up her jacket from the floor. He grabbed her by the arm and practically dragged her across the room and down the hallway. The crowd began to disperse and follow suit.

The Andre lookalike waited for his dancing partner to gather her things. While she did that, he stared at me. He was obviously Greasy Man's muscle, and he wanted me to know it. His date returned to him, and as they passed by me, Andre held his eyes on mine. It was a jailhouse challenge. If I took it, there would be no going back. Only one of us would be left standing, and the other would never get back up. I opted to look at Eric as Andre went by, his eyes never leaving me. I just hoped I'd never see him again.

Eric watched this silent exchange, then said, "Let's get outta here."

We went back to the front dining room, where Eric peeled off to speak again to the owner. The man looked worried, but Eric spoke quietly to him, as he patted him on the shoulder. The anxiety evident on the owner's face began to diminish. By the time Eric said goodnight, the owner was looking relieved.

Back in the car, heading east on Olympic toward Eric's home, I asked, "So, what was that about?"

"Why do you ask?"

"Because whatever you said to that guy included me."

Eric leaned forward and folded his arms on the back of the passenger seat. I glanced over. He was looking straight ahead, as if thinking about how to answer.

"I told him who you are."

I frowned. "What do you mean?"

"I said, 'You see that guy? That's Jake Ferguson. He just got out of prison, and now he works for me. Maybe you've heard of him.'" Eric looked at me. "Guess he had."

I let the words sink in. It was true there was nothing I could do about my notoriety in some circles, but I never figured I would qualify as an enforcer. "So, you used me to threaten him. Is that it?"

"Oh, I didn't threaten him, I just told him who you are. But yeah, the message is, there's an easy way, and there's a hard way. Choice was his." He sat back in his seat. "They want to invest in a small business? Sure, their money's as green as anybody's." He looked at me in the rearview mirror. "But I'll be goddamned if their wise guy bullshit's going to come between me and my profits."

"So those guys *are* mafia."

"Low-level wannabes. He thought his piss-ant investment meant he could stick his hand in the cookie jar.

No fucking way. There's people in line ahead of him. Including me."

"It's not like I could've taken them all," I said.

"I played my ace. Like I said, I didn't *threaten* him. I just told him you were my Luca Brasi and if anything went down, he'd be the first to drop." He laughed. "And he bought it! I swear I could smell him shit his pants."

I shook my head. I knew what a perceived grievance, a show of disrespect, meant to people like that.

"He's got a bulldog of his own, you know," I said. "He was the one eyeballing me on the way out."

"Don't worry. Those idiots couldn't find a tomato in a caprese salad. But just to make sure, I'll have a talk with their benefactors." He paused. "Yeah, I know them too, and those dumbfucks tonight wouldn't make a move without their say so." He yawned. "I'm tired. Take me home."

"Can I ask you something?"

"Shoot," Eric said, his eyes closed.

I had to think about how to say this. "Between Rudy and the other guys, looks like you got a pretty hard-ass crew yourself."

Eric opened his eyes, looked at me in the mirror. "Crew?"

"That's what they are, right? You need something done, they do it."

Eric smirked. "Fair enough," he said.

"So? What do you need me for? Besides driving, I mean."

Eric smiled, let out a small chuckle. "They're ugly. And you're tall, dark, and handsome. You remind me of those twin bodyguards in the last *Godfather* movie. Anybody looks at my 'crew,' as you put it, they think they know what to expect. Then they see *you* . . . and they don't know what's coming." After a beat, he said, "You're just for show. OK?"

"Does Angela know you hang around guys like that?"

He shut his eyes. "I won't tell if you don't."

# CHAPTER 15

**THEN**

**2000**

**Six months before the robbery.**

THE TWO NIGHTS with the Texas Roses are what gave Damon the idea.

"We could make some real *cha-ching* off this," he'd said. "I mean, this town is just busting with horny older women."

He wasn't wrong, if my experience at Bonetti's was any indication. I could easily find my way into the bed of an attractive, willing bar customer at least once a week. Sometimes more. But if Damon really wanted me to do this, then I needed to know what it would do for me, if anything. And if he hadn't lied about how long he'd been at it, then he should be able to share some numbers.

That afternoon we were on the deck of the high-rise apartment he'd just rented in Century City, with its unobstructed view of the famous office tower from *Die Hard*.

I opened my beer. "What are we talking about here?"

He smiled and twisted the top off the tiny glass cocaine vial he always carried with him. "You don't see me living in my car anymore, do you?"

He did a blast using the silver coke spoon he wore on a chain around his neck. He offered me one, and I took it. I sniffed hard and rubbed my finger across my nostrils to clear away the excess powder. That first hit of the day invariably seared the inside of my nose.

Vague as it was, Damon had come up with a kind of plan. "I grew up with this guy. Real operator. Pimps out some of the girls in the old 'hood. Says we can land some here, and some up in Vegas. That way we're never doing business in one place too long." And, he went on, we would work as a team. "We're some good-lookin' dudes, man. Some horny old bitch is gonna want one of us. And we can do it all at Bonetti's. I work the floor, you work the bar. We never miss one that way. In Nevada, we could just troll the nice places until we find somebody. Like those Texans." He paused for effect. "But older." He laughed again.

Once he settled down, I said, "You didn't answer my question."

He sniffed up another spoonful of coke. "One night is five hun' to a grand. We split fifty-fifty."

"Five hundred to a thousand dollars? Are you serious?"

"As a heart attack, my friend. That's the going rate. All-nighters are even more."

If that was true, then I could pack my nose all I wanted. And with a line of good blow, I could fuck all night. In the beginning, anyway. That was before I learned what the long-term effects of cocaine could have on the libido.

"Angela would fucking kill me if she found out."

"You mean kill you for fucking!" Damon laughed again, then raised his hands in the air. "How? You don't live together. You work nights, and she works days. When was the last time she slept over? And what's wrong with a couple buddies taking a trip to Vegas to blow off steam?"

"You've really thought this out," I said.

"It's genius! And all cash. None of that stupid put-it-on-a-credit-card drug shit that coulda' got those guys arrested."

Maybe the coke rush was lending a hand, but my head started to spin with possibilities. Damon held up the spoon, and I took another hit. The phone rang inside the apartment, and he went inside to answer it. I ran everything through my head while I had a minute to myself.

Angela and I didn't cohabitate, and like many struggling young men I knew, I'd used the excuse that I needed to commit to my career before fully committing to a relationship. What a cop-out. Maybe she'd accommodated my immaturity because I might eventually see the light and *grow the fuck up*. Maybe she knew before I did that being a large man doesn't make you any less insecure. Too bad for me that I didn't realize it until I was locked in a cage with no way to do anything about it. But I wasn't thinking about that yet.

"What the fuck!" Damon was yelling at whomever had called. "You ever hear of a job? I have one. I'll pick him up tomorrow."

I heard the phone hit the cradle hard, and Damon came back out on the deck.

"Who was that?"

"My ex," he said as he dropped back into his seat. He looked frustrated.

"I didn't know you had an ex."

"Yeah, well, it's not like that. We're not married or anything. I knew her in school. Bitch thinks I owe her."

"For what?"

He shook his head. "Never mind. What were we talking about?"

I wondered what Damon's ex could want that would make him so agitated. But if his relationship with her was anything like the one he had with his family, I figured it was probably best to leave it where Jesus flang it.

"Making our dreams come true," I said.

My acting dreams had died out some weeks before. That ambition had been like a lighthouse in the fog, guiding me to the next remote possibility. And when that ambition died, the dream died with it. But that would have been news to my family. They understood that since my agent was murdered, I hadn't yet been able to work up the drive to find a new one. They were satisfied that I had a steady bartending job, and that would float me until I figured out my next move. And Angela, bless her, hadn't pushed too hard since Harold had died, either.

I hadn't told anyone, but that casting guy grabbing my dick in the office was the last straw. And then he had the nerve to spread around that I, the "young Eastwood," was a loose cannon. That I had attacked him in his office over some innocuous "misunderstanding." The scumbag was probably just trying to head off some nasty rumors about him. Thankfully, Harold hadn't believed it, but there's always those who will. Gossip like that spreads fast, and Harold's efforts on my behalf would become that much harder because of it. Even though he insisted he thought it was bullshit, it's always bothered me that that was one of the last things Harold heard about me before he died.

*If all they want from me is my body, then I should at least get something in return.* That's what I'd always heard women say. And isn't sex supposed to cut both ways? That's what I told myself. More likely, I was just plain lost, and under the delusion that this was a clear direction I could go in. *Maybe I could make something out of it? Save up, start a business, move away.* Anything but feel like the failure I'd come to believe I was. Sounds so trite now. I was an addict who didn't yet know just how low I was willing to go to feed my addiction.

I took a sip of my beer and looked at the *Die Hard* tower, imagining Bruce Willis triumphing over the evil forces stacked against him. "Let's do it," I said.

The emotional refuge that coke provided me with was just so damn expensive. Spending over a hundred dollars every night for a gram of blow that barely lasted until morning really added up. And the last couple months I'd struggled to make the rent. If I wanted to keep the lifestyle I'd become accustomed to, then Damon's idea was a viable solution with nary a downside. More pussy. More money. More dope. I actually told myself that. What an idiot.

If there's a guidebook on how to do this, they kept it from me. I didn't know my first was even a potential client.

It was a busy Thursday night, customers stacked three at the bar, all dining tables full, and everything was backed up because everyone was taking their time eating and drinking. On a night like that, patience can run short for someone ready to fork over top dollar for a middling meal and a glimpse of a movie star.

A woman came in by herself, not to eat, but to enjoy a relaxing cocktail in a nice atmosphere. She stood and waited politely for a stool, finally snagging a seat when a rowdy party of six were led to their table.

"Good evening," I said. She looked at me through oversized glasses. She had thinning blonde hair, and wore a tasteful floral print spring dress and a cardigan sweater she'd draped loosely over her shoulders. I pegged her for about forty, forty-five years old.

"Hello," she said with a pleasant smile.

"What can I get you?"

"Do you have Vox vodka?"

"I'm afraid not, but have you tried Belvedere? Very comparable and, I think, a shade better."

"That sounds good. I'll have a Gibson, straight up."

I smiled and did my best to hold eye contact. "Straight up, comin' up." If she got the entendre, she didn't show it.

After I silently chastised myself for such a clumsy opener, I set the drink on the bar napkin in front of her.

"Thank you," she said, in a voice that, in the din of the crowd, sounded barely above a whisper.

"You're very welcome," I said, and she immediately averted her eyes from mine. She was shy. And, I thought, a little attracted to me.

"Not many people order a Gibson these days," I said, pointing to the three pearl onions soaking in the vodka.

Her lips turned up a little, and she took a sip. Still, her eyes couldn't stay on mine for longer than a second or two. Before she could put the glass back down, a guy dressed in boots, jeans, a western shirt (snap buttons and all), and a damn kerchief tied around his neck pushed his way to the bar next to her.

"Heineken!" he yelled, startling the woman with the Gibson.

I brought the bottle of beer and a glass and set them on the bar. All he was missing was a ten-gallon hat over his tight blonde haircut. He ignored the glass and took a gulp straight from the bottle. Already he was doing his best to chat up Ms. Gibson.

"I'm new out here," I heard him say. "Just quit my job at the ranch, thought I'd try my hand in Hollywood."

*Yeah, good luck, cowboy. Been there, done that.*

He blathered on about how lonely it can be in LA, and how he just wants to find some friends he can depend on, and who can depend on him "when they need me." He gave her a long stare. "I'm someone you can count on," he said with a country twang I thought sounded forced.

Ms. Gibson nodded politely between sips of her cocktail. The toll of having to give attention to this guy was starting to show. I got called away to mix another drink, and by the time I came back, Ms. Gibson was giving me a pleading look that said "Save me."

Some of these oafs had come in before. Maybe I was hyper-aware now because Damon and I had decided on our own hustle, but this guy was trying to horn in on our territory. And to make it worse, he really thought this aw-shucks act was going to nail it for him. Watching him was like a bad spoof of *Midnight Cowboy*.

I leaned over the bar. "Excuse me, sir." He stopped mid-sentence and looked at me, his jaw drooped open. "I'm going to have to ask you not to bother the other customers."

His face contorted with confusion. "What, you mean me?"

"Yes, sir. Tell you what, your drink's on me, but I'm going to ask you to leave."

"Oh, yeah?" He looked at Ms. Gibson, then back at me. "I think you need to mind your own business."

"I'm the bartender, sir. This is my business." I stood up straight, never taking my eyes off his, as his gaze followed me up to my full height. Looking down at him, I said calmly, "Please leave."

With that, I could see his attempt at machismo wither right in front of us. Ms. Gibson watched silently, her drink held aloft as if floating in space.

"And don't come back," I said, with the finality of a goodbye.

His face fell into disappointment. Without another word of protest, he set his bottle down too hard on the bar, forcing a small plume of beer out the top that splashed onto the wood. We could hear the heels of his cowboy boots all the way to the front door.

Ms. Gibson watched him go, then turned to me.

"Sorry about that," I said. "He should know better than to hit on a classy woman like you."

She smiled, and I could see her cheeks blush in the flattering light.

“Thank you,” she said. Then averted her eyes again. When she took another sip of her drink, I noticed she wasn’t wearing a wedding ring. Then she surprised me. “So, what do you like to do when you get off work?”

Maybe she’d come in looking to connect with a man on a romantic level, or maybe she just needed someone to take care of her physical needs and Cowboy McFuddles had given her the idea, but I never asked. Damon saw us talking and inserted himself into the conversation. Before long, he’d arranged for me to meet her at her hotel, a luxury boutique spot on Wilshire near Westwood. She became my first client. I would see her about every month when she came in from Chicago on business, which had something to do with advertising.

Within a few weeks, Damon started pushing to make those occasional trips to Vegas. Why was a no-brainer. Prostitution is legal in Nevada. Not within Las Vegas city limits, mind you, but that didn’t stop anybody. If anything, unless you hung a neon sign on the Strip, the authorities mostly looked the other way. But I just didn’t think we needed it. Bonetti’s had proven to be a lucrative hunting ground, and those contacts would sometimes refer us to friends and colleagues looking for the same diversions. Besides, I was already lying enough to Angela about the fewer nights we were spending together.

Once we worked out the wrinkles, a typical transaction would go something like this: A single woman, or a pair of friends, would take a seat at the bar, usually to wait for a dinner table. I’d take the drink order, and once I’d delivered it, I’d start some small talk. “Haven’t seen you here before . . .” “Your hair is beautiful . . .” “You can’t be *possibly* be a mother! You could've been in my high school class . . ." Before they'd left, I had their hotel room number or their home address, depending, and a time was set for the rendezvous. Meanwhile, Damon would be running the same game from his waiter position on the dining floor. If I didn't close the deal, but the interest was there, then he would take them the rest of the way.

We kept it going for months. I wasn't getting as much sleep as I should, but what cokehead does? To me, that was an acceptable trade off. The problem I had was my income-to-expense ratio was all fucked up. Thanks to my burgeoning drug use, the more money I made, the more blow I shoveled up my nose. I wasn't saving, or planning, or coming up with ideas for a business. I was just fucking and getting high. The only "acting" I did anymore was moonlighting as a bartender and, though the guilt was already starting to pile up, pretending to be a boyfriend to Angela.

One afternoon I woke up to find a stream of blood had run down my chin and all over my sheets. A blood vessel inside my nose had burst from all the corrosive chemicals I'd snorted through it and flowed uninhibited while I slept. I had a client to see that night after work, so instead of going to a doctor, I took a shower, threw out the sheets, made some coffee, and did some more coke.

Not long after that, I was mixing a customer's Bloody Mary, wondering if doing those Vegas trips just might be worth it after all, and what lie to tell Angela if I did, when I heard Damon call my name. He cocked his head toward the front door. "Look who's here."

Mr. and Mrs. Cavanaugh had just arrived for one of their intermittent visits. They always drove up to the valet in a cherry two-tone Rolls Royce Corniche. In their late fifties or early-sixties, they would both be well-dressed in understated finery that only suggested their wealth, good taste, and conservatism.

Mr. Cavanaugh always wore a tailored suit with a silk tie and stick pin. But his hale physicality was in stark contrast to his wife's frail appearance. Her hair always looked salon-coiffed, and her makeup professionally applied, but she never wore a dress, preferring custom pants and jacket over a frilly blouse. A fine diamond necklace hung around her neck, and an expensive looking handbag always dangled from her elbow. Her one allowance to ostentation was her wedding ring. That thing looked like a museum piece.

"They asked for you," said Damon.

"Who?" I said. "Them?"

"He called me today," he said. "Last minute. Said they'd make it worth our while."

"How'd they even know?" I said. I'd never pegged these two for players.

"Guess they knew who to ask," said Damon.

I looked over at the approaching couple. "I'm not doing him."

"It's for her," Damon said reassuringly. "But he might watch. He offered double."

I felt ambushed. It's not like last minute opportunities didn't present themselves, especially in the workplace, but usually there was some notice before engaging with a new customer. The Cavanaughs had never indicated they were into something like this.

They were a whole different breed from the typical customer that came here. No one knew how or where they'd gotten their money, and they weren't volunteering it. They lived in Riverside, a city fifty miles east of LA, mostly known for light industry. Its economy produced everything from aircraft and automobile parts to food products and medical devices. Hardly glamorous, but obviously lucrative for some.

The Cavanaughs would customarily have a drink at the bar before dinner, and I greeted them as Mr. C. pulled out a stool for his wife. Mrs. C. gave me a longer than usual smile, appraising me as she settled in unlike she ever had before. For the first time, I noticed discolored lines between her teeth, the kind that develop in a lifelong smoker. She ordered her usual, a down-market vodka martini with a twist. He would always have a scotch and soda from the well. For all the care taken in their presentation, they sure weren't picky about their booze.

Not like the Hollywood showoffs we served. One studio executive insisted on drinking his special tequila from a tiny pony glass, but with a martini glass full of crushed ice rimmed with lime wedges next to it. He would take a sip, then chew on a lime wedge, while bragging about the next expected studio hit (that often wasn't). I always got a kick out of teasing the wannabe copycats that would come in all full of themselves and announce, "I want a tequila the way (the studio executive) has his!"

"Sorry," I'd say, with mock confusion. "I don't know the man." And the copycat would visibly deflate, and settle for a beer instead. I admit that, after all the cruel rejections I'd endured, that little bit of revenge felt good.

Mr. Cavanaugh would sometimes betray a hint of impatience or dissatisfaction with Mrs. Cavanaugh. They came to LA every month or two, and their conversations tended to cover the same territory. One time, Mr. C. berated his wife right in front of me. "Do you always have to bore the bejeezus out of everyone?" he'd said, loud enough for anyone nearby to hear. She would shrug, wave her hand like she was swatting away a gnat, and sip her martini.

"You ever get the feeling he's just waiting for her to die?" one of the waiters said to me one night after the couple had been seated at a table. I had to wonder.

The Cavanaughs liked to stay a couple nights at the famed Beverly Hills Hotel, also known as The Pink Palace. In the 1960s and '70s, the hotel had been a center of Hollywood bustle. Many stars, bored between jobs, would lounge around the pool all day, their drinking, smoking, and carousing contributing to an early demise. Starlets would flirt with studio heads and agents, hoping to find that big break (and the bungalows were always available for an afternoon "negotiation"). And every evening the cocktail hour in the iconic Polo Lounge hosted any number of luminaries, socializing, doing business, but mostly being seen. Those days died with the studio system, and the demise of those attached to it. The place was still a first-class establishment, but now it catered mostly to well-heeled tourists and oil-rich Middle Easterners. It was no longer even owned by Americans, but by the Sultan of Brunei.

The Cavanaughs always talked about how much they enjoyed the bungalows, which is where they were staying this night. As they were leaving after dinner, Mr. Cavanaugh came by the bar. "We'll be in bungalow twelve," he said pleasantly, then joined his wife at the front door. She gave me a flirtatious, knowing smile as they left.

Before departing the restaurant, I washed off the night's work in the men's room so as to not smell like a bar rag. Damon was waiting for me in the parking lot.

"I'll drive you," he said.

"Expect this to be quick?" I asked.

"I need my share for something first thing tomorrow." Damon had been like that lately. Ramping up the work, wanting his cash right away. I suspected he was turning tricks on his own, outside our agreement, but I didn't care. I was growing tired of this, and despite the promise, there never seemed to be enough money. There had to be a better way.

Damon steered into the hotel's meandering driveway. "I'd meet you in the Polo Lounge," he said, "but I think they'll keep you past closing. I'll park on Benedict Canyon and wait for you there. Now go give her a night she'll never forget."

I walked through the lobby and headed for the courtyard pool. The eyes of the employees were glued to me as I went by, trying to look like I belonged there. I found my way through the winding paths to Bungalow 12. When I got there, I pressed my ear to the door and listened. No music, no voices, nothing. Maybe they changed their minds and went to bed. I was about to change mine, but I remembered how far behind I was on this month's rent. I knocked lightly on the door.

I heard a swish of fabric, as if someone jumped up from a chair, then footsteps. The door opened and Mr. Cavanaugh greeted me.

"You made it," he said cheerfully, leading with a wide smile. He'd shed his jacket and tie, and his sleeves were rolled up. What looked like another scotch and soda was in his hand. "Please, come in."

I stepped into a sumptuous suite larger than most homes I'd been in (save for the more affluent of my clientele). Much of this business took place in nicer hotels, but this place was off the charts. The furniture, art, and wallpaper were in the French tradition. I could see into a full-sized kitchen (but given the first-class room service, who would ever need it?). A curved wooden staircase led to a floor above.

"Like a drink?" asked Mr. Cavanaugh.

"Just some water, please," I said.

"Of course." Mr. Cavanaugh went into the kitchen. I could hear the refrigerator door open, a bottle top twisted, an ice maker engaged, and ice filling a glass. Mr. Cavanaugh came back with a tumbler of bubbling water. He'd even perched a lemon wedge on the rim. "Here you are," he said, handing it to me. "Shall we?" he said, sweeping his hand toward the stairwell. I followed him up.

At the top of the stairs was the bedroom. More French. More space. And the light was dim, coming only from the nightstand next to the four-poster bed.

Mrs. Cavanaugh was under the covers, the bedspread pulled up to her naked shoulders. She looked even scrawnier, her frame barely forming a rise in the shape of a body.

"Please," said Mr. Cavanaugh, a wide grin of expectation on his face, sweeping his hand again, this time in the direction of Mrs. Cavanaugh. "I'll be over here." He took a seat in a plush armchair across the room. He leaned back and crossed his legs, the striped silk upholstery making only a hint of sound.

I stepped to the bedside, took a sip of water, and set the glass on the nightstand. Mrs. Cavanaugh's eyes roamed my body, her breath gathering steam. She reached out as if to take my hand, but then her thin fingers deftly unzipped my trousers. She'd done this before.

"Take it out," she whispered.

I looked over to Mr. Cavanaugh. He was watching intently, his glass of scotch perched near his lips, as if something had distracted him before he took a drink. I had never had an audience for my services before. Only a client and myself. First time for everything.

I reached into my open fly, and presented myself to her. Mrs. Cavanaugh drew a breath. I could smell the tart aroma of her cigarettes with her exhale. She leaned in and took me into her mouth.

"That's it," I heard her husband say from across the room. "Deeper."

Mrs. Cavanaugh pushed her face into my groin and held it there. I could tell she wasn't breathing. I hoped I'd still get paid if she passed out with my cock in her mouth. She finally drew back, gasping for air. "Come here," she said, and pushed back to make room for me.

"Take off your clothes first," Mr. Cavanaugh said.

I stripped and pulled back the sheet to reveal her naked body. Her flesh hung limp from her bones. I climbed in next to her, and she began stroking me to make me hard.

But her cold fingers, cigarette breath, and general lack of sexiness worked against it. I may have been a gigolo, but my customers always had something attractive, some sexiness, about them. Sure, they were older, but even then, physical fitness in LA was kind of a requirement. That went a long way toward making this work bearable. Unfortunately, Mrs. Cavanaugh had gone far past that point.

"Turn her over," I heard Mr. Cavanaugh say. I looked down to Mrs. Cavanaugh, who was already beginning to move. "On her hands and knees."

I considered reaching to turn off the lamp on the nightstand, but it was too far away to be done smoothly. By the time I looked back, she was already in position, her naked posterior facing me. I got to my knees to position myself for a coupling.

"Now slap that bitch." I turned to Mr. Cavanaugh, whose face was a twisted combo of anticipation and rage. He'd set his glass on the floor, and he was leaning forward, so he wouldn't miss a thing. His vision never moved from Mrs. Cavanaugh. "I said . . . *hit* that cunt!"

* * *

I dropped into the passenger seat. My stomach was still roiling, and I would've booted right on Damon's dashboard, if I hadn't already yarked in the bushes behind the hotel.

"Hey there, buddy," Damon said. "You look like you could use some chicken soup."

My chest was heaving as if I'd just run a marathon. I'd taken the back way out in order to avoid the disparaging stares of the employees in the lobby, and ran the perimeter of the massive grounds to find Damon as planned. My face felt cold to my own touch, and I turned the rearview mirror to confirm my pallid complexion. "Why didn't you tell me?"

"Tell you what?" said Damon innocently.

"That was a rough trick!"

"C'mon, let's go to Canter's and get some steak and eggs." Even in the darkness I could see Damon hoping to evade a confrontation. He reached for the ignition.

"You start this car, and I'll break your fucking arm," I said.

Damon froze, looking straight out the windshield. Then he leaned back in his seat. He seemed resigned to something. "What do you care?" he said, finally. "They pay better."

"I notice you didn't volunteer," I said.

"They asked for you. She likes big guys, I guess." He looked at me. "What did they make you do?"

I looked down into the blackness of the footwell. "He, uh . . . Cavanaugh . . . he told me to hit her." I shut my eyes. "So, I did."

"She OK?"

I could still hear Mrs. Cavanaugh's whimpering under the sheet. "I don't know," I said.

I could feel Damon shrug. "It's not like they didn't ask for it." He tapped me on the shoulder. "I think you have something for me."

I dug into my trouser pocket and retrieved the thick wad of cash Mr. Cavanaugh had handed me as I left. I sliced off Damon's share and shoved it at him.

"Take it easy, man," he said as he dropped the money into his jacket pocket. "All in a night's work."

"Easy for you to say." I was starting to catch my breath. "You shoulda' told me."

"Would you have done it?"

I didn't answer. I'd already decided this had to stop.

C H A P T E R

# 16

## NOW

BY THE TIME I'd dropped Eric and finally made my way home, all I could think of was sleep.

The discovery that Eric's business mingled with syndicate lowlifes swirled in my head, leaving a sense of . . . I wasn't sure what. I didn't like that bottom-feeding goons, and characters like Rudy, had any proximity to Angela. And there was his crew, peopled with characters like Rudy. But it was none of my business, and certainly not my problem. I decided to worry about it after I'd gotten some shuteye.

I'd made a habit of stopping off at my mailbox in the lobby, though if anything came, it was always junk mail, the kind you receive when you move into a new place. Ads for storage units and moving companies. *A little late, aren't you?* I came off the elevator and went straight to the vintage cluster mailboxes mounted in the lobby wall. I opened the tiny metal door. Empty. I closed and locked it, and turned to find the real surprise of that long day.

Carla was seated in one of the cushioned chairs near the lobby's front door. A magazine from the used stack on the end table next to her was in her hands. She was looking at me, and she wasn't smiling, like she usually did when she saw me.

"We need to talk," she said.

Once inside my sparse apartment, Carla slipped off her jacket and settled into the one armchair. My place came semifurnished, and I could see her scrutinizing the used decor. She wasn't impressed, but she also had too much class to comment.

"You want something to drink?" I asked. "I think all I have is water."

"No, thanks," she said. Her tone was flat, without her usual friendliness. It reminded me of Angela's, when I'd first spoken to her. I don't think I could ever get used to that sound of disappointment. "I guess you're pretty surprised, my showing up here."

"I am," I said. "How did you know where I live?"

"You texted it to me, dummy. Weeks ago."

I frowned. Did I? I must have. Maybe while I was waiting on Eric somewhere. Whatever. She got it somehow. "What's on your mind?"

She looked at me incredulously. "You're kidding, right? You have no idea why I would show up unannounced in the middle of the night."

"Did I do something?"

"It's what you didn't do," she replied, so matter-of-fact, I knew I was missing something. It was obvious to her, but a mystery to me.

I looked at the beige carpeting, as if whatever it was might be found there.

"Oh, for fuck's sake!" she said. "You know, I have a master's in philosophy? UCLA. Full ride. That and a quarter'll won't even buy you a cup of coffee." She paused. "Well, maybe not where I work." She let out a breath. "I should have my head examined." She crossed the room to where I sat on the bed, and stood over me with her hands on her hips. "What am I going to do with you?"

She bent and took my shoulders, looking me in the eye. Then she pushed me down onto the mattress, laying her body flat against me. She softly touched her lips to mine. I hesitated, thinking that there must be some return gesture to be made on my part, but God if I could think of anything. So, I let nature lead me. I returned the kiss, and I felt my face flush. *Jesus, my pulse feels like I just ran a three-minute mile.* We held the kiss for what seemed like a long time. I snuck one eye open, and saw hers were comfortably closed. When I felt her lips part, I mirrored the movement with my own. This was the first time I'd kissed anyone since before my trial. It felt natural, my face against hers, but I couldn't get over the sense that I'd forgotten how to do this right. Her tongue was warm and smooth. I felt my body responding to her. So did Carla, and she answered with a rhythmic pulse of her hips.

My breathing increased. I reached up and filled my hand with her breast. Its fullness was soft, and I could feel her nipple against my palm.

Her fingertips caressed my face, and my heart felt like it was about to crack. And that my dick was about to explode.

She gripped my jaw. "Sinking in yet?" she said.

* * *

When my alarm woke me at 6:30, Carla was gone. The glass of water I'd brought her after our energetic tryst was cleaned and dried, and set in the dish rack. I hadn't slept that soundly in years, so I had no idea when she'd left. Even with the truncated night, I felt I'd gotten in more sleep than I needed. A handwritten note was next to the coffeemaker, where I would obviously find it.

*I'm off today but I'll be around later if you want to call. I'd still like to talk to you about some things. Thanks for the lovely night! C*

There was a lipstick kiss under the "C," and when I held the paper up, it smelled like her perfume.

The corners of my mouth turned up into my first unforced smile in some time.

CHAPTER

# 17

A WEEK LATER, THE ringer on the company iPhone shocked me awake like the force of that earthquake my first morning back in LA. I fumbled in the dark for the phone, trying to focus on the screen to see who was calling me at such an ungodly hour.

It was Eric. At 3:30 AM. *What the fuck?* I swiped the screen to answer. "Yeah?"

"I need you to come get me," Eric said. He sounded agitated.

"What is it? You OK?"

"I'll explain later. Just get here. I'm at Pershing Square."

Spanning a full city block, Pershing Square was a landscaped space near the city's center that hosted public concerts and seasonal markets. Eric could easily have a piece of any one of the many nightclubs in the area, but at this hour, the square would be taken over by homeless. Once I'd pulled myself together, it would be less than a five-minute drive.

"I'm on my way," I said.

"North side. By the construction." The line went dead.

As all bars were required to close at 2:00 AM, by now the area looked deserted. Only the sporadic, lonely vehicle traveled the boulevards, the driver usually on his way to or from an odd-hours night job. The marine layer had descended, and refracted through the street lamps, shrouding everything in an amber haze.

I had left in such a hurry, I didn't program the car's GPS, and instead used the iPhone by speaking the destination into it. I followed the blue line on the screen, which brought me to approach the square from the east. I crossed Hill Street and slowed to a crawl, scanning for any movement. The hackles in my neck rose, though there was nothing visual to cause alarm. The tone of Eric's voice had put me on edge.

I was on a one-way boulevard, so I hugged the left shoulder that bordered the square. In daylight, this block would be teeming with pedestrians and honking vehicles. At this hour, it was like a ghost town. I came to a stop next to the construction site. Nearly the entire east side of the square was cordoned off by heavy chain-link fencing. Tall plywood barricades beyond blocked the street lamps, covering this section in dark shadow.

I left the engine running and rolled down the window, the hum of the mechanism suddenly louder than I'd ever heard it. I listened for any sign of Eric, for a sign of anything. Nothing. Not even the homeless were stirring. This wasn't good.

Then I heard footsteps, and Eric rounded the corner ahead of me. He was walking fast, almost running. The Biltmore Hotel, a grand mix of Renaissance, Mediterranean, and Beaux Arts architecture, was directly across the street. Maybe he'd been doing business there? I pressed the button that unlocked all the doors simultaneously. *Brruup.* The rear door opened, and Eric jumped into the seat. He was breathing hard.

"Thanks, man," he said quickly.

"Are you all right? What the hell's going on?"

"Yeah," he said. "Let's go."

I stared at him for a moment, waiting for any elaboration, but with none coming, I put the car into gear. "Straight ahead," he said.

"Eric, what the fuck is going on?"

"I think everything's OK." Eric's breath was easing now. "Something happened. It'll be all right, but we got to go get somebody."

"Who?"

"One of my partners. Rudy's with him."

*Oh great. Rudy.* But Eric's answer hardly cleared anything up. "A partner? You mean one of your crew?" I no longer bothered with illusions that Eric's "partners" were anything but.

"Yeah. Had to set him straight," said Eric, looking at his phone. "It's close. Just straight down there," he said, pointing ahead.

I went through the intersection and clocked the street sign: Olive Street. In the distance, I could see the entrance to the 110 Freeway. Between there and us, on my left, was the big public library. Now I realized where I was.

"Slow down," said Eric. "Turn in here."

My heart skipped a beat. Eric was directing me into an alley, but not just any alley. The *exact* alley where all those years before I had made my biggest mistake. *What the hell?* My armpits began to sweat.

I eased the car into the passageway.

"Stop here," said Eric. "Kill the engine." He was peering through the windows, his head swiveling in different directions. It was like he was expecting something, but he didn't know what.

I could barely breathe. The closest I'd come to this spot since that disaster of a night was from way across the boulevard when I'd first arrived back in LA. I hadn't been able to bring myself to enter this dingy, tragic place, and I'd been going out of my way to avoid it ever since. But what could Eric possibly want here? *Shit. He's my boss, and I need this job.* I reached forward and turned off the engine.

"And the lights."

I clicked the headlight dial from Auto to Off, and the alley went pitch black.

I felt like my mind was reeling into madness. The kid couldn't possibly know what this place is to me. Could he? Unless Angela told him, but why would she do that? That fucking Google will tell you anything, but you have to look for it. This couldn't be anything more than an outrageous, unthinkable coincidence.

"What are we doing here?" I asked, trying my damnedest not to give away my rising alarm.

"We just have to wait. Should only be a minute." Eric's voice had a twinge of serious tension in it.

Then, a single thin beam of white light flashed from the end of the alley. One quick flash. Then another.

"That's it," Eric said. His breathing sounded labored. "Turn on the lights."

I tried to swallow through my dry mouth. "Eric, what the fuck is going on?"

"Turn on the lights, man!"

My fingers rose to the dial. I turned on the headlamps.

In the moments of darkness since we'd arrived, a group of seven or eight men had gathered at the end of the alley. It was Eric's crew, their suits and shirts giving them away. At the apex was Rudy, his buttoned jacket concealing his girth.

In front of Rudy was a man on his knees. His head was tilted downward, as if he couldn't hold it up any longer. His hands were behind his back, and I could make out a patch of blood on his high forehead. Rudy's left hand was on the man's right shoulder, holding him in place.

"Eric," I said, my voice settling into something more forceful. "What the fuck is th—" My words stopped as if someone had flipped a switch, because I was staring into the barrel of a high caliber revolver pointed at my face.

"Balance," said Eric, the tensive pitch in his voice suddenly absent. "This is what you'd call 'balance.' Now flash the high beams. Once."

I was staring into the barrel of the gun, unmoving.

"Jake." My eye-line shifted from the barrel to Eric. "Lights."

I pulled back on the column wand and let it go. The headlamps flashed brighter, then dimmed to normal. "Now what?" I said.

"Now . . . watch."

I looked ahead to the small crowd.

Rudy shook the kneeling man's shoulder. He raised his head, and looked straight at the car's headlamps. A shock of recognition hit me. William Best, my cohort in our one robbery together, our only robbery *ever*, was on his knees in the alley where all our lives had essentially ended. Like me, he was a lot older now, but I'd recognize him anywhere. Bill had been sent to Corcoran Prison to serve his sentence, and I had never heard from him, or about him, again. And now, here he was, at the mercy of my employer.

"Bill . . ." My voice was a hoarse whisper. Then Rudy raised a pistol up over his head, as if to make sure Eric and I knew it was there. To me, the gun's extended barrel looked like a silencer had been attached to it. Then Rudy stepped directly behind the kneeling man, and lowered the pistol to aim it at the back of Bill's head. "Wait. What's he doing?"

"Balance," said Eric again.

I could see Bill's eyes open wide when he felt the barrel touch his skull. Then Bill's forehead exploded in a mist of blood, bone, and brain matter. The last look on Bill's face was one of tragic resignation. His body fell forward with the force of the bullet, landing face down on the concrete.

I turned to Eric. "You motherfucker."

"Yeah," he agreed. He indicated toward the dash with the gun. "Now turn off the lights. Wouldn't want a cop to come by and see this, now would you?" I turned them off.

"You just made me an accessory to murder," I said.

He smiled. "Kind of like the old days."

My mind cranked like rusty old gears. I couldn't string together how any of this was connected. "What is this?"

"You really don't know who I am," Eric said.

"All I know for sure now is you're a killer."

Eric shrugged. "Takes one to know one."

"Who the fuck are you?"

"*Now* we're gettin' somewhere," Eric said, his timbre even and cool. "Ask yourself, Jake, the last time you were here, who else was with you?"

It was like a lightning bolt, as if shot from the sky directly to my head. Why Eric had seemed familiar in a way I couldn't place, because the source was so far removed. By a generation, in fact. "Damon," I said, barely above a whisper.

"That's right." Eric leaned forward, his eyes filling with fire. "Damon!" he screamed. If he'd meant for me to flinch, it worked. His rage quelled as soon as it had appeared. "But I just called him Dad."

# CHAPTER

# 18

## THEN

**One day before the robbery.**

"YOU WANT TO rob the *El Repettos*?"

"Keep your voice down," Damon said. A slow Sunday night at Bonetti's was crawling to a close. We were huddled at the far end of the bar, out of earshot of any customers or other employees (if I wasn't yelling, that is).

"Are you fucking kidding me? They're on the news practically every week. Those guys are the biggest gang in LA. They kill you for looking at 'em funny."

"Which is why they'll never expect it," he said. "Remember my buddy Malik? The guy I grew up with?"

Damon's "buddy" was the one who gave us the low-down on how to be a gigolo and get away with it. "Yeah. What about him?"

"He does a lot of business with them. They're Chinese. He's Black, so he moves their product in his neighborhood so they don't have to."

"Nice work if you can get it," I said.

What *wasn't* this Malik guy into? The last three months had taken a real toll on me. Between the clients I now serviced, the blow Damon always seemed to get from him, and the stress of lying to Angela to cover my ass, I had dropped close to thirty pounds. My face was gaunt, my limbs were losing their muscle from lack of exercise. Solid food was becoming a thing of the past, turning my daily shits into a rancid, bloody stew.

Angela had just that afternoon laid down the law. It was a Sunday, and we had spent the day at the Santa Monica Pier. I'd tried to enjoy myself, indulging in the games she loved to play—the darts, the bean bag toss, the noisy arcade with the pinball machines. Despite the hits of blow I snuck when I thought she wasn't looking, I was able to keep down the hot dogs and ice cream until we rode the carousel. I had to jump off the painted horse mid-ride when I wretched all over it, leaving it covered in vomit. She found me outside dry heaving into a city garbage can.

"It's either that or me," she'd said. I was still leaning over the blue receptacle with the "94.7 the Waaaaaave" radio station logo on it, coughing up half-digested hot fudge and ice cream. She'd had enough of the lonely nights, of worrying about me getting home safely, of not killing anyone while inebriated. Of smelling another woman's scent in my clothes because I was too far gone to cover my tracks by doing my damn laundry. She was done. With the lies. With the worry. With me. With all of it. My choices were to check into rehab or lose her for good.

When Damon presented this insane idea that late Sunday night, I actually thought it might give me the chance to escape this prison I'd put myself in. I'd raised the walls so high around myself, I couldn't even see the sun anymore. All I could see was darkness, and I was desperate for a way out. To blow down the walls of addiction and depravity and hopelessness. And maybe—just maybe—I could prove something to myself, and Angela, at the same time.

But there was no way I could afford rehab. Bonetti's had some decent health insurance, which was great to see a doctor when you get the flu or a dentist if you broke a tooth. But a thirty-day stay in a drug rehabilitation center? That was a fix only available to LA's richest. Or someone who's come into a big wad of money.

"Bill's gonna help us," Damon said.

"Bill?" Damon confirmed my incredulity with a nod. "He's a fucking zero. Dumb as dirt. That's why he's almost thirty and still busing tables."

"He'll do what he's told. And he'll keep his mouth shut, which is even more important." That last part proved to be true; Bill never talked. But he really was thick, so maybe he just couldn't form the words. "It'll be easy," Damon said. "Malik says all the dealers drop off the money they've made in this old building downtown. He showed it to me. They collect everything for the week, and then move it out on Tuesday mornings. That's why we need to go tomorrow."

"Tomorrow?"

"It's perfect. We're closed here, so we don't need to call in sick or anything. And they only have one guy watching it. Maybe two."

"Maybe *two*?"

"That's why we need Bill. You're gonna be outside in your car. He and I go in, subdue the guard or guards, grab the money, and you drive us away."

"What's wrong with your car?"

"My car's a piece of shit. Can't rely on it. And Bill doesn't have one. At least you got the easy part. You just wait for us, and then . . ." He made a swooping motion in the air, like a plane taking flight. "Off we go. They'll never know what hit 'em."

I looked across the dining room, now nearly empty of patrons. Bill was at the busboy stand just off the other end of the bar. He watched us while he stacked dirty plates in a plastic bin.

"Here," Damon said, sliding a thick bindle of cocaine toward me. "That's two grams. Think about it tonight, but I gotta know by tomorrow. Noon at the latest."

CHAPTER

# 19

## NOW

I NEVER EVEN KNEW that Damon had been a father. Eric must have been a preteen by the time the three of us were sent away. Had he been feeding this chip on his shoulder all this time?

A ghostly figure approached the car from the dark end of the alley. Rudy was walking toward us, his silenced pistol in his hand.

"Unlock the door," Eric said.

I did, and Rudy opened the passenger door and got in. He pointed his gun at me.

"Let's go," said Eric.

"Where?" I asked, assuming wherever it was would be the last place I'd see.

"Don't worry, if I wanted you dead, you'd be out there with your old buddy," said Eric.

I turned on the ignition, and the headlights came on. The men at the end of the alley, and Bill's body, had disappeared. I put the car into reverse, but before taking my foot off the brake, I said, "Does Angela know?"

Eric smirked. "I won't tell if you don't."

* * *

Eric sat in my one chair, the same one Carla had sat in only days earlier. Rudy stood next to him, always the servile toady, his silenced pistol trained on me. From my position on the bed, I knew I could never cross the distance between us fast enough. Rudy and his silencer would stop me before I got halfway. Not that I could move, with all the questions in my head weighing me down. *Why didn't I see this coming? How did I miss the connection? How stupid am I?*

They'd both put on surgical masks and hats, Eric a fedora, Rudy a Dodger cap, before we left the car and entered my apartment building. Eric peeled off his mask and dropped it into his hat, which now rested on his lap. I noticed they were both careful not to touch anything with their hands.

"How'd Bill find his way here?"

"Easy," Eric said, unconcerned. "I entered my company in a job placement program for inmates. I use my mother's last name, so no one ever connected me to my dad. If they even give a shit, which I don't think they do."

I felt there had to be more to this story, and I was right.

Eric's voice dripped with arrogance. "You see, Bill got out only a week before you. Can you believe it?" He shook his head. "We had him washing dishes. Wasn't much of a worker, though. 'Fraid he didn't have your aptitude." That smirk again. I wanted to slap it off his face, once and for all. "The trick was making sure you two didn't run into each other, so we just kept you driving around town." He and Rudy shared a laugh at their own ingenuity.

I didn't see the humor. I was still trying to purge the image of Bill's exploded forehead from my mind. Poor guy. Bill Best was such a hard luck case. Whenever I saw him it always seemed to be on the far side of some disaster. Like the time he was so giddy he bought a preowned sports car that he could hardly afford, then crashed it less than two blocks from the dealership. Some guy's lives are just a train wreck.

"You know there's cameras in that alley, right?" I said. "That's how they caught us."

"Disabled," said Eric. "Big difference between you and me. I'm not a cokehead, so I actually plan shit out." He leaned forward. "You know what happened to your friend Damon?"

"No."

Eric's eyebrows went up. "That's it? You're not even curious?"

"We were sent to different prisons. It's kind of a rule that inmates who do crimes together aren't allowed to stay in touch."

"Yeah, OK, but don't you *want* to know?"

"Not really."

"Permit me to enlighten you, anyway," Eric said. "Damon was killed in San Quentin. Stabbed in the showers. Exactly one day before I was going to visit. Already had the car packed."

"Sorry to hear that," I said.

"Are you?"

To be honest, I wasn't. "He must've pissed somebody off," I said. Eric's eyes narrowed. "When?"

"Oh, a good ten years ago," he said. "Surprised you ask, because the word is you might've had something to do with it."

"Are you fucking kidding me? How could I do that?"

"Gangs send messages to other prisons all the time. You sure you didn't ask a favor . . ." He cocked his head. "Or *do* one . . . to get something done?"

"Yeah," I said evenly. "I'm sure."

Eric obviously didn't know much about Damon's propensity for crime. If Damon had stacked up an unpaid debt in prison, say for drugs or gambling, well, that's a barrel of shit you never crawl out of. But ten years ago? It was more likely the El Repettos had finally caught up to him. If the woman he killed that night had been related in any way to a member of the ERs, he may as well have shot himself right then. Saved them the trouble.

Eric looked up at Rudy, who stared silently at me. "Not sure I believe you," Eric said.

"I don't give a flying fuck what you believe. The day we got convicted was the last time I ever saw either of them."

"You mean when you snitched," Rudy said. *Well, what do you know? The Sphinx speaks.*

"They pled guilty," I said.

"After you snitched," said Eric.

I could see Rudy stiffen. You can take boy out of the prison . . . "All right, *Junior*," I said. "Enough of this shit. What do you want?"

"It's time to pay the piper, Jake," said Eric, as if he were making an announcement. "You get one chance to make up for everything you did. And everything you didn't."

It finally dawned on me why they were here, and why I was still alive. At least for now.

"You want me to do a job for you."

"Ding, ding, ding! Very good!"

I decided to push my luck. I mean, what did I have to lose? "I could just go to the police."

"And say what?" said Eric. "I told you, the cameras were disabled. The only person they could prove was there is you." He paused for emphasis, smirked again. "By the ping of your phone. You do know that these things are tracked everywhere they go, right? You've seen those towers with the funny grids around the top?"

I felt the weight of my company iPhone in my jacket pocket. Suddenly it felt heavier. I turned to see my own Xiaomi phone plugged into its charger on the nightstand.

"And any evidence that we were there," he continued, "is looooong gone."

I glanced at Rudy, who was now smirking back at me, too. Must be a company-wide thing, that grin.

"There's cameras here," I said.

"Yeah," he said. "Which has you walking through the lobby with a couple guys worried about getting Covid. Just makes you look like you don't care about your friends . . . whoever they are. And there's none in the elevator or the halls."

Jesus, they'd kept me running all over town, and at some point had even scoped out my building.

Rudy pulled a handkerchief from his pocket and went to the nightstand. With his cloth- covered hand, he yanked the Xiaomi phone from its charger cord. He held the screen toward me. "Open it," he said.

I entered the PIN. Rudy stepped away and handed the phone to Eric.

Eric dialed a number. After a moment, he began speaking in a mocking tone, as if he was me in a panic. "Eric! I don't know what to do. Something happened! Sorry, I'm not making sense. I think I *killed* somebody." He listened for a beat. "No, leave it there." He hung up. "One of my guys is at my house." He powered the Xiaomi down, then dropped it into his jacket pocket. He went back to a mocking tone, but this time as himself. "I don't know, detective. He called me in the middle of the night. He was ranting and raving. I couldn't figure out what he meant, but I thought he said someone was *dead*."

I thought for a moment. "What if I say no?"

"You could. But then Bill Best is going to show up in the worst possible way for you. And you'll be back in Folsom before you can spit. Or, better yet . . . 'Q.' With all of dad's friends." "Q" is short for the San Quentin Rehabilitation Center outside San Francisco. The oldest prison in California, it has the only death row for male inmates, and is usually the last stop for prisoners considered to be the worst of the worst.

"On the other hand, you do what I say, no questions, no arguments, and you might come out of this all right." Eric looked out the window. "Whaddya know? It's gettin' light out." He stood and arched his back like it had gotten stiff. "Heard it might rain today." He shifted his look to Rudy. "That could work for us." Then back down to me. "So, what's it gonna be?"

"What do I have to do?"

"We'll get back to ya in a few hours," he said. "What you need to know is, if you don't play along then . . . well, let's just say I'll make Angie's run on this Earth a lot shorter than it is already." I glared at him. "Don't look so glum. Think of this as a do-over. You should get some sleep. We go tonight." He nodded to Rudy.

Rudy stepped over to me. "This is for Damon." I braced myself as he wound up and swung a haymaker to the left side of my face.

Dammit. That was my good side.

# CHAPTER 20

MY EYES OPENED into sunlight. I sneezed, which set off a pounding throb in my cheek. The last thing I could remember was Rudy punching me in the face.

I pushed myself up from the floor to a sitting position. I didn't know how long I'd been out, but judging from the angle of the sun, I reckoned two or three hours. I guess it didn't rain, after all. The weatherman sure has a great gig. You can be wrong every day and still have a job.

I gingerly pressed my fingertips to my cheek. It stung to the touch. The antipathy I'd gotten from Rudy ever since our initial meeting finally made sense. He had done time, that much I'd figured out. But he'd done it with Damon. That's probably how he met Eric. Hardly mattered now.

I lumbered into the tiny bathroom and looked in the mirror. Lying unconscious on the floor with the left side of my face against the carpet must've stanched the blood flow. My cheek was bruised a deep shade of purple, but much of the bloat had been held back. My left eye was pushed partially shut from underneath, but I could see out of it, and all my teeth were still in my head. Not as bad as it could've been. That Rudy sure knew how to aim a punch.

I went to the kitchenette and collected ice cubes and a hand towel to fashion an ice pack. It gave some relief when I held it to my face. I picked up the iPhone from where I'd left it on the bed. I wanted to talk to Angela, but I wasn't about to use this to do it. I assumed they could track me with it, maybe even listen in.

This fucking thing had been planted on me like a spy behind enemy lines. Handed to me as a gift, followed by a sharp blade in the back. Kind of like my experience with Hollywood. Some things never change. The next time this thing rings will be to direct me to . . . what? It felt like a time bomb in my hand.

Eric had pocketed my Xiaomi phone, which I bet he'd have Rudy dump somewhere easy to find, with the call history and location record pointing straight to me.

10:28 AM on Saturday morning. Carla would be on her shift.

She spotted me the moment I opened the diner door. She began to smile, then I saw her eyes go wide. She set the coffee pot she was holding back on its hot plate, and made a beeline for me.

"What the hell happened to you?" she asked as soon as she reached me. She tucked her arm into my elbow and guided me to a two-top in the back. Normally, she would scurry off and come back for my order, but instead she took a seat in the chair across from me. This was the first time I'd laid eyes on her since she surprised me with that night-time visit a week before. Even with what I was facing, I felt guilty I hadn't reached out.

"I'm sorry I haven't called," I said.

She leaned in and spoke softly. "You didn't answer my question. I mean, it bugged me I haven't heard from you but"—she indicated the contusion on my face—"I didn't want that to happen."

I smiled through the pain. "I like you, Carla," I said, though I had trouble making eye contact with her. "I really like you."

"Look at me," she said, so I did. She leaned in again. "I believe you. I like you, too. And thanks for apologizing, but what the fuck happened?"

"I can't tell you. All I can say is I didn't do anything wrong."

She sighed. "Somebody's got you by the balls, don't they?"

My pulse quickened. "Why would you say that?"

"Because that's what happens. You make a mistake, and you spend the rest of your life paying for it. Look at my brother."

I looked down. "Yeah, that kind of nails it."

A cook behind the line called out. "Carla! Order up!"

"Stay here," she said as she stood. "I'll get you something to eat. You look like you need it."

I watched her walk away. I was going to miss that view.

# CHAPTER

# 21

ANGELA OPENED THE door. "What the hell happened to you?" I ignored the fact that, again, Angela had asked the same question as Carla. I mean, verbatim.

"Can I come in?" I asked.

She hesitated a beat, partly because of the purple splotch on my face, but also because of my tone. I must've sounded like I was on a mission. She opened the door the rest of the way.

"Nice place," I said, stepping into the living room. Angela's one-bedroom apartment was the top half of a Spanish stucco duplex in the flats between Hollywood and the mansions in Hancock Park. A leafy, tree-lined neighborhood with wide quiet streets and Old Hollywood charm. Most of the buildings dated to the early nineteen hundreds. Many were still standing because their wood framing provided a buffer against earthquakes. When I parked the town car at the curb, it reminded me of Charles Bronson's apartment being invaded by thugs in *Death Wish II.* That Bronson sure was a magnet for trouble.

Though she had decorated with the understated taste that I remembered about her, Angela's home felt . . . strained. The wood floors were long overdue for refinishing, and the walls looked like they'd given up hope of being repainted. There was no plush furniture to relax on, or heavy drapes to pull across the large antique paned windows that overlooked the street. The apartment, like the building, felt solid and spacious, but everything in it looked as if it had come from a garage sale or was a sidewalk find. Eclectic, but sparse. Wide archways connected the rooms, and built-in bookcases were topped with matching elegant curves. Angela had filled the bookshelves with everything from popular psychological thrillers to Eastern Philosophy to "How to Win at Chess." She had always liked to read, but even the books looked tired.

Dressed for a lazy Saturday at home in shorts and a T-shirt, she stood barefoot in the open doorway, one hand on the doorknob. "How'd you know where I live?"

"I dropped Eric here once."

She let that sink in, as if she couldn't decide if it was bad news or not. "OK, so?"

"I wanted to talk to you."

"You could've just called." She waited. I probably should've better organized my thoughts. "Talk, already! I'm busy."

She didn't look busy to me, but then I did barge in without warning. "I came to say goodbye."

Angela stared at me. She looked like she wanted to scream, but it was as if something had reached up her throat and grabbed any sound. She finally let out a breath and shook her head with disappointment. "Why?" She wouldn't look at me.

I couldn't come up with anything but my stock response. "I'm sorry."

"I'm sorry, I'm sorry," she said, imitating me. "That's all you fucking say!" She was almost yelling now. "Jesus, Jake, you just got back!"

I stood in the middle of the room, mute, memories flooding my mind: the drugs. The clients. The lies. The deaths. Prison. Shattered dreams. Time wasted. Life wasted. Angela.

The iPhone in my pocket dinged with a text.

"Dammit," I muttered, and looked at the screen:

*astoria midnight*

I dropped the phone back into my pocket.

"Problem?" she asked.

"No. I gotta go." I opened the door to leave.

"Aren't you going to tell me what happened to your face?"

I stopped with my hand on the knob. "Some homeless guy got the drop on me," I lied, and started out the door.

"Jake, wait." She touched my arm, and it hit me like a jolt. She must've felt it, too, because she pulled back her hand as if she'd been hit by static electricity. She looked at the floor. "Do you ever think about us?"

I took a long beat to answer. "Only all the time."

Her eyelids closed, and she gently pushed the door shut, cutting off my clean getaway. She looked into my eyes and touched my swollen cheek. "Let me get you some ice."

"You don't need—"

"I want you to stay," she said, cutting me off. She seemed have a burst of courage, and wanted to push through before it abandoned her. "Just for a little while. The way we used to. Then you have to go."

She took my hand and led me to her bedroom.

# CHAPTER

# 22

My cheek throbbed every time the cargo van pounded over a pothole. I was seated between two members of Eric's crew on one of the two metal benches that ran the length of the vehicle. Across from me were three more guys, including Rudy. He'd occasionally look away, but most of the ride he stared at me. I hadn't officially met the other passengers, but I'd seen them around some of Fly-By-Night's businesses. It felt like a prison transport, though a different kind of confinement.

Big change from that afternoon, when I watched Angela pull her T-shirt off over her head, and we lay together in her soft bed. For two hours it was like it was in the beginning, when we were just two kids finding our way in the world, with nothing ahead of us but the kind of freedom that only the young can know.

I couldn't see who was driving, but Eric was in the passenger seat, his ubiquitous phone in his hand. When we rounded a corner, I saw through the rear window that another van was trailing us with a company name and logo on its side: "SentryCity Security." We'd all donned coveralls with an identical SentryCity logo across the back, and a smaller version of it over the breast pocket. A few of the men were wearing trucker caps, also bearing the logo. On the floor were several large black thick canvas bags, containing what, I couldn't know.

Everyone was wearing pale blue surgical masks that had been handed out to each of us as we entered the van. It made sense. In the post-Covid world, no one would think twice about employees of any company being required to wear them. We'd all slipped them over our faces, hooking the loops behind our ears. With the matching masks and monochromatic coveralls we looked like extras in a Devo music video (had the band ever done a song about the Coronavirus).

The enclosed space and lack of air circulation made for a hot ride. When shafts of light swept over us, I could see glimmering beads of sweat on the foreheads around me, and could feel them forming on my own. I mopped my brow with my coverall sleeve.

We'd been in the van for about forty minutes, the first half on the freeway, and the remainder negotiating surface streets and traffic lights, when I felt the swerve of a sharp turn. After another two or three short jigs and jags, the van came to a stop. I craned to see out the windshield.

We were at a mechanized gate guarding the entrance to what looked like a mobile home park. The lane between the domiciles appeared well kept, swept and orderly, but the lack of streetlamps suggested a low-income area.

Eric's window hummed open. He spoke to someone outside the van, but I couldn't make out what they were saying. After a quick verbal exchange, Eric handed the man an envelope. Maybe a payoff?

Over the idling engine, I heard the gate open, the chains and cogs squeaking and clanking in tandem until it stopped with a clunk. The van crawled forward. Once inside, I could see through the rear window that we were indeed passing tidy mobile homes, arranged neatly at diagonal slants. We sped up for a short distance, took another sharp turn, reversed a few feet, and then stopped. The driver killed the engine.

Eric opened his door and jumped out while the rest of us stayed put. Rudy stared at me.

The rear double-doors of the van opened, and there was Eric, one hand on the door handle, the other still holding his phone. We filed out, and as I hopped to the ground, Eric and I made eye contact.

Had Angela ever looked into Eric's eyes the way she did mine that afternoon? And if she had, what did she see? All I could see in Eric now was a black hole. I wondered what he'd do if I told him that I could still feel Angela writhing under me, could hear her moans, and feel her breasts, her skin, her kisses.

We were at the rear of the mobile home complex. The vans were parked side by side, backed up to the edge of an open paved area. Impossible to tell for sure in the dark, but it looked like an empty parking lot, or maybe a space to keep heavy equipment. By then, it had to be around three am, and all the lights in the homes were off for the night. In spite of the full moon that night, cloud cover had dissipated the available light, blanketing everything in a dull gray haze.

I fell in behind the rest of the crew, but as I passed Eric, he stopped me.

"You stick close to Rudy," he said.

"Why am I not surprised?" I replied, and pulled my arm free. I followed the line of coveralls into the darkness. I heard engines engage behind me, and when I looked back, the vans were driving out the way we came in.

Eric moved to the front of the group, switched on his iPhone flashlight, and led us single file off the pavement into a small field or vacant lot. No one spoke as we crossed, the only sound came from dead weeds crackling under our feet.

We came to a steel cyclone fence I guessed to be around ten feet high. It had several strands of angled barbed wire running along the top. Must be the perimeter of whatever we were hitting. A fence? Really? No lights? No cameras? Pretty old school. Pretty damn lazy.

Eric dimmed the light on his phone, I suppose to draw as little attention as possible, and aimed it toward the fence. Rudy stepped forward. From somewhere, maybe one of those canvas bags in the van, he had produced two sets of three-foot-long heavy-duty bolt cutters. He handed one each to two of the crew, and they went to work cutting an opening in the fence. Two other guys stepped up and loosely draped thick furniture blankets over them. That made a big difference in dampening the sound. The men worked quickly, snapping through steel strands. Before long they'd cut an opening high and wide enough for us to walk through unimpeded.

I would've been last in line, but Rudy fell in behind me as I took my turn stepping through. I followed the group for another twenty or thirty yards, until we came to an abrupt drop. The men lined up along the edge to look.

A storm drain. LA County had built this system of subterranean concrete culverts all across the region. Underneath the city were hundreds of these man-made waterways, designed to replace the natural creeks and brooks that once spidered throughout the county. Fondly remembered by grand and great-grandparents who had spent their childhood summers wading in the mud or catching crayfish in the deeper pools. But during winter rainstorms those bucolic streams would turn into watery avalanches of mud, debris, and rocks, causing millions of dollars in damage, and leaving hundreds dead or homeless.

These smaller drains acted like tributaries to the two major "rivers" and one creek that divert drainage away from the city to the ocean: the Los Angeles and San Gabriel Rivers in the basins, and Ballona Creek near Venice Beach. The system was conceived in response to the devastating floods of the 1930s, which meant many of these tunnels predate current overland structures.

One of the crew dropped his bag and pulled out what looked like two identical aluminum washboards. They each had two large metal hooks on one end and two straight prongs protruding from the opposite. Telescoping ladders. The hooks were to secure it to something solid, and the prongs were the feet, with rubber on the bottom to prevent slippage. He and another man placed the hooks over the edge of the concrete rim, and the ladders extended to the bottom of the culvert.

One by one, using both ladders, we all climbed down. This was starting to resemble a bizarre military operation. Devo meets *The Dirty Dozen*. Once we had all descended, we set off toward an unlit opening that led underground.

The pitch black inside was soon illuminated by the entire crew turning on their phone flashlights, so I followed suit. The fencing above had done its job of keeping the unhoused from setting up camp inside. The relatively fresh outdoor air was soon replaced by the stench of mold and old trash.

These tunnels never received any sunlight, so pools of water could stand for months, collecting insects, animal carcasses, household garbage, bacteria, toxins, and chemicals, basically anything that can travel downstream in a good hard downpour. I covered my nose with my sleeve which, between the fabric and the mask, helped somewhat. I thought of the cloud cover, and just hoped it didn't rain, after all.

After we had trudged around a hundred yards, Eric stopped and flashed his light on a steel ladder mounted into the concrete wall. The narrow beam flickered across it, revealing heavy rust and grime. It could have been installed when the tunnel was built, perhaps as long as eighty years ago. A relic. It must still be here so maintenance crews could have access to this part of the tunnel.

Eric nodded to a crew member, probably the shortest and slightest of all. The man slung his canvas bag over his shoulder and started climbing. As he clambered up, one of the rungs broke loose under his weight, but he nimbly caught himself without falling. Once at the top, he slipped another telescopic ladder from his bag and affixed the hooks to the rim of some kind of opening. Again, gravity did the work of extending the ladder down to us. It draped neatly along the length of the original, barely making a sound when it was stopped by the concrete below. Then the man used it to climb back down.

Now Eric went up. The crew all aimed their phone lights toward him, turning night into a six-foot circle of day. Eric pulled out his key ring, from which dangled his kubotan, a sleek hand-held stainless steel rod originally devised as a self-defense tool for women. Usually about five to five and a half inches long, it's shaped like a steel stick with a point on one end, and rounded or flat on the other. The idea is for a woman who is, say, walking through a dimly lit parking garage, to hold the kubotan in her hand and use the sharp end on an attacker like an ice pick. Weeks earlier, I'd asked Eric about it, and he said he carried it to "put out the eye of any dumbass who tries something." I'd since noticed several of his crew also carried them, including Rudy. iPhones and kubotans. What else could be standard issue at Fly-By-Night Enterprises? Nunchuks?

Eric tapped the round end of the weapon on the hard surface above him. *Kang . . . kang.* After a moment, a tentative reply came from the other side: *Kang . . . kang.* It sounded like one of those naval war movies, when a character taps on a metal submarine hatch.

Light cut through squared lines above Eric's head, and a hatch opened. Eric reached up and pulled himself through. I could make out a second pair of legs. Whispers drifted down to us. Then Eric appeared in the passage opening.

"Let's go!" he hissed.

I waited my turn, then headed up the ladder, with Rudy right on my heels. He was really starting to creep me out. It was like he wanted to keep me at arm's reach at all times.

By the time I hauled myself through the opening, most everyone had pistols in their hands, and were quietly double-checking their ammo load. No one spoke. Rudy came through behind me, stood up straight, unzipped his coveralls, and pulled out his own pistol. His silencer was affixed to the barrel, probably the same one he'd used on Bill Best. I felt a chill.

I stifled my astonishment when I realized the room we'd invaded from below was the security nerve center. Black and white images flickered from large flatscreens, transmitting closed circuit cameras poised at sections outside the building, the main gate, the rear and sides, across the roof. (Too bad they hadn't pointed one down the hole we just came out of.) Other screens were divided into windows of images from inside the building. I counted six employees going about their business in different areas, a number that ticked up when one man emerged from a bathroom. Seven. They appeared oblivious to what was about to happen.

I heard someone wheezing, and turned to see a man in a SentryCity uniform lying on the floor. He was facing my direction, his ankles bound with a plastic zip tie. I couldn't see his hands, but they must've been secured behind his back, likely with another plastic tie. Two strips of duct tape were wrapped around his head, covering his eyes and mouth. The poor guy was sweating profusely, and he was breathing hard through his nose. He had thick hair, and a beard and mustache. I felt bad for him. Removing that tape was going to hurt—if he lived that long. I knew what this crew was capable of.

Eric was hunched over a control board with the employee who'd opened the hatch. He was pointing out different areas, singling out certain people, while whispering information to Eric, who nodded in comprehension. The Inside Man. Nothing like this ever gets done without one. He would know who would be where, what their duties were, when they take their breaks. More importantly, who on the staff would, or wouldn't, be a problem. He must've been the one who had subdued the man tied up on the floor. An inside man is indispensable, and from what I learned in prison, because they're a solid link to the other perps, they're often the first to roll over. Or to be betrayed.

I had to give props to that prick, Eric. Usually, when you hear about a big robbery, usually cut through a roof or a wall, or stormed the front door. Riding in that van, I wrongly surmised we were staging some kind of Trojan Horse scenario. Instead, we came up through the floor, and city planners had unwittingly made it easy for us. In fairness, it would be hard to predict something like this way back when the infrastructure was built. I'd bet the current owners thought this entrance to the city's storm system made a convenient last-ditch getaway for cornered employees in the event of a heist. Eric had found the one direction no one would be expecting us to come from.

Eric turned to face his crew. "OK," he whispered, "you know what to do."

Maybe everyone else did, but nobody'd said boo to me. And I wasn't about to ask.

Eric cracked the door and peeked out, then opened it wide and the crew rushed through. Eric poked me with his pistol.

"You stay with me," he said, "We'll keep an eye on this guy." He indicated the incapacitated employee on the floor. The guy was really wheezing now.

"You mind if I sit him up?" I said. Eric eyed me with suspicion. "He's having trouble breathing."

"Go ahead," said Eric. He sat down in a padded office chair and leaned back. "Then have a seat and watch the show."

CHAPTER

# 23

THE CLOSED-CIRCUIT MONITORS captured every move the crew made.

They all went quickly down a wide corridor, then two of the men peeled off and entered a break room, where three employees were enjoying their graveyard shift lunches. All three were forced to the floor at gunpoint, turned face down, zip- tied and duct- taped.

Two more sprinted to an oversized articulating door at the front of the building. One subdued a lone watchman stationed at a kiosk just inside, dragging him out to the floor. The other crewman went to control buttons inside the kiosk. A moment later, the door silently opened on the screen, revealing the two disguised vans waiting in tandem outside.

The vans backed into the building, stopping side-by-side in the loading area. The crewman in the kiosk closed the door behind them.

On another monitor, Rudy led a handful of men to the end of the corridor, and, moving from one screen to another, they made a hard turn into a room where two armed and uniformed guards were stationed. The entrance to the vault. I could see that one of them had heard something that got his attention and stood up from his desk.

The remaining five crew members rushed him, and though he valiantly tried to fight back, he was quickly overpowered. The other guard moved to close a door between himself and the invading marauders, hoping to lock himself inside a bulletproofed cubicle. Rudy managed to insert the barrel of his gun into the door jamb before it could lock, and the man raised his hands in surrender and backed off.

Then, he suddenly twisted and hit a button on the console next to him. An alarm. But no sound emitted from there or from anywhere. A silent alarm? Had the police just been notified that the SentryCity facility has been breached? The employee would never know, because Rudy fired one shot at his head, and the man dropped.

I rose from my seat.

"Sit down," Eric said, casually aiming his pistol at me. I stiffly sat in the chair. "Well, shit," he said, shaking his head. "The guy should've just gone along."

"What about the alarm?" I said.

"What about it?"

"Didn't he just trip it?"

Eric chuckled. "Our guy's been tripping alarms all night," he said. "The police call, and that phone," he pointed to a sleek, black digital telephone on the console, "is answered every time." He switched his voice to mimic the Inside Man. "'Nothing going on here, officer. Must be another glitch in the system.'" He chuckled again. "By now, I'd say they're tired of making the drive. But if they do, they'll just see another quiet night at the old repository." He paused a beat. "You notice that phone hasn't rung."

My muscles felt like guitar strings pulled so tight they were about to snap. "Why the fuck am I here?" I said. "You obviously don't need me."

He looked at me. "Why do *you* think?" His smirk was back.

"What is this, twenty questions? If I knew, I wouldn't ask, would I?"

He shrugged. "Think of it as finishing what you started."

His calmness in the face of this ongoing robbery was really starting to creep me out. Something was very, *very* wrong with this kid.

"What the hell does that mean?"

"Relax," he said. "You'll find out soon enough."

## CHAPTER

# 24

WITH THEIR PLANNED and practiced heist happening with speed and precision, the whole thing felt like it was over as soon as it began. And I soon learned why I was there: my sturdy back.

Eric ordered me to drag the bound man from the security room. Grabbing him under his armpits, I hauled him out, his heels streaking the concrete floor. I followed Eric to the loading area at the front of the building.

By now, the surviving employees had been gathered together and were lying, bound and taped, by the wall on the floor halfway between the entrance and the wide corridor that led to the vault. One crewman stood watch, reassuring them it would be over soon, and no one else would get hurt as long as they cooperated. After what had happened to their colleague, they behaved themselves accordingly.

The phony cargo vans stood with their back doors open like hungry maws, waiting to be fed. Someone operating an electric-powered forklift moved neatly stacked, shrink-wrapped packages of money from the vault and down the corridor to the vans. The electric forklift sounded eerily similar to the futuristic vehicles in science fiction TV shows from my youth.

Two crewmen used razor knives to methodically cut open the footlocker-sized bricks, then dump out the bundles onto the floor. Next to them was a large pile of brand spanking new black backpacks that had appeared in the time it took me to drag out the security man. Eric directed me to help dump the cash bundles into the backpacks. I wanted to tell him to go fuck himself. *Load your own damn bundles. I'm out.* And then I saw Bill Best's face explode in my mind.

"Fifty bundles each," he said. "Make sure you count 'em right."

A tag on the pack identified it as a "sling bag." One strap instead of two. It was designed to be hooked over one shoulder. With these, a second pack could be hung over the other, so one could carry twice the load without the awkward hassle of tangling the straps. When I zipped opened the first one, I saw the guts of the pack, the sleeves and pockets for stationery, pens and laptops, had been cut out, creating an empty well. All the packs I filled had been altered this way.

If my math skills were anywhere close to correct, the ratio was around two backpacks per man. As this was a repository of cash profits from all manner of businesses, the bills had likely been separated only by denomination. The serial and plate numbers would be all over the map, nothing sequential to identify their origins. No wonder Eric's crew was so loyal, so willing to do his bidding. They were all going to get paid tonight and walk away with a fortune literally on their backs.

I counted out bundles, filled several packs, and tossed them into the van closest to me. The forklift arrived with another load, but before I could start counting again, Rudy stepped up to me. His gun was tucked into his belt, pushing a dent into his girth. Inside Man was with him, and hanging from each of his fists was a full backpack of cash. Maybe part of the plan was for him to leave separately, so he'd already collected his cut.

"C'mon," Rudy said. "We need your help."

I followed them across the loading area toward the security room. We passed Eric, who watched us, his face unreadable, blank. Enigmatic.

Rudy led us into the security room. Inside Man dropped his packs on the floor and stopped at the control console to tap some commands into the system. The monitors all went simultaneously black. Then, avoiding the open trap in the floor, he crossed the room to a reinforced, six-foot high metal cabinet with a manual keypad mounted on its double door. He punched in a code, and the heavy doors sprung open. Inside were modular stacks of coal black electronic gear. Tiny blue and red lights blinked and flashed against the dark metal. Protruding from all of them were three-and-a-half-inch wide removable hard drives. Inside Man started a process of dismounting the drives one by one, and then started pulling them out of their mounts.

"You sure you just can't erase them here?" asked Rudy.

"I did already, but we should take them with us," Inside Man said. "That way, we're sure." He turned to me. "See that pack?" he said, nodding toward the one closest to him. "Bring it here."

I picked up the pack. However much was his end, it weighed a good amount. Two of these on your back could wear you down in a hurry if you weren't in shape. I brought it to him, held it out.

"Open it," he said.

I set it on the floor and unzipped the top. Inside were bundles that I or one of the others had counted out. If the same amount was in the second pack, then he must've gotten an equal share.

As I straightened up, Inside Man grabbed the shoulder of my coveralls and balled his hand into the fabric. The intention was to hold me in place. But whoever had given him that order (probably Eric, maybe Rudy) hadn't counted on my prison response.

It was a martial arts move, something I'd learned from another inmate early on, when I was still finding my way on the inside. I reached up with my opposite hand, and closed my fingers over the top of Inside Man's grip, essentially making him a part of me. Whichever direction I decided to turn, he'd go with me, like it or not.

I turned my entire body—shoulders, torso, legs, everything at once—creating a force that would be virtually impossible for anyone to fight against, no matter their size. Though we were about the same height and weight, my attacker jerked with the velocity, taking him off balance. As I pulled the man around me, I brought my free arm up behind him, my hand finding the back his skull, and slammed his head against the wall. One simple, fluid, involuntary move made in self-defense. Just like in the movies.

I heard two sounds in quick succession—*Phht! Phht!*—and felt Inside Man jerk twice, then I felt his last breath escape through his mask, like a vapor of warm mist on my face.

"Fuck!" yelled Rudy.

He was pointing his pistol in my direction. Even through his mask I could see his jaw hanging open in surprise. He had missed his target. Which meant he had intended to shoot me.

I still had a grip on Inside Man's clothing. I tightened my hold on the fabric and shoved the body at Rudy. A newly-dead corpse is not easy to manage, but with a shot of adrenaline like the one pumping through my system right then, the guy was like a rag doll. I felt his lifeless feet leave the floor, and Rudy took a body block from, well, a body. Rudy went down, Inside Man's limp carcass sprawled over him.

"Hey!" Rudy screamed. "Help!"

I heard commotion out in the loading area. It would only be a moment before Eric and his posse got to me, or Rudy wrestled his gun from under Inside Man and finished me off.

I grabbed the two backpacks on the floor and dropped them through the open trap. I jumped after them, my feet landing on the small ledge between the opening and the step where the collapsible ladder's hooks were still attached. The top half of my torso was still exposed, and I saw Eric and two of his crew appear in the doorway as Rudy pulled his gun free. Eric and his guys were blocked by Rudy and the dead body, but Rudy took aim and fired.

I ducked as the bullet landed in the wall behind me, and felt concrete dust sprinkle my neck. I hugged my knees to the outside rails of the ladder, laid my palms against the sides, and dropped, like a fireman doing an emergency bail-out. I slid to the bottom, picking up speed as I went, and hit the bottom of the storm drain hard.

I grabbed both sides of the ladder and lifted, hoping the telescoping mechanism had locked for our climb into the building. It had. The hooks lifted off the ledge, and I threw the ladder aside. The light coming from above was enough to see the backpacks lying a few feet from me, but also enough for me to be seen. I scooped them up, ignoring a couple of loose bundles that had bounced out of the opening. I swung one pack over my shoulder, carrying the other in my hand, and ran.

I didn't know which way I was going, back toward the entrance or deeper into the tunnel, and I didn't care. I ran as hard as I was able, the two packs bouncing wildly against me.

*Phht!* I heard a bullet whiz past my ear and hit the floor. *Phht!* I felt a sharp bite, a sting low on my left side. A bullet had either grazed me or gone through me, but I didn't have time to check. *Phht!* I felt something nudge me forward. One of Rudy's bullets had hit the backpack over my shoulder. It must have been stopped by the bundles of cash inside it, but it hit hard enough to knock me off balance. I nearly fell, but recovered.

I heard Rudy curse as he lost sight of me in the blackness.

# CHAPTER 25

**THEN**

**An hour after the robbery.**

MY FINGER TREMBLED as I punched the code, engaging my apartment building's noisy security gate to clank open. The living room of someone I'd never even seen was directly above the garage entrance. I held my breath, praying the noise wouldn't wake whoever was up there, making this the time we wound up meeting. I inched my car down the narrow passage into the garage beneath the building.

Dawn had yet to break. We had planned to come here *because* I could park underground. Neither Damon or Bill had a spot where they could hide out of sight of the world, haul the booty inside unseen, split the money, and then make our escape. In fact, my own vague, desperate plan to disappear from my seamy life, and appear reborn in my

Oregon hometown, was falling to shit before it began. I parked in my assigned space, nose to the wall, a feeble attempt to hide the mess of my spidered windshield.

We took the stairwell to the second floor, avoiding the elevator. None of us spoke as we hustled down the hallway, through a fire door, and to my apartment. I had some trouble inserting my key, my hand was still shaking so badly. Damon impatiently reached out to take the key ring from me when the knob finally turned. He muttered some profanity, and we all rushed inside my sparsely furnished single unit.

I was relieved that Angela hadn't decided to show up unannounced and surprise me by climbing into my pull-out sofa bed. She would do that sometimes if she was feeling lonely, or just randy. As if that was the only intangible I had to worry about. After spending some fruitless months encouraging me to cohabitate, she'd accepted that I wasn't as committed to our relationship as she would've liked, and decided to hang onto her own place. My drug use was spiraling, and she didn't want to be around if something bad happened. But I think she would've expected a car accident due to intoxication over a robbery/homicide any day.

Bill made an immediate beeline for my tiny bathroom, not bothering to shut the door. The sound of his retching into the toilet filled the air. It triggered a corresponding nausea in me, but I managed to hold it down. If I was going to boot, I needed something in my stomach.

I went to the kitchenette, poured a glass of water from the tap, and gulped it down, not offering any to the others.

If they wanted a drink, they could fucking get it themselves. I crossed the room and closed the cheap aluminum slats over the one window to block the view. Not that anyone but the guy in the apartment across the breezeway could see in, but that would be one too many.

When I turned, I found Damon kneeling on the floor dumping out the contents of the bags. Wads of cash, crudely bound with rubber bands, were forming a pile. Bill came out of the bathroom, wiping his mouth, and went straight to Damon.

"You know what you fucking did?" Bill said, sounding more forceful than I'd ever heard him.

"I told you to shut up," Damon shot back.

"You killed that lady!" Bill was getting too close to a scream.

"Jesus," I said. "Keep it down! These walls are like cardboard."

Bill looked at me with that sad-sack face he always seemed to wear, but times a thousand. He shook his head.

"The way this is going, her kid probably runs the El Repettos," he said. He looked back at Damon. "You know that, right? They get wind of who we are, we're dead!"

"I said, shut up," Damon snapped. His pistol was in his waistband, ready to be drawn. I couldn't see Bill's weapon, but I was starting to think these two might shoot it out right here.

"It won't matter if they can't find us," I said. "Let's get this done and get outta here."

Bill took a breath, and his nerves seemed to settle. "Yeah, let's do it."

By then, Damon had emptied both bags, and the three of us started dividing the bundles into stacks. Hundreds, fifties, twenties, tens. Before long each denomination had several towers, pressed together in rows to prevent collapse. There were no fives or singles. I recalled hearing somewhere, maybe the local news, that the ERs liked to give those "to the poor," believing the smaller denominations of their drug profits were a boon to the community. Given how fast these stacks were piling up, the ones and fives were probably just too much bother.

It took us about a half an hour to count it all. $397,640. Split three ways, we would each have over a hundred and thirty thousand. Plenty to disappear with. And I still hadn't figured how to explain it to Angela. Or even if I should.

Damon stood up, put his hands on his hips, satisfied. "You got anything to eat?"

I heard a slight creak from the hallway outside. Then the door splintered from the force of a battering ram, followed by the S.W.A.T. team entering, their guns aimed directly at our faces. All three of us instinctively raised our hands above our heads. Looking back, I think, since we'd seen it in so many movies, our response was automatic. We were lowered to our knees, and our hands were cuffed behind our backs.

A plainclothes detective sauntered in. He looked to be about forty, with a military-style buzz cut on his square head. He wore a cropped mustache and had a formidable build. His jacket and shirt collar were open, and he wore no tie, as if he'd been surprised awake and threw on whatever was nearby. He crouched to address us three kneeling would-be robbers.

"I want to thank you guys," he said. "I'll be telling my grandkids how you fucking morons gave me the easiest collar of my life."

The detective's name was Sanchez.

# CHAPTER

# 26

## NOW

I RAISED MY HEAD just enough to see across the field, worried my dark hair rising above the yellow and green foxtails might give me away if anyone was looking.

From my vantage point in the undeveloped lot beyond the trailer park, I could see the typical sunrise activity of a low-cost retirement neighborhood in the San Fernando Valley. A few elderly folks were out walking their dogs or taking their early morning constitutional. No one showed the slightest interest in me or even that anyone knew I was out here.

As it happened, I had run out the way I had come in. The ladders we'd used to climb into the drain were gone, so I kept going until I found another access ladder mounted in the wall about a quarter mile away. Like the one inside the tunnel, it was old and rusty, but its deterioration had been slowed by the magical drying effects of daylight. I climbed up and crept along a path that ran alongside the open channel. The clouds had cleared and, using the moonlight to navigate, I found an opening in the fence. It was at ground level, probably where local teens had pulled it up to do . . . whatever teenagers did now. I threw the packs up and over the fence and crawled through, then made my way into this field, where I decided to wait until daybreak.

I looked down at the holes that Rudy's bullet had torn through my coveralls. There were dried red splotches around both the entrance and exit in the light-colored fabric. The bleeding had stopped, so the wound might be not be that bad, but it stung like a motherfucker. If there was a time to look, this was it.

I peeled off the top half of the coveralls and pulled up my black T-shirt to see the damage. Mercifully, it had only grazed me. A thick red streak about three inches long stretched across the new ring of soft flesh that had recently appeared above my hips. That slug might have missed me altogether if I hadn't developed such a fondness for the hearty meals Carla kept serving me.

The blood had coagulated. Luckily the coveralls had stanched much of the flow. But my blue jeans had a stain at the top seam and a smudge on my leather belt about the length of my thumb. If I pulled the T-shirt down over my waistline, it would be mostly hidden until I could dress the wound and change clothes. But how to do that?

I had to get moving somehow. There was no way I could walk from deep in the San Fernando Valley to downtown Los Angeles. That would take a week. I'd powered off the iPhone as soon as I'd left the tunnel so I couldn't be tracked.

And I couldn't leave a digital trail using something like Uber or Lyft.

I sure could use that Xiaomi phone right now. If only I hadn't left the damn thing sitting out in plain sight, maybe Rudy wouldn't have bothered with it. Sure. They'd seen me use it, taking it had to be part of their scheme. If they hadn't, I could've called Angela or Carla. But I didn't want to drag them into this. That would force them to cover for me, and possibly become an accessory to the crime.

First things first. Angela.

Her boyfriend had tried to have me killed, but I'd gotten away within an inch of my life. So what would Eric do now? Would he take out his frustration on her? Did she know about the shit he was up to? I couldn't believe that. Eric had told me she didn't, and that might be the one true thing I'd ever heard him say. But was she in *danger* because of my escape? And what if I hadn't escaped? What if Rudy had hit his target? How would Eric explain my sudden vanishing act? Would he even bother to? I *was* an ex-con, so a simple "I don't know, hon, he just didn't show up for work," could be explanation enough.

Carla. I couldn't know if Eric or Rudy had connected her to me. I dug through the furrows of my memory, and I wasn't able to find a single instance where they could. But I needed to talk to her, if for no other reason to let her know this whole shitstorm wasn't my doing.

And where were the fucking cops? It had to be two hours since I ran out here. Eric must've rounded up his crew and hightailed it out pronto once I'd gotten away. Whoever hapless Inside Man was (may he rest without peace), he'd managed to keep the police away all this time.

Regardless, other weekend workers would soon be arriving, and then the shit would really hit. It was time for me to go.

The money. The positive was that I had a good pile of it to use however I needed. And, as paper is an inanimate object incapable of plotting to blow my head off, as I assumed Eric and company were doing right now, I could figure out what to do with it later.

I stripped the coveralls off my legs, balled them up, and stuffed them under a loose pile of discarded cans and bottles, broken boards and faded signage, the kind of refuse that tends to gather in an open city lot. The ear loop on my mask had been broken during my wrestling match with Inside Man, and the mask had fallen off completely somewhere during my run. So it was fortuitous to find a dirty, scratched pair of cheap sunglasses that had been deposited there who-knows-when. I blew off the loose dirt and wiped them down as best I could.

Trying them on, I could feel they were completely crooked on my face, probably comically so, but they might do the trick in front of those ubiquitous surveillance cameras (and cover some of the splotch on my face). I set them aside for the moment.

I could count the money later in a safe place, but thought it wise to have a decent wad of cash handy. I laid the two packs next to each other and saw the hole left by Rudy's bullet. I ran my fingertips over it, recalling the force of the slug hitting the backpack. Talk about dumb luck.

I opened the pack and rooted around until I found the wrapped bundle that had stopped the bullet. One hundred tightly wrapped hundred-dollar bills. Ten thousand dollars. And I had two backpacks full of these. Gravity had sent the slug to the bottom of the compartment. I felt around until my fingers found it and, after inspecting it to further marvel over my accidental fortune, threw it away.

I tossed the punctured bundle of cash into the pile of refuse (some bum might soon have his luckiest day ever) and then pulled another bundle and stuffed it into my jeans pocket. I hadn't felt a wad like that since the days I was selling myself, but none of those ever saw a payday like this.

I took out the iPhone. I'd learned enough about these contraptions to know that if I were to use it at all, it had to be quick. I decided to take the chance. I powered it on, opened the GPS app, and found a Metro Link train station about a half mile south. If a scanner, or whatever they use to surveil these damn things, could read my search history, they might assume I'd hopped a train out of town. That could give me some time, should law enforcement be looking for me, and I had to assume that sooner or later they would be. I memorized the route to the station and immediately powered off the phone.

I slid on the old sunglasses, slung the two backpacks, one over each shoulder, took a breath to brace myself, and stood. The loose weight of the bags was a bit awkward, and the padded straps still dug into my skin. The graze in my side came awake with a vengeance, but I'd have to suck it up.

I set off, crouching just low enough to feel unseen. With any luck, I would appear to be just another unhoused man in search of a place to camp.

# CHAPTER

# 27

THE WORLD CHANGES. You change with it or get left behind. But what if you were kept from a changing world?

I had spent years confined behind electrified walls as the world outside spun without me. Now I needed to catch up, but without being noticed. In prison, the way to do that was to keep your nose clean. No drugs, no gambling, no debts. Do your time quietly. That was a lesson from in there that I could use out here. Don't draw attention. I'd made that mistake before and wound up losing years of my life.

Not getting noticed today, like then, means not going home. The building's cameras would record me. These fucking cameras. In the time I'd been away, surveillance had become total. So where could I go now?

In the few months since I'd returned to LA, I'd been coasting on the good graces of those around me. I'd learned how to navigate the city again by way of the freeways and boulevards, but outside of downtown, I hadn't spent a lot of time walking the neighborhoods. I wished now I'd gotten to know the surface streets more intimately, like anyone who makes their home in the city.

Maybe I could go back to the hostel where I'd first landed? Only Carla and my parole agent, Sanchez, knew which one it was. And thankfully no one aside from me knew about Carla. But a hotel would be better, one of the many that dotted the streets of downtown. And there was no law that said you couldn't still pay your way with paper money. Not that credit cards had become my main form of currency. I'd mostly only used my one debit card for the few businesses I'd seen that had gone straight up cashless. But the discount clothiers on Los Angeles Street were always happy to accept untraceable, nontaxable cash.

I scanned the Metro station from across the street. No cops were present. There was a sparse open platform that had a decorative facade meant to evoke an adobe outpost. I went to the corner and took a spot behind a small group of people waiting for the walk signal. When the light turned green, we all moved as one, me keeping pace and doing my best to blend in.

I broke off when the others went directly for the platform, and I went past the ticket kiosks. Each had a glass eye mounted above the console. A camera lens, no doubt. I stepped up to a small information booth.

There would be a camera here, as well, but I assumed if I made a purchase at the kiosk, I would have to enter a destination, and I wanted to avoid leaving a specific trail. I tapped on the glass of the booth to get the attention of a middle-aged woman inside, who was engrossed in a paperback.

"Hi," I said with a smile. "How much for one ride?"

The woman kept her eyes on her book as she answered. "Dollar seventy-five. You can get it at the kiosk."

"All is have is cash," I said, apologetically.

The woman looked up to speak, but stopped when she saw the sunglasses hanging askew on my face. She looked like she was about to laugh, then I think she saw the bruise on my cheek and stifled it.

"It takes cash," she said.

"Can't I just do it here?"

"Dollar seventy-five," she repeated, shaking her head. I slipped a hundred-dollar bill through the window slot. She glared at it, as if the mere sight of it insulted her. "You don't have anything smaller?"

I shrugged. "Sorry."

She snatched it up, muttering something about how she "won't have enough now" and opened a drawer beneath the counter to make change. Then she testily punched some buttons in the countertop, and a ticket popped up through a thin slot in the Formica. She shoved the money, topped with the ticket, under the glass.

I took the cash and ticket. "So how far north can I go on this train?"

"Lancaster," she said. "About an hour."

"Do I transfer anywhere?" I'd taken enough trains prior to my employment at Fly-By-Night Enterprises to know that was required on some routes.

Starting to look truly annoyed, the woman said, "Straight shot." Then she leaned forward, enunciating every word. "But if you want to go further . . . you can get a ticket . . . at the kiosk. There's a map"—she pointed—"over there, too."

She leaned back and resumed her reading, ending the conversation.

"Thanks." I adjusted the straps crisscrossing my chest, and went toward the platform. When I'd arrived in LA from Folsom, I'd walked outside the bus station in the middle of the night only to find a taxi stand with no taxis. I worried I'd have the same kind of luck on an early Sunday morning in the Valley.

I passed the kiosks to let the cameras see me head toward the platform, then pivoted onto the boulevard and crossed over the median to the opposite side of the street where, miracle of miracles, I spotted a single, banged-up taxi. Apparently one of the last that still lingered near public transport hubs. I waved to the driver, who returned a small nod, and I dropped into the back seat, placing the packs on the floorboard. I passed a hundred-dollar bill through the cash slot in the partition.

"I want to go to Hollywood," I said to the cabbie, hoping he didn't have a problem with taking a fare on a thirty-minute ride over the hills to the basin.

The grizzled driver turned to stare at me, then down at the hundred poking through the plexiglass. The old man wore thick glasses and looked like he hadn't slept or bathed in a week. His once-bright Aloha shirt was threadbare and faded. I saw his bushy eyebrows rise, and he looked at me suspiciously.

"That should cover it," I said. "Including tip."

The man snatched the bill and started the car, not bothering with the meter.

# CHAPTER

# 28

I DIRECTED THE CAB into the alley behind Angela's building. When I was in the business of selling myself, I'd had to hurry out a back door more than once, usually a few steps ahead of an unsuspecting—and unexpected—husband or boyfriend. I figured Angela also had a rear stairwell, an alternate way in and out. I figured right.

I checked to see if I had bled through my shirt onto the car seat, and was relieved I hadn't. The wound had coagulated well. Guess those multivitamins Carla had suggested paid off. I slipped another hundred through the slot. "There's more if you wait for me." The old man took the money and shut off the engine. The combustion sound was replaced with birdsong.

This early on a Sunday, the air felt cool, the neighborhood peaceful. With the freeways and roads practically empty the trip only took about twenty minutes. I dragged the packs out and carried one in each hand. I checked both directions down the dusty throughway for anything or anyone out of place, then deduced which of the rear doors was

Angela's. One flight up, and the door on the end should be her kitchen.

I sneaked up the wooden stairway, my feet as light as possible on the boards, and peeked into the apartment. It was hers, all right. I recognized the colorful potholders over the stove. I had to take the chance, dropped a pack, and rapped on the window pane in the door. I pressed my ear to it. Nothing. I rapped again, harder. I was afraid I might break the glass, but this was the only way to get her attention, if she was even here. I prayed she hadn't spent the night at Eric's or, worse, that Eric had decided to come to her.

"What the fuck!" I heard from deep inside the place.

I rapped again. I heard shuffling, then Angela peeked through the kitchen window. Once she recognized me, she shook her head, and opened the door.

"What the hell! Do you know what time it is?" Her hair dangled in sexy curls around her face, and she was wearing an oversized T-shirt.

My thoughts steered me back to her bedroom the previous afternoon, and I secretly pictured how she looked under that shirt. "Are you alone?" I whispered.

"What?" She looked at me like I'd lost my mind just in the last twenty-four hours (and maybe I had). "Of course I'm alone! What do you want?"

I dropped to a knee and opened a pack, pulled out two bundles of cash, and handed them to her. "Go to a hotel. Now. Don't tell anyone. Don't go to work tomorrow—call in sick or something. And don't talk to Eric at all. You can't trust him. Please. I'll explain later."

She looked at the money in my hand. "Jake . . . what the fuck—"

"Just do it. Please!"

She stared at me, as if she was trying to determine what was true, and what wasn't. When she finally took the cash, her hand was trembling.

A wave of guilt swept over me, and goddamn if it didn't feel just like the guilt that had begun to consume me all those years ago. The guilt I never wanted to feel again. "You'll go," I pressed. "Right now. OK?"

"Yes," she said to the money in her hand. The she looked up. "I'll go."

I picked up the packs and started down the steps, then stopped halfway. "I'm sorry. I promise I'll be in touch as soon as I can."

I rushed back to the alley and found the cabbie waiting right where I'd left him. Twenty-eight minutes later, he dropped me at Fifth and Main, two blocks from the original hostel, my first home back in LA.

* * *

I had begun the weekend as a free man. By early Sunday morning, in the eyes of the law and civil standards anywhere, I was a criminal. By the time the sun rose that Sunday morning, I was a fugitive. And all of these for the second time in my life.

My parole agent, Sanchez, had certainly logged the hostel as my first home, but I'd updated him when I secured my apartment several blocks away. I couldn't know if Sanchez had kept a record of the hostel, if for no other reason than to have a paper trail if one of his charges decided to go off the reservation, so to speak. I didn't think it could happen that quickly, but what if someone had already connected the dots to my first postrelease residence? I decided to keep some distance between myself and the hostel. Better safe than sorry.

What I really wanted was to see Carla. She would be on her shift by now, slinging hash to hungry customers. Probably too busy to talk to me at this hour, anyway, so that would have to wait. Too bad. I sure could use a look into her green eyes right now. That always felt safe. But refuge would be elusive for a while yet. I cut down 5th Street and made a hard right onto Los Angeles Street, even though nothing would be open at 8:30 on a Sunday morning.

I worried Angela might not heed my warning that Eric was not to be trusted. She might decide to confront him herself (or worse, his favorite hitman, Rudy). But I knew, given the chance, I would gift her with some more of this cash, hopefully help make her road to recovery possible . . . if there was one.

So many goddamn unknowns. I didn't know when I could talk to Carla. Or Angela. Or if Sanchez was a detail freak. Or even when I could put on a clean shirt. However, there was a 24-hour CVS on the next corner that was certain to be open. I could at least get some basic first aid for the graze in my side. When I reached the corner entrance, I took a quick glance around, adjusted the cheap sunglasses on my face, and went in.

If only whoever was in charge of the radios in these places would learn how to tune one. Scratchy music filled the empty store, the volume magnified by the lack of customers at this early hour, rendering the muzak unrecognizable. It was like some drunk wanted to hear his favorite station but was too hammered to nail the signal. If I had to listen to that all day, I'd just as soon jump off the building than work in it.

I grabbed a hand-held shopping basket from the stack inside the front door and found the First Aid aisle, located adjacent to the pharmacy. The lone pharmacist, wearing glasses and a black Covid mask, was robotically filling prescriptions. I gathered up Bactine, Neosporin, Extra-Strength Tylenol, a packet of gauze, cotton balls, and a box of large breathable Band-Aids.

I went to the snacks aisle and stocked up on protein bars and a couple single use bottles of fruity energy drinks from the cooler. Next, I went to see what clothing might be offered.

I was shit out of luck when it came to any pants my size, so my blue jeans would have to be innocuous enough. Then I spotted a three-pack of gray cotton T- shirts. Maybe one of these would ease up on the heat. The black one I had on was like a heat magnet, sucking up sunlight, and sending my sweat stinging its way into the wound. And to the touch, it felt like it had soaked up enough blood to feed a shark. A clean pair from a three-pack of black briefs in my size would feel pretty good, too. I'd just pulled a lightweight windbreaker off a hanger and had started for the cashier when something else caught my eye.

I picked out a new pair of mirrored aviator sunglasses from a rack at the end of the aisle, checked them in the small vanity mirror. I placed the crooked set I'd been wearing all morning in the empty space, my gift to any unhoused person who couldn't afford new ones. If one wandered in and found them, who was going to stop him if he walked out with them on? On my way to the cash register, I snapped off the price tag and tossed it in the basket with the rest of my goods.

The last item was an impulse buy. At the register was a display of boxes, each holding ten surgical-style Covid masks. Those could come in handy. I selected a box and set everything one by one on the counter for the young cashier. She glanced up at me when I handed her the tag for the sunglasses (perhaps to check the veracity of the purchase). She was gracious enough to avert her gaze when she saw my facial bruise. I opened the box of masks and pulled one out, then paid from the bundle of cash in my pocket.

"Would you have a men's room I could use?" I asked.

Her cheeks dimpled as she looked up. "It's just for employees."

I leaned in. "I understand," I said, as if she'd just confessed to something. "It's just that I've been on the road for a while, and I have to get going again." I removed the sunglasses, making real eye contact with her. Unlike with the Metro ticket agent, I was hoping the swelling on my eye might elicit some sympathy. "And . . . I did just buy all this stuff."

A shy, impish grin appeared with her dimples, and I noticed her cheeks had flushed. I'd surprised myself. I could still muster one remaining talent from my acting days: My charm.

"OK," she said, and pointed toward the rear of the store, nearly whispering now. "The code is five seven five three. Just don't take too long. My boss is coming in soon."

"Thank you," I whispered back. "I'll be quick, I promise." I swept up the plastic bag with my purchases and hurried across the big store. I glanced at the pharmacist who apparently didn't notice, or didn't care, about the customer hurrying toward the employee bathroom.

I had to move fast. The cute cashier could easily identify me now, and I didn't want her to get into trouble on my account. I punched in the code, heard the mechanism click, and stepped in, locking the deadbolt behind me. I did my business and washed my hands thoroughly.

I stripped off the smelly T-shirt, opened my belt, and stripped off my 501s and underwear. I got a better look at the graze in the mirror. It was a good thing I picked up the first aid supplies. If I let this go untended for too long I'd have a nasty infection for sure.

I pumped the liquid soap dispenser, mixing the gel with warm water from the faucet, and pressed my hip against the sink to reduce spillage. I grimaced as I swabbed the wound. "That fucking hurt," I heard myself say. I pushed out a breath to brace for more, then set about rinsing it clean, scooping handfuls of water until the suds disappeared.

Dousing a cotton ball until it was dripping with Bactine, I braced for the next jolt of pain I knew was coming. I swabbed the disinfectant into the bloody rivulet, repeated the action twice more, each time with fresh cotton, and used paper towels from the dispenser to mop up the excess.

Then the Neosporin went in, enough to even the divot with my skin. I topped that with a folded piece of gauze, and fixed two of the large Band-Aids over it to hold it in place.

By the time I was done pulling my jeans on over a new pair of skivvies, the pain-relieving effect of the Neosporin was setting in . . . somewhat. I cracked open the Tylenol and chewed several, cutting the bitter taste by washing them down with gulps from one of the energy drinks.

After fastening my belt, I opened the pack of T-shirts and pulled one on. I stuffed the remaining two into one of the packs. I dampened my hands and finger-combed my hair into some semblance of a style, then stuffed my discarded T-shirt into the trash can, covering it with used paper towels.

Lastly, I patted my jeans pockets to make sure nothing had dropped out while I'd worked on the wound and felt my wallet in my back pocket. A thought struck me, and I pulled the wallet out, a vintage leather number that Carla had found at a flea market and gave to me one random morning.

"You need a place to keep important stuff," she'd said. I'd opened it to find a black and white photo of a laughing and beautiful Carla, taken in one of those amusement park photo booths.

Now, I pulled out a forgotten business card. There was a phone number printed in matching font below the name, but scrawled on the back was a personal, very private, cell number, one for "special friends." Friends like me. I slipped the card into my front pocket.

I took a last look in the mirror. My face was passive . . . serene. It mirrored an undeniable sensation that I couldn't recall ever feeling before. A wave of tranquility moved through me.

With my new belongings stowed, I left the bathroom. As I passed the cashier on my way to the door, she tapped her wristwatch while sending me a playfully disapproving look. I waved a goodbye.

"I'll remember you in my will," I said, and her dimples smiled back.

As I stepped out into the morning sun, I recalled the old saw that every day is a new day. Each one filled with possibility, but especially for those able to make their own choices, and to take their own actions.

It was then I realized that I'd been fooling myself. Despite what I believed, until this morning I had been no more of a free man than I was in prison. I may as well have been following the crowd to the chow hall, going to where the state told me to. Where Carla told me to. Where Eric told me to. Or Rudy. Nothing more than a prisoner.

I had been yearning for salvation, a deliverance, a kind of forgiveness, which I thought could only come from Angela. The day before she had let me know that she might, finally, absolve me of the hell I'd left her in so long ago. But now, she was facing another kind of fresh hell. The cash I had with me could be my chance to clear the decks of my guilty conscience. Maybe that was just a prison of another kind, but I wouldn't know until I reached the end of my new plan.

I might have been on the run, but at that moment, I was free. I knew what I would do next, and that it was no one's idea but my own. The outcome was unpredictable, and I might lose everything I'd waited for all these years, but at least it would be my choice.

I needed to find a working phone booth and call the personal, very private, number of my former prison mate, the Ghost.

# CHAPTER 29

**THEN**

**Two months after the robbery.**

"HELLO AGAIN, MR. FERGUSON," the District Attorney, debonair in his tailored gray suit and trim beard, addressed me in the witness stand.

I'd been here all morning. My testimony was stretching into the afternoon, and the other side hadn't even started their cross-examination yet.

"Let's pick up where we left off before lunch," he said, glancing at the two men at the defendant's table. "What happened when your colleagues exited the building?"

I was dressed in a cheap suit and tie. My discount dress shirt didn't allow for much air flow, so I was sweating into it. Before long, I'd be mopping my brow with my sleeve. I could feel Damon and Bill watching me from the defendants' table, waiting for my testimony like everyone else in the packed courtroom. I allowed my eyes to drift to them and met their stares (in Damon's case, more of a glare), then looked back to the D.A.

"They got in the car," I said.

"And then you," said the D.A., leading the story, "being the getaway driver, drove them away from the scene?"

"Yes."

"And where were you going?"

"My apartment."

"And what would happen once you got there?"

"The plan was to divide the money, then we would split up."

"With the expectation that you would never see each other again?"

"Yes."

The D.A. smiled slightly. "And yet, here you are, on trial, with those same two men. Isn't that right?"

I took a deep breath. "Yes."

The D.A. straightened up at the lectern, took another glance at the defendants' table, then turned back. "So, what went wrong?"

I needed to clear my throat. "We had been recorded leaving the scene. The police got my license number, and they came and arrested us."

"Caught you red-handed, as they say?" The D.A. allowed an upward lilt at the end of his sentence so that it sounded like a question.

"You could say that."

"Yes, I could, but would *you* say that?"

"Yes."

I had reiterated this so many times already, even given a jailhouse interview to the *LA Times* when the news broke that, rather than stand trial, I would proffer a guilty plea and testify against my codefendants.

"We're getting ahead of ourselves," the D.A. said. "Let's go back to the alley. You were behind the wheel with the engine running, and Mr. DeSanto and Mr. Best got into the car. Is that correct?" *Jesus, why don't you just tell it? Fucking showboat.* The D.A. was making the most of this, intending to slice another prominent notch into his bow ahead of the coming election.

"Yes," I answered. "I was in the car, and they got in with the bags of money, and I took off."

"What time was it then?"

"Three-oh-nine AM."

"That's pretty precise. How do you know that?"

"Because I looked at the dash clock right before they came out. We were supposed to be gone by three-oh-five."

The D.A. turned to the jury. "So, up to this point, things were basically going according to plan, but now you were running a few minutes late." He paused, took a deep, rather dramatic breath, then indignantly crossed his arms. "Something happened because of that small delay, didn't it?" The jury was hanging on his every word. The guilt or innocence of all three of us would come down to this moment of testimony. "Yes," I said.

The prosecutor turned back to face me, even took a couple steps toward me for emphasis. "So, what went wrong?"

I cleared my throat again and swallowed. *My kingdom for a sip of water.* "We hadn't taken the bus schedule into account. There was a stop just outside the alley on the corner of Olive Street." The D.A. waited for me to continue, wanting these specific words to come only from me. "We, uh . . . well, I hit the gas as soon as I knew they were both in, and I picked up speed pretty fast. I was going to come out of the alley onto 5th Street and make a left to the 110 Freeway, but a bus had just dropped off a woman on Olive where I couldn't see her. She walked across the alley entrance right as I was coming out . . . and I hit her."

"Go on," prodded the D.A. He had coached me on this portion of testimony.

"She, uh . . . she went over the hood and hit the windshield, then went all the way over the roof. I stopped the car, and when I looked back, I thought for sure she was dead." I started rubbing my damp palms together.

"And what happened next?" the D.A. asked, this time with some force.

"Damon . . . uh, Mr. DeSanto, got out of the car. He walked over to her and shot her. Twice."

The D.A. nodded grimly. "*Where* did he shoot her, Mr. Ferguson?"

"In the head."

"Both times?"

"Yes."

"And where was this woman looking when Mr. DeSanto shot her"—he turned to the jury—"twice, in the head?"

"At Mr. DeSanto."

"So, she knew what was going to happen to her?"

"Objection!" Damon's court-appointed attorney jumped from his seat. "Calls for speculation."

"The witness observed the murder take place, Your Honor," the D.A. said without turning his head from me. "Nothing 'speculative' about that."

"Overruled," said the judge in her thin, raspy voice. She was a slight, pointy, sixtyish gray-haired woman who, behind her rimless glasses, reminded me of a bird.

"Thank you, Your Honor," he said, then turned his attention back to me. "Did you have a clear field of vision of the murder as it happened?"

"Yes."

"So, you're certain she was looking directly at Mr. DeSanto when he shot her?"

"Yes."

The jury shifted in their seats. My testimony was making them uncomfortable. Or angry. Or both.

"You found out later that the murdered woman was named Clementine Esperanza, isn't that right?"

"Yes, I did."

"Mrs. Esperanza was a kitchen employee, yes? A working woman who had to come home late because hers was the job she could get. Isn't that right, Mr. Ferguson?"

"I guess so."

"But she wasn't the only one hurt by all this, was she?"

I hadn't expected that question. "What do you mean?"

"Mrs. Esperanza was a grandmother to her daughter's two small children. She would often look after the kids when her daughter needed help, like so many workaday folks just trying to get by."

"Objection," said Damon's attorney. "Relevance."

"Your Honor, I'm simply illustrating how Mrs. Esperanza's untimely death affected people besides Mrs. Esperanza. She had a family who loved her, who has struggled mightily to make ends meet ever since."

"Overruled."

The D.A. looked back at me. "You are aware of the family's challenges since she was killed, aren't you?"

For the first time since I was sworn in, I looked at my feet. "Yes," I said.

"Is the man who shot Mrs. Esperanza in the courtroom right now?"

"Yes, he is."

"Would you point him out to us, please?"

I pointed at Damon, who was still glaring at me.

"And the third man in the car that night, your other colleague in this robbery, is he also in the courtroom?"

"Yes," I said, and pointed to Bill Best.

The D.A. directed his next line to the defendants' table. "May the record show that the witness has identified the defendants, Damon DeSanto and William Best." He turned his attention back to me. "Mr. Ferguson, have you been promised anything in return for your testimony, such as a reduced sentence?" The D.A. clearly wanted to shoot down any accusation of preferential treatment before the other side had a chance to make one.

I hadn't expected that question, either, but I was grateful to be asked. "No. I haven't."

The D.A. pointed at Damon and Bill. "Weren't these men your friends?"

I looked directly at them. "Yes," I said, though it felt like I was talking about someone else.

"Then why would you testify against them?"

I scanned the gallery, hoping to catch sight of Angela, but she'd apparently kept her vow not to attend the trial. "I just wanted the money. I didn't want to hurt anybody. I made a mistake, and somebody got killed. That wasn't supposed to happen." I had to stop for a moment before continuing. The weight of the truth of what I was about to say was hitting me for the first time. "So I can try to make up for doing something wrong by doing something right."

"I bet your friends over there aren't too happy with you, are they?"

"No."

"Can't make an omelet without breaking a few eggs, right?"

I looked down again. "I guess not."

"Had the robbery been successful, you intended to go back to Oregon, correct?"

I nodded. "I wanted to start over."

"Thank you, Mr. Ferguson. The court appreciates your cooperation and your testimony. No more questions, Your Honor."

"Very well," said the judge. She was about to say something else, maybe take a recess before the defense began their cross-examination, but the D.A. stopped halfway to his table.

"I'm sorry, Your Honor, just one more question, if I may?"

The judge sighed. "Go ahead," she said, resting her head on her hand.

"Mr. Ferguson, you testified this morning that you're not from Los Angeles."

"Didn't you say you had a question?" asked the judge, starting to sound impatient.

"I do, Your Honor. Just quickly laying the groundwork."

"Move it along," she said.

The D.A. returned his attention to me. "At the time of the crime you had been 'self-employed' as an escort to wealthy older women, and you had hoped, if successful, this robbery would free you from that lifestyle." The D.A. paused and, per his established courtroom style, let the silence hang in the room a moment. "But you didn't come to Los Angeles to be a gigolo or a thief—"

"Objection!" My court-appointed attorney abruptly, *finally*, rose, his thick glasses nearly falling off his pudgy face. "How does my client emigrating here *years ago* from his hometown have any relevance to the facts of this case?"

The D.A. spoke confidently, his eyes locked on me. "Goes to motive, your honor. Mr. Ferguson has insight into the motivations of the accused."

The judge considered for a beat. "I'll allow it."

I steamed. Despite my full and unfettered cooperation, the D.A. still intended to make me look as bad as he could. "I came here to be an actor."

The D.A. nodded. "So, despite the sordid choices you made after the failure of your quest for fame, and your tragic attempt to escape them," he smirked, "I guess you finally got your name in lights, didn't you?"

"Objection! Badgering!"

"Withdrawn, your honor."

Typical. Here in the center of the entertainment universe, anyone who's not in it never passes up a chance to denigrate anyone who is . . . or wants to be.

* * *

"Do you have anything to say before I pass sentence?" the judge asked.

I stood before a packed courtroom, referring intermittently to notes I'd made on a sheet of legal paper. I'd had two weeks to think about what I would say when this moment arrived, and to wonder and worry about my future, or what might be left of one.

"Yes, Your Honor," I began. "I came here to be a movie star. Instead, I'm in this courtroom. In a misguided attempt to feed my drug habit, I sold my body. When I became desperate to escape that life, I took part in a crime that resulted in the death of an innocent person. The time I've spent in jail has forced my body, and my mind, to be rid the substances I craved so much before all this happened, and with that cleansing has come clarity. I now understand my reasons for being involved in this stupid crime, and the choices I made that brought me here today. The simple truth is, I have no one to blame but myself, and I accept whatever punishment you deem appropriate. Thank you."

The judge must've decided that "appropriate" meant that I didn't deserve any leniency, because she didn't give any. It didn't matter to her that I'd testified against Damon and Bill, had taken responsibility, and incriminated myself in the process.

Under the Felony Murder Rule in force at the time, Bill and I were each sentenced as if we had personally pulled the trigger: twenty-five-to-life. And that came with no guarantee of a parole review. As for Damon, it was simple timing that saved his bacon. California has had a mishmash of on again- off again state and federal rulings and moratoriums on the death penalty for decades. Otherwise, Damon

DeSanto would've received it, for sure. Instead, he pulled the big one for that time: life without the possibility of parole. Damon and I managed to listen stoically as our sentences were handed down. Bill cried.

We were sent to separate correctional institutions; Damon to San Quentin, Bill to Corcoran (Charles Manson's last home), and me to Folsom State Prison, ending what any of us had ever known of freedom.

# CHAPTER 30

**NOW**

"WHAT A PLEASANT surprise!" Pierre's French-Canadian accent lilted through the phone.

The Ghost hadn't answered my first attempt to reach him on his personal, very private number, as is the expected protocol in his line of work. I left a voicemail to ring me back at the decrepit phone booth I found on Los Angeles Street. The city may have only spared this one along with the increasingly sparse amount of working public phones because most residents in this area hover at or below the poverty line. It took Pierre all of two minutes to respond.

"Thanks for calling me back, Pierre," I said. "I was afraid you might've left town already."

"I wish that were so," he replied with a chuckle. "Between expenses and the, uh . . . exclusivity of my endeavors, business could be better. But then, we would not be talking now. I hope this means I will see you."

Twenty minutes later he did.

Located in the Arts District next door to a Hauser & Wirth gallery, the popular, upscale Manuela restaurant attracted a well- dressed, artsy crowd. Just the kind of place Pierre liked. I was concerned I might stand out in my uncool T-shirt and Levis, but the season was changing, and autumn was making its usual slow arrival to the Southland. My new windbreaker shouldn't stand out too much, so I threw it on before going in (though I wished I'd bought a hat while I was at it).

I entered the restaurant just after its ten AM opening time. To me, the large open air dining area looked as if "urban" and "rustic" had birthed a patio for a child. It was bookended by a brick wall that hid it from the busy street on one side and a working garden with clucking egg-producing hens in stacked cages on the other.

I spotted Pierre seated at an outdoor corner table, well away from the modular bar and, therefore, any prying eyes and ears. As I got closer, I could see his ruddy beach tan, which in prison had faded to its native North Country alabaster, was back in full. I dropped the packs under the table and hooked my foot into the shoulder straps. Despite the shade provided by the abundant flora and the wooden canopy above, I kept my new sunglasses on.

I was grateful to find Pierre had ordered a cappuccino for me, and I took a gulp. Pierre smiled at how I ignored the customary approach of sipping the coffee.

"In need of a lift?" Pierre said dryly.

"Been a long night," I replied, and waved to a waiter, indicating I'd like another. "Sorry, Pierre, but I'm in a hurry."

"Isn't everyone?" he said, with an easy smile. He leaned forward. "I am curious why you called."

"I need The Ghost."

Pierre's smile faded. "Jake," he said, his voice lowered. "What are you doing?"

"You know I won't tell you that," I said, downing the last of the coffee. "Isn't that how you do things?"

"Then you realize what my next question is."

"No," I said. "I'm not a cop. You want to check me for a bug?"

"I would be stupid not to."

I unzipped my jacket and held it open, then I glanced around. The row of planters next to our table offered adequate coverage, so I raised my T-shirt, exposing my bare torso.

"What happened?" asked Pierre, seeing the large bandage on my side and the thin red line that had seeped through it.

"You're back to questions I can't answer." I said, lowering my shirt.

Pierre nodded. He understood the game as well as anyone, and he knew not to push it.

A waiter delivered my second cappuccino. "Ready to order?"

Pierre kept his gaze on me another moment, then looked up. "We'd like a few minutes, please."

"Of course. Take your time."

Pierre paused for the waiter to leave ear shot before continuing. "I would need to know the requirements of the task to provide the right tool."

"Come in hot, and come out in one piece." I took a beat. "Alone."

"How many?"

"Could be a couple, could be a roomful." I watched Pierre for any change in his demeanor. All I picked up was a sense that he was doing his best not to imagine the aftermath of my "task."

Finally, Pierre said, "That can be very expensive."

I leaned over and pulled the zipper on a backpack, opening it just enough for The Ghost to see inside. "I think I can cover it."

Pierre straightened up. He smiled. Despite his aversion to violence, nothing leavens a natural born criminal like money.

"The food here is quite good," said Pierre. "I hope we have time for breakfast."

CHAPTER

# 31

PIERRE DROVE THE two of us in his Model S Tesla. I almost laughed when I saw it. These cars had become so ubiquitous in LA you'd think it was a requirement for residency.

This town has always had a penchant for automotive status symbols, like the past fads of the Mercedes 450 SL or the new generation Thunderbirds. I hadn't been in one of these yet, and I took in the interior, if that's what you could call it. Between the rectangular steering wheel, and the control panel that looked like a giant iPad mounted in the dashboard, there was practically nothing to operate. It felt more like an aircraft cockpit. I decided that Pierre, despite his complaint that business was slow, was doing just fucking fine, thank you very much.

We negotiated the Arts District's cobweb of streets, the original warehouses and factories now converted to trendy lofts and boutiques. We came to the spectacular 6th Street Viaduct, a new construction of futuristic concrete arches girded on both sides by concentric cables.

I recalled the previous bridge as the scene of a dazzling shootout and car chase in the movie *To Live and Die in L.A.* (and maybe also a Madonna video?), but this was my first time seeing this architectural marvel. I wondered how I could have missed something so huge . . . and so beautiful.

As we glided down the far side of the bridge into Boyle Heights, I was startled to see that Pierre didn't even have his hands on the steering . . . thing.

"What the fuck?" I said, imagining us careening through the guardrail and landing upside down on the 101 Freeway.

Pierre just smiled, then took the wheel as we came to the end of the bridge span.

Boyle Heights was another historic area I had neglected to ever visit. Once one of the most ethnically diverse neighborhoods in LA, shared by Japanese, Mexican, and Jewish communities since the late 1800s, it was the childhood home of gangster Mickey Cohen.

Remnants of its heyday still stood. The Breed Street Shul, Mariachi Plaza, the original Sears and Roebuck Mail Order Building, and even County General Hospital (used for decades in the opening credits of the daytime serial *General* Hospital). The community became what is now overwhelmingly Hispanic not due to overt racism, but to real estate redlining, which allowed the Jewish, Irish, and Japanese residents an avenue to different areas, but not the Latinos. I couldn't recall anyone even mentioning Boyle Heights as a place they'd heard of, let alone visited.

Pierre followed the main drag into what looked to be the town center, then pulled the Tesla into a strip mall parking lot, took a space facing the boulevard, and watched the passing cars. I looked around. Most of the storefronts had yet to open for business.

"Are we there?" I asked.

Pierre shook his head. "I want to be sure we made the trip alone," he said.

My eyes went to the street. "Who would've followed us?"

"Hopefully no one."

After a few minutes, Pierre seemed satisfied. He backed out and drove us into the residential neighborhood behind the mall. A few more turns, and he pulled into the driveway of a decrepit Craftsman home nestled halfway down a quiet, tree- lined block.

"Pardon," Pierre said, reaching over and opening the glove compartment. He retrieved an automatic garage door opener. He clicked it once, and the small garage door opened, exposing an empty space. It looked so narrow, I wondered if the Tesla could even fit. Pierre slowly maneuvered the car inside and, with another click, the garage door shut.

I had to squeeze out between the car door and the wall. The only light streamed in from a single small window in the wall next to me, and I could see into the kitchen of the house next door. Behind the lace curtains framing the glass, I saw a stout Hispanic woman working, perhaps making Sunday brunch for her family. If she'd noticed me, she didn't show it. I retrieved the packs from the rear seat.

Pierre opened a door that led to the backyard and morning light filled the garage. I followed him outside, squinting against the sun. The savory scent of refried beans and stewed pork drifted from the kitchen next door. I inhaled, relishing the aroma. That lady next door could really cook. But I had to cut the pleasant olfactory moment short when the sun hit my eyes, and I pushed my index finger under my nose to head off a sneeze.

The yard was larger than I would have expected, surrounded on all sides by a high ancient hedge. I was beginning to understand why Pierre had chosen this spot. Talk about blending in. We crossed the brown dry yard to an outbuilding by the back fence. It looked like it had been meant as a guest house, but the few windows had been covered with thick plywood sheets, fixed in place with a combination of heavy nails and steel brackets. No one was breaking into this place without some serious determination.

Pierre opened an app on his phone and tapped in a code. I heard a lock inside the door clunk. He opened the door, waved me inside, and closed it behind us.

Pierre flipped on an overhead light. He punched the app again and a large bolt slid back into place. The unit was sparsely furnished. It could work for a young single person just starting out, but it was obvious no one had occupied the place in a while. It had a simple coffee table and chair, a kitchenette with a toaster oven, and a smattering of cups, plates, and utensils on a tiny counter and shelf. An old two-seater sofa stood in the center of the small room, holding down a ratty area rug. Pierre pushed the sofa aside and pulled up the rug beneath it, exposing a trap door in the hardwood floor.

Pierre punched another code, and the same whir and clunk sound emanated from below. He pulled up a steel ring recessed in the wood and swung open the door. An earthen smell rose up, bringing with it the unmistakable scent of gun oil.

"Watch your step," Pierre said as he climbed down into darkness.

I left the packs behind and followed, carefully finding the steep stairs one at a time. I steadied myself on the opening of the trap until I had to let it go and use the stairwell. As I ran my hand on an old wood banister, a tiny sliver found its way into my palm. I heard Pierre pull a loose chain, and with a click the subterranean room was illuminated by a bare bulb in the ceiling. I was only halfway down, my eyes still adjusting to the dim amber light, but I could see what Pierre had been so careful to hide from the world.

The walls were a marketplace of death.

Fully automatic—and highly illegal—machine guns of every caliber. Pistols, both revolver and slide action. Long guns in the form of shotguns, rifles, and a few collectible musket loaders. Covering one full wall were weapons devoted to mass killing: grenades, a handheld rocket launcher, oversized ammo magazines to give an attacker an edge in a firefight. A fricking bazooka! On the opposite wall were neat rows of the weapons that had given The Ghost his nickname. Solid gold guns of every type—the kind you see confiscated from drug lords and leaders of powerful street gangs.

This hole in the ground held enough kill power to stage a coup or control the inner city of any major metropolis. I wondered if the El Repettos were still in business, and perhaps regular clients of The Ghost. But I kept that curiosity to myself.

"Jesus, Pierre, how the fuck did you do this?"

"It was already here," he explained. "A bomb shelter, built when your country was afraid of nuclear attack." He looked around at his handiwork. "I think I would call it a 'useful irony'? Certainly fortuitous." Pierre swept his hand in the air. "See anything you like?"

I raised my eyebrows. "I wouldn't know where to start."

Pierre thought for a moment. "I believe I have just the thing."

# CHAPTER

# 32

MY HAND SHOT out to grab the Walther I'd left on the nightstand. I fumbled to get hold of the gun and it dropped to the floor, bouncing toward the door. Miraculously, it didn't go off. *Nice move there, Tex.*

I had jerked awake from a nightmare: Eric and company had somehow tracked me down, gotten into this flimsy SRO hotel room, and were aiming their weapons at me. In my dream Inside Man and the dead guard from the SentryCity heist were beside me. Both were alive in my mind, but their faces said they knew what was coming.

I pulled in a series of deep breaths to calm myself. Amazing that even at my age, a dream still had the power to terrify.

I sat up and looked toward the window, sensing the awakening city beyond the blackout shades, the light stubbornly creeping in at the edges. For the world out there, it was just another Monday morning. For me, it might be the day that everything ends.

This was beginning to feel too familiar. Less than six months before, in a room much like this one, I was awakened by an earthquake. Today, it was a nightmare. The rooms looked eerily similar (but at least I had my own bathroom in this one). If I looked out the window, would I see another bum taking a dump on the sidewalk?

*Why the hell did I come back here? Because the law said so. That's why.*

I'd checked in late the previous afternoon. Pierre had dropped me on Los Angeles Street, where knock-off clothiers were in full Sunday swing, and I'd picked out more new garments. Then I searched the surrounding area for a cash-friendly SRO of some kind. With all the gentrification in downtown LA, many of the flophouses that used to be here had been forced out, but a few remained. I found this one off 7th Street, next to St. Vincent Court. The irony of this dump being only half a block from the Los Angeles Athletic Club, one of the most exclusive gyms in the city, didn't escape me. I supposed most people didn't notice it on their way into LAAC or St. Vincent Court, with its charming brick walkway and Middle Eastern restaurants.

I had arrived with packs of cash on my back, and a bag of new duds in one hand. In the other, was a hard-sided case containing the wares I'd bought from The Ghost. These included the Walther PPK (which made me feel a tad like James Bond), recommended by Pierre over the 9mm Glock I'd considered. He explained that the recoil on the Glock was so strong I could drop the gun before getting off a second shot. The .380 Walther would still do the job, but was more likely to remain in my grip. And, of course, I also had the main item I hoped would get me out of this mess alive.

I'd settled in, showered, redressed my wound, and gave the desk clerk a hundred bucks to arrange for some groceries to be delivered. By then, the SentryCity Security robbery was all over the news, leading every local newscast, and making its way into the lead stories of twenty- four-hour cable channels.

Helicopter footage accompanied every story. The compound looked untouched, but the anchors were breathlessly recounting the event: the daring entrance from under the building, how the alarm and surveillance systems sent bogus signals and then were disabled, and the discovery of two dead employees.

Newscasters reported one of the men shot dead was a twelve- year employee of the company. They went on to say he had been head of security for the facility, and would have the required knowledge to manipulate the alarm system. The other victim, the guard, had not been named publicly, pending notification of next of kin.

Early estimates put the take at around twenty million dollars. I thought I'd heard that wrong, but then the anchors repeated it, themselves clearly stunned by the amount. Perhaps SentryCity was inflating their losses to pressure the insurance company for repayment? I'd known some guys who had done just that, embezzled, reported higher losses, then killed their colleagues to avoid discovery, only to be convicted of murder.

But twenty million made a crazy kind of sense. I'd finally had a chance to count the take from the two backpacks. I'd been hauling around a million bucks, cash. Multiply that by the potential amounts carried out by each of Eric's crew, and that number of twenty mil would be pretty close.

What would Pierre have done if he'd known just how much I'd actually had with me? For all of his loyalty and gratitude, I think he would have left me lying dead in that underground bunker. I pictured him sipping champagne in a first-class seat all the way to the South Seas, his new surfboard checked with his luggage below.

I ate one of the bananas that had been delivered the night before with the rest of my supplies while the in-room coffee pot percolated. I was glad for the sleep I'd gotten. The preceding thirty-six hours had been exhausting (understatement of the decade) and had pushed me into a deep slumber. If that damn dream hadn't happened, I might still be out. But I was awake now, and I wanted to make the most of this time.

I didn't bother with the TV or the digital clock radio by the bed. This morning, the only sounds I wanted to hear were my own thoughts. I knew what I had to do. I'd conceived the plan all the way back in that forgotten field yesterday.

And it had to be today. The sooner the better.

Eric had to know, that with me in the wind, his chances of evasion were thinned considerably. But with close to twenty million dollars at his fingertips? With that kind of money, even after paying out his crew, a person could truly disappear. I recalled the Italian restaurant I'd driven Eric to the night I learned he had underworld contacts, how that scene looked to me like a West Coast *Goodfellas*. Would Eric pull a "Jimmy Conway" and start taking out members of his gang in order to enrich himself? The murders of Inside Man and the guard sure made me think it more than likely.

I unplugged a new Xiaomi phone I'd bought the day before at the same place Carla had sent me to when I'd first met her. I knew by now a device of this kind wouldn't be traced to me. I could make necessary calls from it, at least in the short term. And though I'd powered it down, I held on to the Fly-By-Night company iPhone. It might come in handy.

I'd check on Angela shortly, once I was on the move. And I would make time to see Carla.

Yes, I knew what to do. I just didn't know if I had the balls to do it.

# CHAPTER

# 33

"THAT WAS *YOU?*"

Despite the din of busy weekday traffic, I could hear Angela through the phone just fine. I was at the curb outside the diner, faced away from the crowd leisurely waiting for their names to be called for their turn at breakfast.

"I was there, but it wasn't *me*," I countered. "It was Eric. And that prick, Rudy."

"Oh please, Jake."

"It's true, Angela. Eric's into some bad shit. I watched them kill somebody the other night. And they tried to kill me."

"What are you talking about?"

"You really don't have any idea the shit he's up to?"

There was a pause, and I thought I heard a heavy sigh. "Maybe I had an idea," she admitted. "But what do you mean he tried to *kill* you?"

"You saw the news? Two guys dead?"

"Who hasn't?"

"One of those guys was supposed to be me."

"Oh, God! Jake!"

"I think they planned to leave my body behind, like a fall guy. Rudy missed. But with my record, I'm a logical suspect."

"But you work for him. Wouldn't that just lead back to him? Why would anyone do that?"

"You'd have to ask him. All he really has to say is he tries to give these guys a second chance, but he can't watch them every minute."

"What do you mean? What 'guys'?"

I squeezed the bridge of my nose with my thumb and forefinger. "I can't believe you don't know this. Eric's company is in some program to give jobs to ex-cons. One guy they hired was Bill Best, my partner from the . . . the thing that sent me away. They killed him, too. I saw it happen." I felt myself getting worked up, so I took a breath to calm down. "Eric's father was my other partner. He died in San Quentin."

"Jesus," she said. "Wait . . . you mean . . . *Damon*?"

"Yeah," I said.

"Wasn't he the one—?"

"The one who pulled the trigger, yes." I expected her to react to that, to say something. When nothing came, I said, "Your boyfriend's been thinking about this for a while. Makes me wonder how he found his way to you."

She stayed quiet. Was she asking herself the same question? "I never imagined he could do something like this," she said.

"Well, if I've learned any goddamned thing in this life, it's that people do all kinds of scary shit."

"What are you going to do?" Now she sounded worried. Frightened.

I thought a moment. "Has he tried to call you?"

"Yes, but I haven't answered. He tried a few times yesterday. Not today. Not yet, anyway."

"He doesn't know where you are, does he?" I said, feeling a twinge of panic.

"No! You were such a dick about it, I haven't told anybody. Not sure I should even tell you."

"*Don't* tell me," I shot back. "I don't want to know."

"You didn't answer my question, Jake. What are you going to do?"

"Turn off your phone. Just check it every now and again like you have been. I'll get in touch again when I can."

"Jake, what are—"

I ended the call before she could finish. When I turned around, Carla was watching me from inside the diner, her hands on her hips, her face so cryptic I couldn't tell if she was happy to see me or about to carve me up like a strip of bacon in an omelet.

I went inside.

CHAPTER

# 34

"TAKING MY BREAK," Carla called to a old cook, who nodded without argument.

She grabbed my wrist and guided me to the rear of the diner, down a hallway toward the bathrooms, then she took a turn into a storage room that held dry goods. She closed the door, crossed her arms, and looked at me.

"Start talking," she said.

I thought lightning bolts might shoot from her eyes and strike me dead.

"I can't stay," I said, finding it harder to speak than perhaps I ever had, but I forced out the words. "I wanted you to know that I wish things had been different for us."

I may as well have said her mother just died. Her gaze shifted from anger to sadness. She took a seat on a large box marked "Baking Flour" and her eyes dropped to the cement floor.

"You got jammed up, didn't you?" She waited for an answer until she decided she'd waited long enough, and looked up. "Didn't you!"

"Yes," I admitted. She looked away, as if I repulsed her. "But not because I wanted to."

"Nobody ever *wants* to," she said. "Just ask my brother. He says it happens all the time. Your old buddies show up because they want you for one *last score*!" The disgust wrapped around those last two words was unmistakable. She shook her head. "You didn't come to me." It wasn't a question.

"It happened fast."

"Is there somebody else?" she blurted. "I mean, I thought we had something pretty good. Could'a been, anyway." I didn't answer. I couldn't. "I thought you trusted me."

"I do," I said, and I meant it. I hadn't trusted anyone in years, and the feeling surprised me. "I just don't want you to get hurt."

"So, that's it?" she said.

"Yeah," I said. "I'm sorry." She started to say something else, but I cut her off. "And don't ask me what I'm going to do."

CHAPTER

# 35

"THIS IS COMPLETELY untraceable. You could drop it where you stand and, as long as you don't leave fingerprints, it's impossible to link to us."

My conversation with The Ghost the day before kept running through my head.

"And you may want to practice with it," he'd advised me.

Practice? I didn't have time to go to some gun range or out in the woods and *practice.* So instead, I stood in the middle of my small room, the strap slung over my shoulder to help keep the gun in place, and repeated the action of twisting its three magazine tubes.

The IWI Tavor TS12 is considered one of the best, and most lethal, short range shotguns in the world. Easy to carry, easy to load, and easy to fire. I had to admit it felt good in my hands. The hardest thing to get used to was wearing surgical gloves to prevent powder burns and fingerprints.

"See the switch inside the trigger guard?" Pierre had asked. I turned the gun to inspect the front of the curved metal guard and saw what looked like a button. "It's remarkably simple. You press that button to turn the magazine. The magazine is made up of these three tubes." He pointed to three narrow silos that created one cylindrical mechanism running nearly the length of the barrel. "You will feel it automatically reload a shell into the chamber. You just shoot until the tube empties, then press and turn. Shoot, then turn again."

I shrugged. "OK. So what does that mean?"

"It means you can fire up to fifteen rounds without reloading. Just turn the magazine every five shots by pressing the switch. Five in a tube if you use two-and-a-half-inch shells. Or four if you use three-inch. You expect to be in close quarters, yes?"

"Probably."

"Then I recommend the two-and-a-half inch so you have the extra ammunition. Sixteen with one preloaded in the chamber, which I also recommend. The heavy-duty recoil spring combined with the lighter load ammunition will reduce the kick even more. You could fire this with one hand. Truly. Except you will need both to turn the tubes. That is the one drawback to this weapon."

For a native Oregonian, it was practically a birthright to have experience with all manner of weaponry. Our family Christmas Day ritual was to tear open presents, have a big breakfast, then the guys would head to the gun range. One year, my uncle, a Vietnam veteran, brought along a Bushmaster PDW or Personal Defense Weapon. It had the same "Bullpup" design as the Tavor, and when I fired it at twelve years old, the kick nearly knocked me on my ass. Something I never forgot. But it also seared the basics of how to use it into my memory.

*Like riding a bicycle. I hope.*

Pierre went on to babble about specs and research, how the Israeli company that developed it had taken about four years to get it right. Their main goal was to make it 100 percent reliable. It was fully ambidextrous, so a leftie like me could use it as easily as any right-handed shooter. The 12-gauge shotgun's use of construction materials meant it weighed only nine pounds. You had to account for a little more when fully loaded, but even still, a fit soldier (or hit man) could carry it for hours without it becoming a nuisance. And at less than a yard long, with that strap over your shoulder to suspend it, the Bullpup design meant it could be hidden under a roomy jacket or long coat. That was advantageous, given the weather was beginning to cool.

"OK" I said. "If you can buy it at any gun show, what makes this one so different?" I asked that, not because I thought I'd save a few bucks by heading to the nearest NRA convention, but because Pierre's products were supposed to be unlike any others in the world.

"This," he said, and held up a black metal cylinder with rings spaced about an inch apart.

"Is that a silencer?"

"No," he said with a grin. "It's a suppressor."

"Potato, pot-ah-to."

"Exactly. And this," he held up another item, also round and black, but much shorter, "is called a choke."

Pierre took the gun from me, and with a few twists of his wrist, securely mounted the choke on the end of the barrel, then he screwed the suppressor onto the choke. Overall, it lengthened the shotgun by about a foot. "This gun has been customized from existing items on the market. No one else has this. It drops the decibels significantly. To a neighbor it may sound like someone had punched a wall. It will give you a better chance to go undetected, and hopefully, escape."

"How much?"

"For you, my cost only. Five thousand dollars." Pierre must have read the "you can't be serious" look on my face, because he went on to explain, "You were a friend to me when I needed one." He aimed the Tavor at the wall of his bunker, as if he were going to fire it. "You really should practice with it at least once. Weapons like this need a 'break-in period' for the user to become familiar with its quirks."

"Quirks?" That was a term that I'd typically apply to a used car. "I'll do what I can, Pierre."

Then he gave me a look I had never seen from him before. "I will always call you my friend," he said. "But you understand, I can never grant you another favor."

I looked down at the weapon in my hands, felt its weight, and imagined its purpose.

I nodded. "We're even."

Having taken the morning to familiarize myself with the gun and its mechanisms, I'd gotten to the point where I could, with a quick push of my thumb to release the action, swivel the magazine left to right. As promised, each time the breach would open for a shell to pass, the gun would automatically load a new one into the chamber. It was a stunning piece of machinery, designed to do nothing but kill human beings. Pierre told me it had been marketed to the general public as a "self-defense" weapon. I supposed that could be true . . . if your home was ever invaded by the Delta Force.

I pulled on a lightweight autumnal transitional overcoat I'd included in my wardrobe binge the day before. I'd also chosen a pale blue dress shirt to go under it, offset with a sharp black tie and a pair of sleek gray slacks. Lastly, I set a new straw Panama hat on my head. Its narrow brim would allow me to drop my chin and not impede my vision, but make it difficult for any surveillance cameras to get a clean look at my face. Lesson learned.

With the new outfit and the gun's oversized case, I hoped to come off as just another salesman hawking his wares to the surfeit of merchants on Hollywood Boulevard.

I used my new favorite mode of transport: a cab that takes cash. I gave the driver a hundred- dollar bill and had him drop me at the corner of Hollywood and Ivar, one block west of Vine Street.

Any time of year, fabled Hollywood Boulevard is teeming by late morning, and today was no different. I headed east, making my way through tourists. The businesses on this stretch were hardly on the higher end of what is already a lower class of market. Barkers in tchotchke shop doorways compete with each other for attention and commerce, shouting and gesturing that only they have the best cheesy souvenirs.

The boulevard's lone strip club anchors the center of this block, and has certainly influenced the tone of it all. Fast food purveyors promise "sinful pizza" and "tipsy tails." Whoever came up with the slogan emblazoned on the club's awning, "1000s of Beautiful Girls & 3 Ugly Ones," probably had trouble hanging on to a significant other. The posters out front featured the women who worked there. One of them, pictured in a scanty electric blue dress, reminded me of the buxom woman I saw in Eric's office the first time I came to the Astoria. For all I knew, it was her.

Several homeless men were scattered along the curb.

Some were lolling over the terrazzo inlaid with brass stars that made up the Hollywood Walk of Fame. I had to smile at the irony that the star for the hated gossip columnist Hedda Hopper was covered in grime and located smack in front of the sleazy strip joint. The crazy and the immortal, all gathered together. Talk about the highs and lows of Hollywood.

A few homeless guys pleaded for donations, but most simply stared straight ahead, muttering unintelligibly, as if watching a horror movie only they could see. A private screening for the mad. Just the sight of these broken souls ignited my secret fear, the one that drove so many of my worst decisions, to evade joining them in this nightmare of an existence.

I turned the corner onto Vine which, just beyond a corner parking lot, would bring me to the Astoria. There was no way for me to know if Eric—or any of his crew—would be inside, but I had to start somewhere. With the addition of a Covid mask and my new sunglasses, I felt secure enough to walk the frontage of the hotel.

On either side of the building were steel entrance gates, blocking access to all but deliveries and workers. Both were closed, and neither had a keypad or a traditional lock that I could see. I resisted the temptation to try opening one, not wanting to alert security, and I knew I couldn't risk walking through the front door, or even the valet parking garage. Chances were too high that one of Eric's crew could be there.

I didn't break my stride as I glanced over the top of my aviators into the Astoria's garage, and then the lobby, seeing nothing unusual or anyone I recognized. I kept going until I reached the Avalon Hollywood nightclub next door and turned into its deserted entryway.

Built in an ornate Spanish Baroque style, the Avalon began as a playhouse in the 1920s. I had first known it as the Palace, and it had been featured in a few movies I'd seen. I once brought Angela here to see Big Head Todd and the Monsters, making her a fan for life.

It would be hours before it opened for business, so I decided to bide my time under the Avalon's awning, out of sight of the hotel's cameras. I put the case down and used it for a chair.

Directly across Vine, next to Capitol Records, the faces on the Hollywood Jazz Mural smiled back at me. Nat King Cole, Ella Fitzgerald, Chet Baker, Billie Holiday. Music figures both gifted and tragic. Funny how we eulogize those whose talents and lives we exploit and exhaust. That was the experience for many who would make it in Hollywood—to be exalted, then left depleted.

I suddenly felt tired. I couldn't know how, or *if*, my plan would work out. I didn't even know what I would do next. This stretch of Vine was empty compared to the crowds just around the corner. An occasional pedestrian would stroll by, perhaps a guest of the Astoria, or maybe a tenant of the modern, geometric apartment buildings that had sprung up nearby in recent years.

The loud whine of an engine broke through the traffic noise, and a large refrigerated food truck, one of the many wholesale restaurant food purveyors you often see blocking curbside traffic, passed by and I heard it brake to a stop. I peeked around the edge of the foyer to see it had parked in front of the Astoria.

The emergency lights started flashing, and the driver dropped out of the high cab onto the street, right where Rudy had passed off the company car to me all those weeks ago. The driver pressed a button on his key fob, and the truck locked with a beep. He jogged into the lobby of the hotel. A minute later, the steel gate nearest to me opened, and the driver emerged from the walkway that ran along that side of the building. Dangling from his hand was an orange traffic cone, which he dropped on the concrete, using it to prop open the gate.

From my vantage point at the AVALON, I watched as the man rolled a flat dolly loaded with a palette of foodstuffs onto the hydraulic lift at the rear of the truck. Obviously a delivery for the Astoria's kitchen. He punched a button on a controller dangling from the truck's inside wall, and the lift lowered him and the dolly to street level. He rolled the dolly off, closed up the truck, and repeated the locking ritual with the key fob. Then he steered the dolly onto the sidewalk and through the gate, leaving the traffic cone where it stood . . . and the gate open.

I admit, this felt something like kismet. Or fate. Whatever you want to call it. I opened the case, took out the Walther, and slipped it into my outside coat pocket. I shut and hefted the case, lowered the brim of my hat an inch or so, and headed for the walkway. I stopped, glanced inside, saw no one, and turned into it.

Halfway down the building a side door had also been propped open with a kickdown door stop. Delivery Man must've come through here. I slowed just enough to take inventory as I passed by the opening.

A hallway wide enough to accommodate a dolly the size of the one Delivery Man had just pushed through. To the right, I could hear the clanging bustle of the kitchen. On the left, a little further down, was a freight elevator. All the way at the end was another open door which led to the garage. I could see a uniformed valet, busily sorting through tickets at a stand.

I'd rather not encounter any humans, so I hustled to the rear of the building. Nothing back there but a narrow walkway separated by a low brick wall from the hotel's power supply. Its monotone hum filled the space from behind a chain fence. There was another higher wall beyond the power grid at the edge of the property. I couldn't see a way inside the building from back here.

This might be my only chance, so I returned to the open delivery door, took a breath, and went inside. I passed the kitchen, where the staff was debating which produce to use on that night's menu. I hoped no one would notice the man with the long coat and hard-sided case, trying to look like he knew where he was going. I reached the freight elevator and pressed the Up button.

A tall man in a white smock and chef's toque stepped out of the kitchen. "Can I help you?" he asked. I couldn't place his accent but he looked Latino.

"Hi," I replied. I took off my sunglasses to give my best "friendly salesman" vibe, but kept the mask in place. I slid my hand into my pocket and felt the Walther, then indicated the case. "I have a meeting upstairs. They're thinking about changing the lighting on the roof." Hopefully I hadn't just lied to the guy who also had a say in the restaurant's decor and not just the cuisine.

He nodded. "It could use an upgrade." He definitely sounded South American, but no way I could identify exactly where. "Can I see them?"

*Shit.* "You know, I would, but I have to get 'em out, set 'em up, then put 'em back in to take upstairs. And I'm running late."

"I could call them for you," he offered. "We can use my office to see how they look in the dark." Any other time, this guy would be a salesman's dream.

"Thanks, but I'm just gonna go where I'm told."

The elevator opened. I stepped in and pressed six. I heard his footsteps coming my way, so I pushed the Close Door button.

"It's no trouble. I'd like to see what you have—"

"Thanks!" I said again as the gap between the doors began to narrow. "I'll have dinner here soon." The closing door stopped any further conversation.

*Now I'm fucked.* That chef might very well call whoever would be in charge of redesigning the fucking lights, and when that person said they had no fucking plans to change the fucking lights on the fucking roof, they would fucking start looking for me. But this wasn't about me. I had to keep going.

The door opened and I rushed into a hallway that doubled as a work station of some kind, outfitted with tables and cabinets. To my right was a mini-version of the kitchen downstairs. To my left was the way out.

I went through a pair of swinging double doors into a large open space the hotel uses for events and parties (hence the mini-kitchen). No staff was present, but I couldn't expect to be alone for more than a few minutes.

I knew the sixth floor was one floor below the roof, one floor above the corner suite in which Eric and his crew had set up their office.

I went around a big square bar in the center of the elegant room to the far corner. This put me at the rear of the building, which faced another Hollywood landmark, The Roosevelt, once a grand hotel, and now a retirement home. A row of arched windows offered a partial view of the LA Basin. I turned the handle on the last window by the wall and pushed it open. The window frame was hinged at the top, so the heavy glass opened outward from the bottom.

I poked my head out and looked down to the room directly below. The window for that room was also open, though it was hinged at the side. Perched on the ledge, someone was having a smoke, holding his cigarette just outside the room. I couldn't tell who it was, but by the way he was angled, I could see a piece of his shirt and slacks. He was dressed in the crew's uniform of black pants and white dress shirt.

The room was occupied, but from up here I'd never be able to tell how many more were in there. And though the Roosevelt blocked some of the city noise, I couldn't hear any voices coming from the room.

A wind gust blew between the two buildings, taking my new hat with it. *Dammit.* I watched it glide over the wall at the side of the property and float toward Hollywood Boulevard. They don't call the space between tall city buildings "wind tunnels" for nothing.

I shut the window and locked it, then crossed to the opposite end of the wall, to a marked stairwell. In case of emergency, every building has an alternative exit to the elevators, and by law those doors remain unlocked at all times.

Looking through the rectangular window above the knob, I scanned the walls for cameras. The door into the stairwell was equipped with a small rectangular window. I looked through the industrial glass into the stairway and scanned the walls for cameras. I could see none from here, so I opened the door and checked the ceiling above me. Astonishing, but this stairwell may be the one corner of LA that didn't have a fucking camera on it. No sounds emanated from above or below.

I eased the door shut and went down one flight to the fifth floor. As soon as my foot hit the landing, I heard a door open, followed by footsteps coming up the stairs from a couple flights below. The acoustics of the cement surfaces bounced sounds all around me. I held my breath as my hand found its way into my coat pocket and wrapped around the handle of the Walther.

I peeked over the banister. A man in a white waiter's jacket balancing a tray of covered plates on his shoulder was rounding the corner from the second to the third floor. I heard him mumble something in Spanish. He disappeared under the landing. I heard a door open and shut. Then silence.

I must've held my breath longer than I thought because I found myself gasping for air. I could feel my pulse pounding in my neck. I looked out the stairwell door window into the fifth floor hallway.

Eric's office would be directly to my left, in the corner suite. I turned the doorknob and froze. A fashionable young couple emerged from a room halfway down the hall. The woman brushed back her long tresses, hung the Do Not Disturb placard on the knob, then joined her partner who had gone to call the guest elevator. After a moment, the elevator rang its arrival, and the doors opened.

Inside was a blonde woman in a skimpy yellow dress and high heels. She was accompanied by a man wearing a black suit and a white, collared shirt. The telltale garb of Eric's crew. I vaguely recognized him, another beneficiary of Fly-By-Night's job program for ex-cons. The man took the woman by the elbow, guiding her out of the elevator, and they started down the hall, passing the fashionistas.

The departing woman noted the arriving woman's dress. The yellow-clad woman kept her head high, expressionless behind her oversized sunglasses, as if she wanted the other woman to see how unaffected she was by the perusal. She and the crew member continued in my direction.

The fashionistas stepped into the elevator car. The departing woman made a face. She pointed to the other woman, looked to her partner and whispered something. He stifled a laugh. As the doors closed, he reached over and squeezed her butt, and she jumped in surprise.

I drew back from the window so the crew member wouldn't spot me (though he seemed more focused on the woman than he was on being watched). I had to think fast. I drew Pierre's business card from my wallet. I clenched it between my teeth, and slowly turned the doorknob until I felt it quietly unlatch. My other hand was on the Walther, just in case I had to throw down right here. I angled my head and fixed my gaze on the suite's door. From this position, I would be unseen by them, but I would see them arrive and enter the room. I prayed the man didn't take it upon himself to check the stairs.

They came into view as they arrived at the suite. The crewman tapped a key card on the digital reader in the door, and the lock clicked open. I watched him open the door for her. He turned to let her pass, and I recognized him by the scar above his eye. Jesús, I think his name was. His eyes dropped to her ass as she passed him, then he followed her inside, letting the door swing shut on its own. It was now or never.

I pulled open the stairwell door, and took the few steps to the suite, one hand still on the Walther in my pocket. I snuck up to the door frame, snatched Pierre's card from my teeth, and slipped the cardboard rectangle over the strike plate. To my surprise, it worked. The door closed with a *thump*, the bolt having been blocked by the card. I hoped Jesús, or whatever his name was, didn't notice the door didn't make its usual locking sound. I listened for anything that would indicate he was coming back to check.

After a moment, I went back into the stairwell and opened the case. I wriggled my fingers into a pair of surgical gloves I'd stashed inside, then I peeled the sleeve of the overcoat off of my left arm, looped the strap of the Tavor over my shoulder, and lifted the shotgun out of the case. I screwed the suppressor onto the choke I'd premounted on the barrel. Then I pulled the coat back on, letting the drape of the garment conceal the gun. I rose, and the Tavor's barrel ran parallel to my legs, neatly hidden under the coat. That would help with any security cameras in the hall. They may have overlooked installing them in the stairwell, but they were damn certain to be out there.

I went out and faced the suite, careful to keep my left side toward the stairwell wall, where no camera could see. I drew back my coat and took hold of the Tavor's grip. I placed my right palm against the dark wood. It felt like a portal into a black hole.

I pushed the door open.

# CHAPTER

# 36

As I'd remembered, the door led into a short entry hall, a closet on the left, the bathroom on the right. The bathroom door was open, and the light off, so I could safely assume no one was in there taking a crap. The main living area of the suite was to the right, and the bedroom to the right of that.

Pressed into the corner, parallel to the wall on my left, was one of the hotel's rolling brass luggage racks. Piled on it was a stack of black backpacks, the same kind we used in the SentryCity heist. Six or seven were stacked on the base, and a few more hung from the garment hanger. From the looks of them, they still bulged heavy with cash. They must belong to the men stationed here. I had to assume the rest of the money was long gone, divided among the other crew members.

I could hear a couple of men's voices. They were conversing easily, chuckling about something, probably their own jokes. Muffled music, smooth jazz, was coming from somewhere. The other side of a wall or closed door.

I felt my knees unconsciously bend into a defensive crouch. Due to their bantering, the soft music, and the open window letting in the city noise, they hadn't heard me enter. That didn't last long.

Pierre's business card had fallen silently to the carpet, and without it to stop the lock bolt, the door clicked shut behind me.

"The fuck was that?" I heard one of the men say.

"Is somebody here?" a second voice asked.

I could feel my temples pounding. I had to force my breathing to slow, or else I'd sound like I'd just run a race. I lifted the barrel of the Tavor. The swish of my coat sounded as loud as the closing of the door. Jesús poked his head around the corner of the wall, his jaw hanging open in curiosity. His eyes popped at the sight of the shotgun. I fired.

*Phoom!* The sound of the gun surprised me. People are so conditioned to expect a deafening explosion from a weapon like this that I glanced down to see if the gun had misfired, like the sawed-off shotgun that keeps failing Mel Gibson in the *Mad Max* movies. The smoke drifting from the suppressor's nose told me it had worked just fine, but the gun had a stronger kick than Pierre had described. The Tavor jerked back, and my front hand lost its grip on the magazine. Gravity took over, pulling the end of the barrel downward. Panic rose inside me. I quickly pulled up on the weapon to aim again, expecting Jesús to charge. Then I saw the top half of his head had splattered against the wall behind him, and he collapsed to the floor, his jaw still open in surprise.

Someone inside my head screamed *Move!* I rounded the corner, leading with the Tavor. The other man, who must've been the smoker I saw from the floor above, was staring at the red-stained wall. He looked like he was trying to decipher if the brain matter sliding down the paint was real or not. He saw me, reached behind his back, and pulled a pistol from his belt. I couldn't let the raw sound of a gunshot tip off the hotel—and everyone in it—to what was happening here. I fired twice. *Phoom! Phoom!*

The smoker took both shots in his midsection and he went down. I stepped over to make sure he was finished, and had to hold down a surge of vomit when I realized his body had been cut into halves, barely connected by strips of flesh and organs.

A door opened behind me, and the room filled with a melodic saxophone solo. *Fuck!* With my system racing in a feverish rush of adrenaline, I'd forgotten about the bedroom.

"What the hell is going on out—" Rudy. I swung around.

He was standing in the open doorway in a tank top, an erection tenting his boxer shorts. He looked at what was left of one of his men, then to the other, and then to me.

"What is this? Who the fuck are you?"

He didn't recognize me. Had the sight of his mangled crewmen already sent him into some kind of shock? Some deep trauma where he wouldn't recognize his own mother?

If anyone ever asked me why I chose this moment to take this particular action, my answer would have been an unequivocal "I have no fucking clue." Maybe I just wanted the guy who'd tried to shoot me in the back to know that I'd managed to show up again, like a bad dream on a bad acid trip. I lowered the mask from my face.

Rudy's eyes went wide. I guess after he'd missed his chance to kill me, he figured that he'd never see my face again. That I would've kept running, as far away as I could. He sure as shit never expected to see me here, in his "office," right when he was about to get laid. His eyes lowered to the Tavor.

"Wait!" he pleaded. He pointed to the backpacks piled on the rack. "You know what's in those. Take 'em. All of 'em! Just get outta here!"

I aimed the shotgun. With his girth, there was no way I'd miss. That's when I saw beyond him into the bedroom. The woman who'd arrived with Jesús was on the king-size bed. Her yellow dress was in a heap on the carpet. She'd pulled up the sheets over her lingerie-clad body. Even with the shades pulled in the darkened room, I could see the terror on her face.

Rudy used the opportunity to lunge at me. He grabbed the barrel of the Tavor and twisted it, away from his body and down toward the floor. We couldn't have struggled long, but it felt like forever. Time slowed down.

I couldn't know if it was caused by the sex he was about to have, the shock of the bloody cadavers in the room, or the realization that he was next, but his plump body was already damp. His face was close to mine. Thick sweat beaded on his forehead. The salty drops shook onto my face with every desperate twist and jerk, stinging my eyeballs. Our eyes locked, as we wrestled each other for control of the gun.

Rudy's eyes flared with hot rage. It was the kind you see in a prison yard fight, in a man who believes survival is only possible through violence.

*The only way out is through*, I heard from the distant hollows of my memory.

I matched Rudy's prison rage with a prison move. I reared back, taking advantage of my height, and brought my forehead down with as much force as I could muster, landing a head butt to the bridge of his nose.

His nasal cartilage was no match for the hard bone of my skull. I felt his fat proboscis crumple, and his blood spatter my face. He held his grip, but he weakened just enough for me to torque the gun. When I sensed the barrel close any part of his physical body, I fired. *Phoom!* The buckshot took off the bottom half of his left leg, just below the knee, and he dropped like a bag of rocks. At this close range, the pellets went all the way through into the furniture behind him. A table tipped over, now also missing half a leg, sending glasses, bottles and empty plates to the floor. This gun could really do some damage.

The rapid pounding in my temples had grown, traveling to my neck veins and behind my eyes. My nape and shoulder muscles had tightened into snarling balls of sinew. I kicked Rudy in the face, knocking him onto his back, and squelching his yelps before they could start. Blood ran unimpeded from his open wound, pudding on the carpet.

The expended shells had left remarkably little gun smoke in the air. Rudy was writhing on the floor. As I stood over him, his eyes opened, and he glared up at me. His entire body was shaking in agony.

I kneeled, covering his mouth with my free palm. "It's funny, this is the first time I ever used this damn thing." I pressed the end of the barrel to his cheek. Panic replaced pain in Rudy's eyes as the steel touched his skin. He sure as hell never expected me to pull anything like this, either.

"Where's Eric?" I lifted my hand from his mouth. Rudy's body convulsed and tears ran over his ears. "I'm not going to ask again."

His jaw was shaking as much as his torso, but he managed to put the words together. "Wi . . . with your girl . . . your girlfriend."

I felt a shiver vibrate the base of my neck. "He's got Carla?" I couldn't believe there was any way they could know about her.

Confusion appeared on Rudy's face. "Who the f-f . . . fuck is C-Carla?" I relaxed some. Rudy forced himself to speak. "Angela. He s-said . . . he had to . . . finish that."

I pressed the barrel harder against his cheek. "You mean finish *her*?"

He managed to shake his head slightly, as if there could be no other answer. "Loo . . . loose ends, man."

I nodded. "Yeah, I've heard of those." I moved the barrel to his temple. "I'd say this is for Bill. But it's really for me."

Rudy's breathing slowed, and his eyes shifted to some blank spot in the ceiling. It was as if he knew he'd reached the end of his road and accepted it. Even welcomed it. He had the same resigned look that Bill Best had the night Rudy killed him.

"Do it," he said.

You know how in the movies when a character says to the villain, "Death is too good for you"?

I pulled the trigger.

## CHAPTER

# 37

I FIT THE MASK back over my face and went to the bedroom doorway. The hooker hadn't moved from her spot on the bed, and she was visibly trembling. Poor thing. When she'd been engaged to see to Rudy's needs, I doubt it occurred to her that she'd watch his head get blown off. What she'd just witnessed must've sent her into shock.

"Please don't kill me. I won't say anything. I swear!" She was practically hysterical, but at least she was communicating. That meant she could probably take instruction.

"Be quiet. Don't move." I went and grabbed one of the hanging backpacks off the rack, came back and tossed it on the bed. "That's for you."

She looked at it, not understanding. That was OK, she would soon enough.

I went to the nightstand next to her and yanked the phone cord from the wall. "Where's your cell phone?" I asked, trying to speak as gently as I could over my own pounding heart.

She tipped her head toward the end of the bed. I saw a purse on the floor next to her yellow dress. I picked up both, tossed the dress to her, and found her smartphone inside the purse.

"I'm going to shut this door," I said. "You don't move until I tell you. If you make a sound, I'll kill you. You understand?"

Almost imperceptibly, she nodded her head. With the blackout curtains drawn, the room was as dark as a cave. The overhead light was on a dimmer. I turned the knob, adding a soft glow to the room. Taking her purse with me, I closed the door. I wasn't really going to kill her, but she didn't know that. I needed a few more minutes to pull my shit together.

I looked out the peephole. Nothing and no one that I could see. I opened the door to check down the hall. Deserted. I flipped the privacy latch to prevent the door from locking behind me and retrieved the gun case from the stairwell, moving as casually as possible for the sake of the cameras. Just another registered guest who'd forgotten something. Believe you me, nonchalance is no small feat when you've just made three corpses.

I hung the Do Not Disturb placard on the outside knob as I came back inside. The room smelled of gun smoke and blood. I cracked open the bedroom door. She was still on the bed, but had managed to slink back into her dress. The backpack sat where I'd tossed it.

"Open the bag," I said.

"Are you going to kill me?" she asked in a nervous whisper.

"Not if you do what I say."

She slowly reached out, pulled the bag to her, and zipped open the top. She looked inside.

"Show me," I said.

She spread the opening. Yep, inside were bundles of stolen SentryCity cash.

"I'm only going to be a few more minutes. You're going to walk with me out of here. When we get to the street," I pointed to the pack, "that's all yours. And you'll never see me again."

I left her to contemplate her future, however long it may be.

I went to the bathroom and stripped off my mask and shirt, wet a towel in the sink, and quickly wiped off any blood spatter I could find on my face and hands. Thankfully, there wasn't much. In the closet I found what had to be backup clothes for the crew. Several sizes, black and white all over. I took a shirt and jacket that was close enough to fit, and pair of pants that, though loose on me, would have to do.

I switched into them, making sure to gather my wallet, cash, and phone. I checked myself in the full-length mirror on the wall. With my sunglasses on, I could pass as a made member of Eric's crew. I tucked the Walther into my belt. The loose pants were a blessing when it came to hiding a gun.

I pulled two fresh masks from a stack of extras I'd stashed inside my overcoat pocket. I put one on and set the second one aside. I stuffed my bloody garments in a plastic laundry bag I found clipped to a pants hanger and tossed it onto the luggage rack.

I removed the suppressor from the Tavor, stowed it in the case, and closed the lid. I balanced the case on the luggage rack, hid the hooker's purse under one of the backpacks, and rolled the rack into the hall by the front door.

When I went back to the bedroom, I found her counting the bundles in the pack. She stopped with a jerk, like she'd been caught doing something she shouldn't. I held out the extra mask.

"We're leaving now," I said, using my size and the door to block her view of the living area. "You're going to put this over your eyes and I'm going to lead you out. I'm only going to say this once. You're going to leave it over your eyes until I tell you. Once we get to the hall, I'll let you know, and then you can pull it down over your mouth and nose. And you're gonna leave it on until we're outside. You don't want your face on camera. Understand?"

There was her micro nod again. "I didn't have one when I came in."

I let out a hard sigh. "Just do it. For fuck's sake."

She must have sensed my diminishing patience, because she got off the bed, picked up the backpack, and hooked it on her elbow. Then she fit the mask over her eyes, though she had some trouble, given her trembling fingers. I felt bad for her. Unless she took an amnesia-worthy bonk on the head someday, these memories would last forever.

"Give me your hand."

I guided her to the doorway and led her through the suite, ensuring she avoided stepping in the pools of blood or tripping over a severed extremity.

By the time we got to the door, my own hands were shaking. Either courage or stupidity (or both) had brought me this far, but I was beginning to lose my nerve. I needed to get in touch with my cojones again. I drew in a deep breath and let it out.

"The only way out is through," I heard myself say.

"What?" said the hooker, her eyes still covered, her voice too loud.

"Never mind," I said, putting on my sunglasses. "Let's go."

## CHAPTER

# 38

I GUIDED HER INTO the hallway with one hand, pulling the cart with the other. I put on my sunglasses, as the door clicked shut. "OK."

She slipped the mask down to cover her nose and mouth, tucking it under her chin. I gave her a moment to let her eyes adjust to the light.

"Remember, leave it on 'til we get outside."

"I heard you the first time." The snark in her tone surprised me. What do you know? This chick was tough. But I understood. You have to be tough in her line of work. Those of us who have sold our bodies for fun and profit tend to build walls around ourselves.

"You're going to stay next to me all the way out." I pulled open my jacket to show her the Walther. "I don't want to hurt anybody else, but you know I will if I have to."

How was she going to argue with that? If she'd spent time around characters like Rudy, she knew there were people in this world with nothing to lose. And after what she'd just seen, I was probably one of them.

The suite was as far from the elevator as it could be. Every step I felt as if a door would swing open, and Eric and what was left of his crew, or a passel of cops would storm out, guns drawn, and we'd all go down in a blaze of bloody glory.

At the elevator the hooker jabbed the Down button a few times, as would anyone in a hurry, but her reasons were pretty obvious. I let it go. The doors opened with a ding. Inside was a regal middle-aged woman. She smiled and stepped to the side to make room for the incoming couple and their rolling luggage cart, which I pushed to the center of the car. The two of us took our place on the opposite side, the cart separating us from the other passenger. The woman's eyes scanned the packs on the cart.

"Checking out, I take it?" she asked. Her tone was friendly, and her voice refined and pleasant. She could've been an on-air host for NPR.

The hooker looked at me.

"Yeah," I said through my mask. "Time to go."

"Interesting luggage you have there," the woman said.

"Actually, these belong to my boss. He lives here."

Her eyebrows went up. "Oh," she said, her curiosity rising. "Lucky him. What could possibly be in all these, I wonder?"

I pointed to the left side the cart. "This half is methamphetamine." I pointed to the right. "That half is cocaine. We keep the heroin in the case. You want a hit?" I felt the hooker stiffen.

A nervous laugh escaped the woman and her cheeks flushed. She looked like she was desperately searching the recesses of her mind for a witty rejoinder, but the possibility that I wasn't joking got in the way.

With another ding, the elevator opened. The woman gave us a cursory smile and rushed out without wishing us a nice day.

I rolled the cart, and the hooker shadowed me as I steered it toward the lobby. She was being as cooperative as I could hope for, but I still kept one eye on her, while the other was on the front door past the reception desk. The sunbaked street beyond felt like the pot at the end of the rainbow.

The same young man and woman who'd directed me to the roof my first visit here were on duty. They both smiled as we approached.

"Good afternoon," the man said. "Would you like a valet to help with your luggage?"

*If he only knew . . .* "No," I said. "But could you call a cab?"

"Our pleasure," he said, and his colleague immediately lifted a phone and punched a single number.

"Thanks," I said.

"Of course," said the man.

He pushed a button hidden behind the counter, and the front door hummed open. Automation. Out here, it's for convenience. On the inside, it's to keep us controlled and confined.

I pushed the rack outside, and the hooker dutifully stayed next to me. We came to the curb, and I turned to her. She was looking at me intently, I suppose wondering what my next demand would be. That she'd been so acquiescent through all this told me that "demand" was a constant in her life.

I picked up her purse from where I'd hidden it and took out her phone. "Sorry. I can't have you making any calls just yet." I handed her the bag.

She grabbed the purse. "Yeah, I get it."

I nodded to the weighted pack dangling from her arm. "Don't spend it all in one place," I said. The strap was chafing the inside of her elbow, but I don't think she noticed. She seemed unsure which direction to take. I pointed up the easy grade of Vine Street. "You should go that way. Fewer people."

But she looked past me to busy, tourist-laden Hollywood Boulevard. It was like it was calling something to her that only she could hear.

I met her eyes. "I've been where you are. It's your damn life. Do something with it."

She took off her mask and pushed a loose lock of hair behind one ear. Her brown eyes were bloodshot, and I realized she couldn't be more than twenty-two, twenty-three years old. She was pretty enough, in a plain midwestern sort of way, but she looked tired for someone her age. Worn out.

"Go on," I said. "Get outta here."

She hefted the pack over her shoulder and, instead of going the direction I suggested, walked past me toward Hollywood. I watched her go. It felt like the teeming crowd might swallow her up, never to be seen again. This town does that to you.

A dingy white minivan, my cab, came to a stop at the curb, and the side door popped open. I rolled the rack to the car, and I saw that the food delivery truck had left. I had no idea how much time had passed since I'd arrived.

The cabbie helped me load the packs, but I took the gun case and laundry bag to my seat. I got into the van, shut the door . . . and froze. In all the excitement, I had forgotten to pick up Pierre's business card. It had dropped to the floor after I used it to block the suite's door latch from locking.

I debated if I should invent an excuse to go back for it. Too risky. I'd also not taken a key card, so someone would have to open the room for me. Besides, a cleaning person, or one of Eric's crew, could've walked in there already. It was a miracle I'd gotten this far. I gave the driver an address. *Sorry, Pierre.*

As we pulled away, one of the homeless guys I'd seen mumbling to himself earlier staggered down the Walk of Fame.

He was sporting a new Panama hat.

CHAPTER

# 39

THE HOURS AFTER leaving the Astoria were busy.

First stop, my roach hotel. I surprised another cabbie with a hundred-dollar bill (man, does *that* ever work like a charm), and this one even helped carry the packs to my room. He even risked getting a ticket by double-parking on 7th Street, then offered to spot me a falafel at St. Vincent Court. Any other day I would've taken him up on it, but time was short, and I needed to complete my next errand. Besides, when I thought of what I'd left behind at the hotel, my stomach did a pirouette, so I politely declined.

I stashed the money and the gun case, then I carried one of the packs three blocks to the nearest post office. There, I found a box big and sturdy enough to hold the pack and addressed it to Carla. I knew her first instinct would be to turn it in to the police, but I hoped she'd reconsider and use the money to make her life, or someone else's, a little easier. In the end, that would be up to her.

The black and white duds I'd taken from the hotel closet had worked as far as they needed to, but I caught myself in a storefront window and decided I looked like a maître d'. I couldn't afford to stick out at all now. I went back to my room, showered, and changed into some of the other clothes I'd bought the day before. The packs were piled neatly on the single bed.

The Tavor had served its purpose. I unloaded it and returned it to the case. I collected all the shells into a plastic bag. The Walther found a spot in my belt under the black jacket, the one crew garment I'd kept since I didn't have another. With its center button closed over a black T-shirt and blue jeans, I looked like any other denizen of downtown LA. Add the Covid mask and sunglasses, and I was virtually invisible.

Then I called Angela. She answered on the first ring.

"Is that you on the news again?" Her voice was pitched high with stress.

"What news?"

"Something happened at that place where Eric hangs out."

I was afraid the bloody scene at the Astoria could be going public by now, but I couldn't guess how she'd react if she knew I was behind it. I decided my best approach was to feign ignorance and change the subject. "You mean the hotel? Have you talked to him?"

"What? No! Goddammit, Jake! What did you do?"

"Has he called again?"

She paused. Maybe to catch her breath. Maybe because she realized I wasn't going to talk about what she wanted me to. "Yes, he called," she said, calming down. "A few more times. I didn't answer."

"You haven't gone home?"

"I'm still at the place you paid for. Thanks, by the way. I've had nothing but room service and hot baths. Even got a massage."

"Glad you like it," I said dryly.

"But I have to get back to my life, sooner or later."

"Do you have your car?"

"Yeah, in the valet. Why?"

"Take down this address. I won't be there, but I'll leave the key at the front desk, if you can call it that. The guy there will help you. You'll need it."

"Help with what?"

"You're picking something up."

"Jake, what the hell—?"

"Please, just do it. It'll make sense later. If this goes the way I hope it does, you can go home tonight. Tomorrow latest."

"I think I'll stay over again, if it's all the same to you." I could hear her fumbling for a pen and paper. "OK, where am I going?"

I gave her the address, told her to wait ten minutes, and hung up. I filled my empty inside pockets with bundles from one of the packs. You never know when you might have to grease someone's wheels.

I filled my empty inside pockets with bundles from one of the packs. You never know when you might have to grease someone's wheels. I grabbed the gun case, shells and laundry bag, looked around to be sure I hadn't forgotten anything, and left the room for the last time.

At the front desk, I gave my one key to the clerk and told him I had a friend coming to pick up some merchandise from my room, six or seven backpacks. She'd need help carrying them to her car, and I would be very appreciative if he could help her do that. I slid two hundred dollars across the desk to him. He put down his cigarette and hot tea long enough to scoop it up, and expressed his gratitude with a wide smile that featured stained and blackened teeth.

I left the small lobby, crossed 7th Street and dropped the bag of shotgun shells into a garbage can. Then I ducked into an alley and deposited the gun case and laundry bag in a dumpster. I figured Angela would need about thirty minutes to get down here, so I ducked inside a convenience store to wait and watch.

I browsed the aisles, picking out a few items. On schedule, Angela's Prius pulled up to my hotel. She dropped some coins into the meter and went inside. Less than ten minutes later, she came out, accompanied by the desk clerk, both of them loaded down with packs. She folded down the rear seats, doubling the trunk space, and they stuffed the packs into the empty space. She thanked the man, and he waved a goodbye and went back inside the fleabag hotel.

I expected Angela to drive away, but instead her head pivoted back and forth, as if she was trying to spot someone who might be watching her. Her eyes scanned across the storefront, and I drew back behind a revolving stand filled with greeting cards espousing the charm, glamour, and beauty of Los Angeles.

Either she had decided no one was watching, or if someone was, she needed to get out of there. She methodically switched on her turn signal, made sure to look over her shoulder for any oncoming traffic, and carefully pulled out and drove away. Funny how certain things can make you behave. A sudden death in the family can make you overly polite to complete strangers. A sudden windfall can make you act as if everything in the world is suddenly a threat. For Angela, it was the latter. She had seen what was inside those packs.

I paid for my goods, some protein bars and energy drinks (I seemed to be living on those lately) and left the store. I walked to the corner and turned north on Grand. As I walked, I tallied the separate tasks of the vague scheme I'd come up with earlier:

1. Get the money.
2. Get money to Carla.
3. Get money to Angela.

Three down. One to go.

## CHAPTER

# 40

IT TOOK ME about fifteen minutes to walk the half mile uphill to the Museum of Contemporary Art. It was closed Mondays, so I knew I'd have some privacy by the long, narrow reflecting pools behind the building.

Carla had told me about it, explaining that most people went to the Disney Concert Hall down the street. They'd make their way behind that massive stainless steel structure to the Blue Ribbon Garden and marvel over a concrete flower sculpture inlaid with repurposed shards of blue glass. Sure, that was something to see, but she was spot on when it came to MOCA's quiet pools being a superior location to recharge and reconnect with yourself.

It had become my favorite spot in LA, a peaceful space in the heart of the city, where I could think about my next moves, what I wanted for my future, and how to solve my problems. I'd never come here with her or even thanked her. Maybe when she opened that box I sent, she'd forgive a lot.

It was time to make the call.

"Hello, Eric," I said when he answered.

"Surprised to hear from you." His voice sounded pristine coming through my Xiaomi phone. I pictured him incessantly logging onto his iPhone, trying to stalk my Fly-By-Night cell, only to be frustrated that I'd shut it off over a day before.

"Thought you'd be halfway to China by now," he said.

"I would be," I replied. "But my passport expired about twenty years ago."

"I'm still surprised."

"Yeah? And I thought you woulda pussied out and run like the little bitch you are."

"Wow. The ex-con's starting to grow a pair. About fucking time."

I pictured him with that annoying smirk, and fantasized smacking it off his face. "I think we should meet," I said.

Eric paused before answering. "Now, why would I want to do that?"

"Because you don't like loose ends. Just ask Rudy." I paused for dramatic effect. "Oh, wait. You can't."

It was like I could feel his grin fade through the phone line. "So, Rudy's off to the Great Beyond," he said. It wasn't a question.

"Probably a little warmer where he is."

"All right, tough guy. What do you have in mind?"

"I know just the place."

* * *

At three AM on a Monday, downtown LA is a graveyard.

Most restaurants and bars are closed Monday nights, giving their staffs a much-needed break after busy weekends. By nine PM, the streets are quiet. By midnight, they're nearly deserted. By three, you're alone. But then, that's the logic we'd used the first time I'd been here.

I had hoped for some of that famous marine layer to come in. I thought a nice Humphrey Bogart fog shrouding everything in a mist might give me an edge. No such luck. The night was crystal clear.

I waited patiently. Eric was late, but I expected that. He would scope out his options before making himself known, see if the place was crawling with cops. He had no way of knowing if I'd already confessed to the Sentry-City heist and was working with the police. For all he knew, there could be an APB out for him, and he wouldn't even be able to leave the city. It was in his best interest to find out.

LA in the Fall brings cold nights. It's the proximity to the ocean. Outsiders rarely know that, thinking it's all warm and sunny, even at midnight. I didn't dare go back to the roach hotel to get more clothes, so here I was in just my jeans and T-shirt, and a dead man's jacket. I was starting to shiver. I turned my collar up over my neck and cupped my palms to warm them with my breath. Maybe Eric was waiting for me to get hypothermia.

I huddled against the filthy brick wall at the end of the alley, where fire escapes, that had hung there since the 1930s, offered a chance at deliverance. Sometimes it worked, sometimes it didn't. From here, I could see all the way to the entrance, to the spot where I killed my first person. That poor woman all those years ago.

The truth was, I hadn't told Angela everything that day on the beach, when she wanted to know how I'd made it through prison. As guilty as I'd rightly felt way back then, the night I ended that woman's life opened something in me that I never knew was there, and didn't really discover until I was incarcerated: When necessary, I was a violent man.

My size often carried the day. Any inmate who wanted to know how they'd stack up against me, how's the saying go? "Fuck around and find out." Yes, I kept my nose mostly clean, keeping to myself at the library, working out on the yard, reading in my cell. Respect is a big deal on the inside. Show respect, and you'll dramatically decrease your odds of confrontation. Disrespect will get you a shank in the kidney. I learned to show respect, whether the receiver deserved it or not.

There was that one guy, the one who came at me in the yard. After I'd punched him out, I thought things would quiet down, but it soon became clear that he was looking for an opportunity for revenge. In his mind, he'd been disrespected. Twice. And, it was in front of the whole prison. I had to pay.

The mistake he made was threatening to get to me by getting to Anthony, my friend and prison mentor. I wasn't about to let that happen. There was no way old Anthony could fend off an animal like that. I made promises to other inmates, jobs I would do in exchange for allowing me free movement at a certain time. I did the same with a couple of corruptible guards, and then I made my move.

I caught him coming out of his job in the wood shop. I thought it was a *respectful* irony that I used a shank made from a spoon, like the one he'd tried to use on me. Again, my height and strength gave me an advantage. I came up from behind, wrapped one arm around his neck, and sank that homemade blade into his chest, right to the hilt. He was dead in less than a minute. I eased him to the hallway floor, in a blind spot from the cameras. That was another lesson I'd brought in with me: Don't be seen, so you don't get caught. And I wasn't. But I never figured out how I'd dissed him to begin with, either. That's a side of prison life that I *didn't* share with Angela.

It's funny, how intense the love I can feel for someone is. I ascribe it to why I'd wanted to be an actor so long ago. Actors are emotional beings. They feel more deeply than most, and they need ways to express it. I've come to believe that when actors put their efforts into a script, it's a way to get rid of a stockpile of concentrated feelings that can build up. Gotta put it somewhere, right? But it's been too long now for me to know, for sure.

That love lives inside me, like an organism, side-by-side with my capacity for savagery. I've learned I am willing to eviscerate anybody if I feel they're a threat to someone I care about. And in prison, I learned that I always have been.

When I was first arrested my biggest concern was that Angela might somehow be implicated. She wasn't, she had no part in it. But I turned on my friends to be sure she'd be safe. Today, I killed three people, then I gave lots of money to Carla, and even more to Angela. Why? To protect them from harm in the only ways I had available, that's why. And now, here I was in this alley, ready to protect them both from that prick, Eric.

Is this how mothers feel about their children? Is it their willingness to do anything to protect their offspring . . . gouge, maim, kill . . . that gave rise to the legend of the ferocious Mama Bear? I'll have to ask a mother sometime. I don't really know any, anymore.

Headlights sent beams of white light against the walls, and a sedan, much like the one I'd chauffeured Eric in, entered the alley. The first thing I noticed was the empty license plate holder below the front grill.

I didn't hide. No need. I wanted him to see me.

The car crept to a stop about halfway down, right about where I'd parked the night I watched Rudy murder Bill Best. The engine and headlights died, leaving the tinted windows black in the dark.

Finally, the driver's door opened, and the dome light came on. Unless someone was lying flat in the backseat, Eric was alone. He got out of the car and shut the door. He looked up and around, then at me.

"Aren't you afraid the cameras will see you?" he said. He had that fucking smirk on his face.

I took the Covid mask off and stuffed it into my jacket pocket. "Doesn't matter if they do." I stepped away from the wall, letting him see the Walther PPK in my hand.

"So it's like that," he said. "Showdown at the OK Corral." If Eric was feeling any nerves, he wasn't showing it.

"Call it whatever you want."

He held up his hand, and I responded by aiming the Walther at him.

"Easy, tiger," he said, raising both hands. "I have something for you." He opened his palm to show me his key fob.

It wasn't like the one I'd used. This one was larger, and had a keypad instead of the usual two or three buttons. "Maybe we can come to an agreement. Then we go our separate ways."

Something he'd said to me earlier that day rang in my head. "Now, why would I want to do that?"

Sure enough, that smirk flattened. That almost made this worth it. Almost.

"OK," he said. "I might have gone a little too far with you."

"You think?"

"You came out all right."

"I got lucky."

He shook his head. "I underestimated you. Someone else wouldn't have thought to grab the money before they ran. Someone else wouldn't have gotten the drop on my boys. Especially Rudy."

"Yeah, Rudy. What was he to you, anyway?"

He shrugged. "Just another convict that needed a job."

"No. It was personal for him. Was he your daddy's bitch or something?"

Eric's eyes narrowed, and his chin rose slightly, like it does when you get your back up. I'd hit a nerve.

"Oh, I get it," I said. "Damon was Rudy's. What was it? Love at first buttfuck?" Eric stood frozen, his chin still angled upward. "It's OK, Eric. It happens."

Something started coursing through him. His eyes, his posture, his breathing, the tension in his body, it betrayed something bigger than prison, than punks, than friends turning on each other. There was something other than the fact that his father was a gigolo. A thief. A killer. Hell, for all I knew, it was all of it, but whatever it was, it had led him to me, and to this moment.

"In that warehouse, you said you were going tell me why I was there. Then you tried to kill me."

He tried to work up a grin, but whatever was going through his mind made it difficult. He settled for a quip. "Best laid plans," he said.

"C'mon, nobody here but us thieves. Now's your chance to get it off your chest. What's this about?"

His eyes started to shimmer. He swallowed, as if words he wanted to say, but never could, had gathered in his throat like a dry lump that he couldn't decide whether to ingest or expectorate.

Finally, he spoke. "He wouldn't have been there at all, if it wasn't for you."

"None of us should've been there. There's nothing about that night I wouldn't take back if I could."

"You didn't have to turn on him."

"He didn't have to shoot an innocent woman in the face, either."

He blurted, "You put him up to it!"

It was all coming together, the mystery revealed. "Is that what he told you? That it was *my* idea?" I couldn't help myself. I laughed. "Jesus H. Christ, kid. Your old man may have been the biggest asshole that ever lived."

What he'd forced of that smirk disappeared altogether.

"What happened, Eric? You go on welfare? Your mother kill herself? What?" Eric's eyes were locked onto mine. "Hey, I'm sorry if you had it rough, but I've had a little time to think about this, too. And if it wasn't for *him*, I may have never gotten hooked on drugs, never sold my dick, and I *never* would have followed him into this alley."

"Is that right?"

"Yeah, that's right," I said. "You have no idea how many lives got ruined, just so Damon DeSanto could make a buck. Fuck him."

I could see his demeanor waver, as if the lie he had built his life on was shaken by a truth he had never heard before. But he wasn't ready to give up on it yet.

"Don't you want to see what I have for you?" he finally asked, his arms dropping to his sides.

"Not really."

"You should. Before she suffocates." Now I froze. "You didn't really think I'd come here without some kind of collateral, did you?"

"Angela?"

He nodded with satisfaction. "In the trunk. *And* that nice pile you gave her today." And here came that smirk. "Thought you woulda kept more of it." He cocked his head. "Unless you didn't think you'd need it."

I aimed the Walther at his head. "Open it. Now."

"Hang on, there's a code. You should know that the guy that set it up said you get three tries. If it isn't done right, it locks, like a phone. She'll be trapped, might run out of air. She's been in there a while already."

"Then get on with it."

"As soon as we come to terms."

"What terms?"

"I sure wasn't gonna be left with much after you cleaned out my office today. Kudos, by the way."

"Thanks," I said, impatience rising.

"Now, fact is neither one of us is going to be able to stick around. So, I take what's right here in the car . . . *and* the car . . . and you get Angie. How you make your way out of town is your problem."

My heart rate sped up. Given the lengths this junior psycho had already gone to avenge his fantasy father, I couldn't imagine what he could have up his sleeve now. But then, I had the gun. I cocked my head to get him moving, and we went to the rear of the car, he on one side, me on the other. I kept the Walther aimed at him.

"Tell you what," he said. "I'll even throw in a bag. One for each of you. That should be enough to get you to Mexico, or Brazil, or some fucking place. Shot at a new start."

If she was in there, he had me. Again. I leaned over the trunk. "Angela? Can you hear me?" Three or four pounding thuds came in quick succession, followed by a woman's muffled voice saying something I couldn't make out. *Goddammit.* "Open it. And if I don't like the looks of her, I take you out right here."

He nodded. "Understood."

He looked at the fob. "OK, let me see if I remember this right." He started punching numbers, a sequence of five, six buttons. A beep came from the car, but the trunk didn't open. "Nope, that's not it."

I fine-tuned my aim of the Walther. "You get one more try."

He looked at me. That smirk. "Two, according to my guy. Three tries and it locks up for good."

"One," I said, cocking the hammer back.

"OK, OK." This time he punched slowly, carefully, voicing each number. "Five, six, two, three . . . *four.*" On the last button, the car beeped a different tone, and the trunk lid clicked open. Eric reached for the lip.

"Hold it," I said. He shrugged, and backed off. Keeping the Walther aimed at Eric, I reached down, hooked the fingers of my free hand under the lip, and lifted.

Inside was Angela. Hair tousled, still dressed in the jeans and lightweight leather jacket I'd seen her in earlier. She lay tightly nestled in a divot among the backpacks I had given her that afternoon, her eyes circles of fear.

I was relieved to see she looked unharmed, so it took me a moment to register that she had a .25 caliber Beretta in her hand. And it was aimed at me. She sat up slowly, her eyes and that barrel trained on my face.

# CHAPTER

# 41

ERIC LAUGHED, A single "Ha!" He clapped his hands once, and reached out for the Walther. "OK, chief, I'll take that."

He slipped the gun from my grip. I looked back and forth from one to the other, I don't know how many times.

"Still don't get the 'planning' thing, do ya'?" said Eric, aiming my Walther at me.

He was right. My talent for looking ahead was never very strong. Even the plan I'd come up with over the last couple of days was just a vague strategy I'd hoped would work out. My capacity for forethought was sometimes like reading a faded old map, the lines too blurry to follow, so I would just make it up as I go.

"Thanks, doll," Eric said, and chuckled again. He seemed almost giddy. He kept talking, something about not expecting her to make it this easy for him, that he'd make sure that she was rewarded, shit like that.

I wasn't paying attention. I was too busy staring at Angela, still aiming that gun right at me, and trying to comprehend her betrayal. Some part of me expected an explanation or apology, though I knew neither would come.

She stared back at me, her chin quivering. Then something shifted. Her eyes glanced to Eric, who was still focused on me. Her apparent fear had changed. I couldn't describe what it was at the time, but now I would call it "resolve." She swung the gun toward Eric and fired.

The bullet hit him in the left side, where his shoulder and pectoral meet, and he went down. The Walther in his hand fired when he hit the concrete. The bullet cut through my jeans, and barely missed my shin. I heard a chunk of brick dislodge as the bullet ricocheted off the wall behind me.

The ring of gunshots was replaced by the sound of Eric moaning. He writhed on the concrete, his clothes scraping underneath him. He lifted his head and looked at Angela with wide-eyed shock. His hand shook as he raised the Walther in her direction.

Angela pumped the trigger twice more. Eric jerked with each hit, one to the center of his chest, the second to his cheek. Splatter escaped from behind his head, and he slumped flat on his back. He was dead.

I struggled to absorb what had just happened—Angela in the trunk, among packs stuffed with money, a gun in her hand, shots fired. Her lungs were heaving, and her arms looked stiff, as if they'd gotten stuck with both hands aiming the gun. There would be more bullets in that thing, and for a moment I thought she might use them on me.

Instead, words came out of her in a scream. "He was going to kill you! He was going to show you the money and then kill you! He told me!" Her words poured out in a rush, like she couldn't stop them. "He knew where I was the whole time! He followed me and took the money. He said he'd hurt me if didn't help him." Her teeth chattered inside her jaw, as if an icy wind had drawn all warmth from her, leaving her shivering.

I stepped to her and held out my hand. She looked at my open palm, then gently set the Beretta in it. Her hand was shaking so badly I thought the gun might accidentally go off.

"He hid it in here," she said, meaning the gun. "He was afraid you'd search him so he couldn't have it on him." I hadn't gotten around to searching him, but I was impressed that he'd thought of it. Her gaze drifted to Eric's lifeless body as her voice trailed off. "I just couldn't let him hurt you . . ."

I picked up the Walther. With it in my confident left-handed grip, and the Beretta awkwardly in my right, I must've looked like a cartoon gumshoe. Armed and dangerous in a dark city alley. With a gun moll. And a dead body.

We had to get out of there.

* * *

The marine layer had finally arrived.

If the cameras had recorded everything, I'd be identified the instant someone reviewed the footage. But it didn't matter.

With the trunk lid open, Angela couldn't be seen by the cameras pointed toward the street from the rear of the alley, and the ones at the entrance mainly covered the sidewalk, not the length of the passageway.

I turned the dome light off, then gave Angela the Covid mask I'd stuffed in my pocket. I instructed her to put it on and to tuck her hair under her jacket.

"Keep your chin down," I told her, helping her out of the trunk.

She seemed fragile, unsteady, so I guided her to the passenger seat and shut the door. I transferred the packs to the rear seat. Then I lifted Eric and dumped him into the trunk. No dead body is easy to move by yourself so, for once, I was grateful he'd kept himself good and slim. I took a last look at him, his eyes still open in surprise, his lips parted as if in midsentence. *Kid, you really didn't see this coming, did you? Don't feel bad. Neither did I.*

With the key fob in my pocket, the car started right up. I backed out of the alley onto an empty 5th Street and drove into the night. The license plates, mounting screws, and the screwdriver Eric used to take them all off lay on the passenger side floorboard under Angela's feet. At this hour, it'd be easy to find a quiet spot and remount them. But a car creeping through deserted LA streets at any time will always look suspicious, so I found an empty parking space on Flower Street and screwed them on as fast as I could.

I figured the freeways would be the safest route from Point Homicide to Point Safety. I cruised onto the downtown interchange and took the 110 Pasadena north toward the Hollywood 101. That would be the fastest route to Angela's neighborhood.

She'd been silent since her postmurder outburst, staring out the window as we went under the tangled downtown cloverleaf.

"We have to hide this," I said, meaning the cash stacked behind us. "Then I'll take you home." I wasn't sure she heard me, or if anything could even puncture the trance of shock that had seized her.

"I have a storage unit," she said, staring out the window. She looked at me in the dark. "Take the Glendale exit."

I left the 101 at Glendale Boulevard and followed her directions north. We passed Echo Park Lake which, on this moonless night, was a black abyss. The boulevard took us into the area once called Edendale, so named in the early 1900s by a group of radical communists who strived to create a utopia.

As we approached an unlit Burger King sign she said, "Turn in here."

I made a right just before the fast food business and, after driving up a short uphill grade, we came to a large steel gate topped with razor wire. She pulled out her phone, did some tapping, and I heard a "beep" from the direction of the fence. The gate slid open to the left, and I drove through.

She pointed me to a two-story brick building with a sloped roof set between two newer, three-story structures.

We stopped by the third of several articulating doors fronting the building. Her storage unit.

Without a word, she got out of the car. I followed suit as we stepped to the locked unit.

"I need some light," she said.

I pulled out my Xiaomi and clicked on the flashlight. She thought for a moment, maybe trying to remember the order of numbers, then spun the dial on the heavy-duty combination lock hanging from the door's latch, right, left, then right again. The lock dropped open, and in one smooth action she removed the lock and slid the latch. She bent and pulled on the handle at the base of the door, and it rolled open with a noisy clang. She went in and pulled a thin metal chain hanging from the center of the room. A single bulb flicked on above us. Its white glare made my pupils contract so quickly it hurt.

"Can't this be traced to you?" I asked.

I thought I saw a small shake of her head in response. "It was my mother's. It's still under her name." I waited. That didn't add up for me. "Her maiden name," she continued. "She got it to hide some things from my father." Ah, right. Angela's old man was an abusive dickhead. Couldn't blame her mother.

The side walls were lined with plastic bins and cardboard bankers boxes. Against the back wall was a wardrobe rack holding clothes wrapped in clear plastic garment bags. From their bulk the clothes looked like they might be Angela's winter wear. There was an empty space through the middle of the unit wide enough for a person to move, where you could see everything that had been stored. She'd made it easy and convenient to find whatever she wanted.

"You can put them here," Angela said, indicating the empty center space. Her eyes were hollow. She seemed to be operating on autopilot.

"I'll get them," I asked.

I lugged the packs in two and three at a time, lining them up in the center. She pulled the chain to switch off the light, and we went outside. After I'd closed the articulating door, Angela reattached the lock.

I noticed a plaque set into the wall that I'd missed when we'd arrived. It was a commemoration from the City of Los Angeles, designating this building as a cultural landmark. A storage building now has cultural significance? Even if it was the first of its kind in the US of A, wasn't that going a little far? I looked closer. The inscription read:

MACK SENNETT STUDIOS—1912
ONE OF THE FIRST MOTION PICTURE
STUDIOS IN LOS ANGELES
HOME TO THE KEYSTONE COPS

Mack Sennett's successful silent film company had helped make stars of Gloria Swanson, Roscoe "Fatty" Arbuckle, and Charlie Chaplin, as well as the aforementioned Keystones. This very building had been ground zero for one of the most storied and successful movie companies of its day. Or any day.

Many of the stars it helped launch, like Chaplin, credited this studio as their salvation from a life of poverty and strife.

* * *

I brought Angela to the back door of her apartment. She was still moving with the deliberate intention of someone who had to choose every step they made, however short or fundamental. At the top of the stairs, she stopped, staring blankly through the glass panes into her kitchen.

"Do you have your keys?" I asked gently.

She drew a breath, as if she'd been startled awake from a deep sleep, and pulled her key ring from her pocket. I suddenly realized that she didn't have a purse with her, not even when she collected the money from the roach hotel. Angela always liked to keep things simple.

I took the keys from her, opened the door, and ushered her in. The round vintage clock over the range said it was just after four-thirty am. That's a time of night that has significance for me, and I was happy to have spent most of my previous two decades sleeping through it. Seeing it then, I half expected a S.W.A.T. team to break down Angela's door. I needed to get moving, get back in the car, and drive the incriminating evidence away from here.

She had gone ahead of me into the apartment. I found her sitting in the dark on the living room sofa.

"You checked out of the hotel?"

She nodded.

"Did anyone see Eric there with you?"

She shook her head. "No. He called me in the room and told me to get my car and meet him."

"He called you?"

She nodded. "On the hotel phone." She stared straight ahead. "He even knew my room number. He called the front desk, and they put him through. He was smart that way, always covering his tracks."

*Not smart enough.* Something didn't add up. "I never asked you where you met him."

"On a dating site, where else? Boy, did he ever put on the full court press." As she spoke her eyes drifted to the ceiling and down again. "And I fucking fell for it. Jesus, how lonely does a girl have to be?"

"And you never thought he was up to something?"

"I'm not stupid. Not hard to tell guys like Rudy aren't model citizens." She looked up at me. "But I swear, I didn't know who Eric was. Not until you told me." She looked away. "Now it makes sense."

"What does?"

"His wanting to meet you. *Hire* you." She shook her head. "God, he played me!" She brought a hand to her mouth to head off the sob that was trying to get out.

I looked out her large window to the street. The leaves between the building and the streetlamps cut shadows across the panes. The lamps added a dim amber glow to the old room. Despite the trauma she'd just endured, and the tears welling in her eyes, she looked lovely in that light.

"You should get some sleep. You have anything for that?"

She got to her feet. "I have some pills." She sniffled and wiped her palm across her face. "Are you leaving?" Her tone suggested she didn't want me to.

"I have to get rid of the car." I figured she could put that together with the dead body in the trunk without me saying it out loud.

She nodded slightly, and started for the bedroom, then she turned to me. “Will you call me later? When you can, I mean.”

“I’ll try,” I said. “I’m not sure we should talk anymore, though.” It killed me to say that, but sometimes you have to fall on your sword.

CHAPTER

# 42

I DROVE THE SEDAN east, back toward downtown. I'd read an article recently about the lakes that dotted LA. In it was a quote by a sociologist named Harvey Molotch that Los Angeles "can only be explained as a remarkable victory of human cunning over the so-called limits of nature." He was referring to collecting and keeping the water that is so desperately needed here.

Echo Park Lake, Silver Lake, Rowena and Hollywood Reservoirs, all these and many more with their peculiar beauty, function, and history, both giddy and tragic. And then there was the Lake at MacArthur Park.

Once a third larger than it is now, the city met its growing transportation needs by bisecting the lake, extending Wilshire Boulevard right through it. Eventually, the smaller of the two ponds created when it was severed by the new street, was filled in and covered with grass. It had become known as the centerpiece of what was essentially a thirty-five-acre homeless encampment, but the recent ICE raids had considerably thinned the itinerant population.

Now it was home to only the most desperate—hopeless addicts, teen runaways, the mentally, physically, and spiritually broken. At only fourteen feet deep, the lake has been drained several times for different reasons, and every time hundreds of handguns and other weapons would be found on the bottom.

Sounds like a perfect home for someone I know.

Arriving at the lake was like something out of a low budget horror flick. Tents and lean-tos were visible as soon as I reached the edge of the property. Wilshire Boulevard takes a slight bend as you arrive on the north side of the park, the design meant to retain as much of the lake bed as possible. I followed it to the corner of Alvarado Street and braked for the red light. I took the opportunity to scan the area for cops.

The nighttime marine layer had formed a thick mist that hovered over the water. The green space between the street and the lake was dotted with tents and people, many of them motionless in drug-induced stupor. Some were slowly moving in the dark, lighting crack pipes, or carrying their meager belongings to what I supposed was a safer spot than the one they just left. Surprisingly, the gender count seemed to be about fifty/fifty, men to women.

A right turn on a red light is legal in California, so there was nothing stopping me from ignoring the light, but with a corpse as my only passenger, I decided to be extra careful. When the light went green, I turned right.

I came to the corner at 7th Street and was surprised by the darkened sign for Langer's Delicatessen. I used to go there when I needed some fatty protein to quell a raging hangover. I'd order the "#19" sandwich: pastrami,

Swiss cheese, and coleslaw with a swab of Russian dressing on soft rye bread. I was happy to see it was still in business.

I made another right onto 7th and slowly trolled the periphery. The sidewalk is separated from the park on the three other sides by a low wall, but over here there's only the curb. I could jump the car over it, but I didn't want to risk breaking an axle and getting stuck halfway (any more than I wanted to be pulled over and searched). Halfway down the long block, I found what I needed.

There was an entrance in the curb that had been blocked on the far side of the walk by a row of four-feet high steel poles set in cement. This must've been used as a maintenance entrance for vehicles to access the park, but at some point it was decided to block it permanently. The good news for me was that I could use the entry section of the curb to drive onto the sidewalk, go past the poles, and then just turn into the park.

I swerved a hard right into the entrance, stopped, back up a few feet, then cranked right again and slowly guided the sedan between the poles and an old elm tree on the grass median by the street. The sedan fit through easily. I maneuvered the car across the grass, past the tents, and the gawking denizens, steered back onto the unused concrete drive, and continued down an easy grade to the lake.

The brakes squeaked to a stop at the water's edge. I put the car in Park and left the engine idling, then I pressed the armrest buttons and the windows lowered with a hum. By now, people were starting to realize the automobile that just drove off the street, across the grass, and down the slope was not a city crew come to fix a problem in the middle of the night. It actually wasn't supposed to be here, at all.

I reached over the seat and retrieved the backpack I'd left on the floorboard where Angela wouldn't see it. I figured with all the cash sitting in her storage unit, she could get by without this one. I pulled on a mask, got out, and looped the strap over my shoulder. I stiffened when I felt the eyes on me. I braced myself for a charge of desperate druggie thieves wanting whatever was inside that pack, no matter if they could use it, eat it, or sell it. I imagined the brutal response of the crowd if any one of them was lucky enough to take it from me, and then open it where others could see what was inside.

I looked around, giving my best Clint Eastwood squint (which I doubt anyone could see in the dark, but it made me feel better). I don't know if it was my imposing size, my deliberate machismo, or that they were just plain confounded by the presence of this decently dressed masked man, but no one lunged at me. I dropped into the driver's seat, my left foot still on the ground, and pushed my right foot down on the brake pedal. I punched the transmission into Drive and rose out of the car with one easy move.

The car jerked into motion and, under its own power, clunked over the cement rim. The lake bed had been lined with asphalt years before to keep the water from flooding the new subway tunnel that ran below it. The nose of the car hit the water and sank until the front tires met the hard bottom. The rear wheels rose off the ground and spun. That kicked the all-wheel drive mechanism into action, and the two front wheels engaged, pulling the car into the water. The rear wheels touched again as the chassis dropped even with the lake's rim, and they finished the job, pushing the car the rest of the way in.

I watched as the murky green water swiftly poured through the open door and windows, taking the car to the bottom. That "sweet green icing" from that famous song named after the park must have flowed into the lake, because the visibility couldn't be more than a couple of inches. I swear any diver unlucky enough to do a search wouldn't be able to see a damn thing until he ran into it, and might even die from exposure to toxins. Hard to believe people still fished out of here, but then hunger is one powerful motivator.

The car would sit down there until someone released the city funds required to remove it, if they ever found out about it. The city's relations with the unhoused can be precarious, at best, and I didn't expect any of the witnesses here to report an incident that would only bring more police scrutiny. Until then, it would lie on the bottom, and thanks to all that sweet green icing, unseen, with Eric hidden inside. I tossed the Walther and the Beretta as far as I could toward the lake's center. I heard each make a quiet splash in the darkness. *Plop. Plop.* Despite my family's affinity for them, I never really liked guns, and after today, I hoped I'd never need another one.

In the distance, far beyond the palm trees across the lake, the silhouette of the downtown skyline was taking shape as the deep blues and purples of the horizon appeared. The sun would be up soon. It made me think of what Dorothy must've seen the first time she saw the Land of Oz across the field of poppies. *Just don't pull back the curtain.*

As I walked up the grade toward 7th Street, I passed a streetlamp with a surveillance camera mounted on top. Below the camera was a sign: "Notice: All Activities Monitored by Video Camera." No kidding.

I needed some time alone, so I crossed the street to the less populated side and wandered for a while. The sun rose. The one thing you can count on in an unreliable world. If it came to it, I could take refuge from the police in the crush of rejected humanity in the park, but I doubted I would.

I knew if I was caught they'd never let me come back here, or let me go anywhere. I was hungry, and I wanted to hold out until Langer's opened, try to get in one last #19.

C H A P T E R

# 43

I'D AWAKENED TO a subtle *tick . . . tick . . . tick* filling the room. It felt like something looming, waiting to catch me off guard. It was unsettling, and I knew why.

Time passing.

Inevitable. Unstoppable. Irretrievable. You get used to it in prison. You'd better, or your next stop is a psych ward, where you're kept under control by being drugged into a stupor.

My thoughts went to that first morning back in LA, waking to an earthquake that left me fearing for my life, right when I finally had the chance to start over, to try to correct the past. How wrong I was.

Once I'd left MacArthur Park, I didn't have long to wait for Langer's to open. Sitting at the counter with a million dollars at my feet, I was certain the LAPD would pick me up any second. But, with any luck, the pastrami would be ready, and I wouldn't be limited to the breakfast menu. No breakfast could stack up to anything Carla would bring me, but I didn't think she'd want to see me. So, Langer's.

And as luck would have it, the #19 was as ready first thing in the morning as their Western omelet.

By the time I was ready to leave, the only LAPD in sight were busy with overdoses and turf-fights in the park. I finished my sandwich and took a cab ride downtown to Union Station.

The historic terminal had been featured in a lot of movies. *Blade Runner*, *The Way We Were*, *The Driver*. My favorite was *Boiling Point*, when a young Viggo Mortensen, the building's Art Deco facade beautifully lit in the background, takes out a guy in the front parking lot with a deft crowbar-to-shotgun move.

I bought a train ticket to San Diego which, after a scenic ride down the coast, put me there by early afternoon. Then, another cab to the border crossing. Politics being what they are, the way into the US is far more scrutinized than the way out, and I simply walked into Tijuana along with tourists and day-workers. No one bothered to check my pack, though I was ready to be cuffed if they did. I exchanged some cash for local currency and was in a decent hotel by dinnertime.

The next morning, after picking up yet another new set of clothes in the hotel gift shop, I hopped a bus to Zihuatanejo.

I'd gotten the idea to go there because Anthony, my Folsom "Brooks Hatlen," had pushed me to read that Stephen King story, *Rita Hayworth and Shawshank Redemption*. It was sound logic for Andy Dufresne to plot his escape route there all the way from Maine. Good enough for Andy, good enough for me.

* * *

The ticking clock had a cream-colored face with lush black Roman numerals, encased in a round shell of antique wood. An intricate carving of a Golden Eagle, the country's national bird with its wings spread, topped it. A good foot in diameter, it hung above an elegant mahogany desk by a picture window. When seated at that desk, I'd swivel in the chair and have an unobstructed view of the ocean. I swear, I could just stare at the Pacific all day and get nothing done.

Big change from that low rent hostel I'd landed in only a few months earlier. That felt like eons ago.

Time.

The morning after I'd reached Mexico, my conscience had gotten to me. I had tried repeatedly to contact Angela. I'd even downloaded and learned the various secure messaging apps—Telegram, WhatsApp, Signal. No matter how many times or ways I tried, I couldn't connect. It was like she'd just up and vanished. I needed to keep moving, so I headed farther south.

Even after doubts had begun to form in my head, I'd kept trying to reach her, mainly out of my lingering guilt. I'd already abandoned Angela once in this life, and I didn't want to do it again without a proper goodbye. I even hoped for a video call. That way, she could see my face as I apologized one last time for how things had turned out. It would be taking a chance, but I figured if she was being monitored, it would take too long to cut through the red tape down here to alert the local authorities in time to catch up with me.

Looking back, I think my guilt had a way of making me willing to do almost anything, if I thought it gave me a path to redemption. I could finally earn that deliverance I'd longed for. Angela had seen that longing, and she'd used it against me.

After a couple of weeks in Zihuatanejo, I reached out to Carla over Telegram. I was worried that Sanchez might contact her, as I had shared her info with him in case of emergency, but his name never came up. She spoke cryptically, but managed to make me understand that the US Post had safely delivered my "gift." She expressed her sincere surprise and gratitude at my "thoughtfulness" and then astonished me by suggesting she join me. I was overjoyed.

She was due any minute, so I pulled myself off the finest sheets I'd slept on since my misspent youth and grabbed a quick shower. The in-room coffee was better than just about any I'd had anywhere else, so I didn't bother with room service. I would wait until she arrived, then we could order in whatever she wanted. Or we'd go out, if she wasn't too tired from the trip.

I was standing in front of the mirror, having just finished drying my hair, when I heard a knock at the door. It was a practiced signal. *Knock . . . knock . . . knock-knock . . . knock.* That meant the coast was clear, that she hadn't been followed. I figured the towel I was wearing around my waist was cover enough, so I opened the door.

Carla looked me over, and I stared back, letting her fill my eyes. Then she said, "So, you gonna invite me in?"

"Sorry," I said. "I forget my manners when I see you." I stepped aside, and she entered with two large roller bags.

She stowed the bags inside the door, went to the middle of the room, and looked around. "I thought we were supposed to make the money last," she said.

"I thought we could use a little vacation first."

She smiled back. "Nice towel, stud. You gonna wear that all day?"

"Your wish is my command," I said. I pulled the fold holding it to my waist, and let the towel drop to the floor.

She blushed, but she didn't look away. "He'll be here soon," she said. "He wanted to stop in town first."

"And you didn't go with him?"

She shrugged. "I wanted to see you."

"Well, we better hurry up then."

"He won't be here *that* soon," she said.

Afterward, she slid off the bed and went to the shower to rinse off the tropical heat. I called down to order some lunch from room service.

"Now that I've seen that tub," she called from the bathroom, "I think a couple days' R&R could be good."

* * *

The knock on the door made us both jump, even though it was the code we'd all agreed on. Carla and I had spent the rest of the day just hanging in the room, enjoying the view, being together. Carla looked through the peephole, then opened the door to a man who appeared to be a few years younger than she. There was a striking resemblance between them.

"Jake," she said. "I'd like you to meet my brother, Anthony."

I smiled and came over to greet him. "One of the best people I ever knew was named Anthony," I said.

Anthony smiled back and shook my hand. "I'll try to live up to that."

We took seats on the veranda, and watched the setting sun turn the blue sky bright orange. I'd brought out cold Mexican cervezas for them and a ginger ale for me. I'd cut some lime wedges, and we prepped our drinks with the citrus boost. Then we toasted and took a celebratory drink.

"So, you think you can find it?" I asked.

"You mean the money you gave her?" Anthony chuckled and took another sip of his beer. "Already did. It's right where you thought."

"Can it be done?" I asked.

"In a word," he said. "Yes."

"Wait," Carla said. "Isn't Switzerland supposed to be the safest place in the world to hide money?"

"Not really, sis," Anthony said. "If the money is made from a crime that is also a crime in Switzerland, then it's fair game." He laughed. "Nobody with any experience uses Switzerland anymore. It's a lot safer in a place like Panama or Russia."

"How'd you find it?" I asked.

"The same way rich criminals do anything," he said. "Bribe somebody."

I looked to Carla. "I thought we didn't want to get him involved?"

Before Carla could chastise her little brother, he said, "*I* didn't bribe anyone. I called in a favor."

I thought of the Ghost. The "favor" he did for me cost a few lives. I hoped that wasn't the case here.

"It helped that you didn't just want it for yourself," Anthony said.

Carla gave him a side-eye. "You're sure you're in the clear?"

"Oh, yeah, I'm good," he answered. "I have no plans, or desire, to go back to that life. I've had my fill of the penal system, thank you. This was a favor for my big sister and her boyfriend. End of story."

I shook my head. This was an unexpected turn of events, to say the least. "How the hell did she move literal bags of money from California across the Atlantic Ocean?"

Anthony sipped his beer. "Well, there're lots of ways, and she used most of them. It was a combination of money laundering and legit businesses. She and her guy set up a couple of shell companies to move some of it, which is typical. But once she had the cash, she started using other methods common to smugglers." He started counting them on his fingers. "Bought thousands of prepaid phone cards, shipped those overseas, then sold them." Another finger went up. "Bitcoin to move it on the dark web. That might account for a lot of it." Another finger. "Did some smurfing by setting up multiple bank accounts, but you can only do so much of that 'cause, as anyone knows, you can only deposit under ten grand at a time. She probably did that with whatever small change was left." He dropped his hand. "She even used a Hawala."

"A wallet?" Carla asked.

He smiled. "A Ha-wa-la," he said, enunciating the syllables. "Basically, you give money to someone in one country, then someone over there gives that amount to whoever you're sending it to, minus a small commission. The Hawalas figure out payments between themselves. It's legal, but there's an informal, underground system, too. She would just send it to herself wherever she was going, and collect it once she got there."

Carla and I looked at each other, shook our heads. Pretty ingenious.

"Obviously," Carla said, "she didn't come up with this overnight."

"Hardly," Anthony said. "But it adds up quick. If you think ahead, you can move it in a few weeks. Remember, cartels send hundreds of millions every year using systems like these, and there're plenty more ways to do it. End of the day, I'd say she got between eight to ten million dollars. That's small potatoes, probably wouldn't even get flagged. All she had to do then was send it to the one account in Geneva." He leaned back and faced the ocean, the amber glow making him look almost beatific.

"Where is she now?"

"Who knows?" Anthony said, squinting into the last of the sunset. "Doesn't matter, though. She has to surface to get the money. Even if she tries to move it somewhere, the bank will just wait for her, and then hand the case over to the Swiss police. Interpol's got their eyes out for her, too."

"Jesus," I said.

He looked at me. "Eric had planned to take you out. Now that she's skipped, I suspect that was her idea."

"Yeah," I said dryly. "It's occurred to me. She also told me Eric had chased *her*. But once I really had a chance to look at everything, I think it was the other way around."

"I think you're right." Anthony thought for a beat. "What tipped you off, anyway?"

"I'm not sure," I said. "I can't really nail down one specific thing, but if I had to, it would have to be how willing she was to take all that money off my hands. Twice."

"That follows," Anthony said. "She would've taken care of Eric once they got wherever they were going, but then you went and made it easy for her. It's not like she was infamous or anything. She had no criminal record, no social media. Not hard for someone like her to disappear with the right papers. And she'd collect either way."

"A win–win," I said.

Carla fixed her eyes on me. "What did you ever see in that bitch?"

I returned her gaze. "Seemed like a good idea at the time. Now I know a good thing when I see it."

She smiled at me, then looked at her brother. "Can you stay a while?"

"Just tonight," he said. "Parole lets me come into Mexico for forty-eight hours. I'll go back tomorrow to check in."

I looked out at the fading horizon. I don't know why, but the sunlight hadn't given me an urge to sneeze.

I knew that I would never see Los Angeles, or America, again. I can't say that upset me. Carla didn't seem to mind, either. Officially, I am now Stephen Markowski, Canadian born, touring my bucket list of destinations. Carla is now Rebecca (Becky) Sanderford, also Canadian. We're from Nova Scotia, and she's my fiancée, if anyone asks. With some sound advice from her brother, Anthony, and our new identities, I think we'll do all right.

"Funny, I don't miss it now that I'm gone," Carla has said of our home country. "Besides, I don't think we're meant to live in just one place or do one thing our whole lives. And hey, I always wanted to live abroad."

After much of my life spent in an environment that was as much an extension of the mindset that put me there,

I couldn't agree more. And with close to two million dollars between us, we should be covered until we find a place to land. In the Folsom library, I'd thumbed through a lot of travel books, and Tunisia always interested me. Great cost of living, safe cities, beautiful beaches, good education system, and many of its people speak English. More importantly, there's no extradition treaty with the US.

I never really wanted to see my name in lights, anyway.

# ACKNOWLEDGMENTS

WHEN YOU SIT down to write your first book, the words tend to flow relatively freely. Years of ideas are finally unleashed onto the page, fueled by the simple joy of writing for its own sake. And then one day, finally, you have a book. It doesn't matter if it's good or not, it's a book, and you wrote it. Of course, every aspiring novelist dreams of the day his or her first novel is published. When that day comes, it's one you will never forget. It is a splendid, frightening, and unforgettable experience. What you don't know is how hard writing your second book is going to be.

Hollywood Payback is that book for me. I had no idea how difficult it would be to meet a deadline, let alone finish another novel. But I can tell you this: It would never have happened without the faith, support, and encouragement of people I can never repay.

Liza Fleissig is, in a word, incomparable. Her ingenuity and determination is a stellar example for anyone. As my agent, she expertly guided me to realize my dream of becoming a published author. Every effort she makes for me, and all of her clients, is to enrich them as people and artists. Dignity is foremost with Liza. Her tireless work for authors to be valued in a world that routinely tries to undermine any creative person is unparalleled. I am blessed to be a client of hers and of Liza Royce Associates.

Crooked Lane Books. So many imprints get slammed by current or former authors (and I suppose for good reason) but to me CLB is the ideal of what a publishing house should be. My editor, Jess Verdi, only has the goal of making your book better. And mine is, thanks to her. She and her team always say what they're going to do, do what they say, and then go far beyond, all to help your book succeed in a noisy, confusing market. Everyone at CLB has afforded me the freedom to write what I feel, and to never stand in the way of that. The kindness and generosity that publisher Matt Martz has fostered at this company is a Godsend. My sincere thanks to you all.

Captain Robert John Burke of Engine 7, OBFD (yes, that Robert Burke, from countless films and TV shows, is also a fire captain) gave me indispensable advice on how my protagonist could escape a deadly situation. My hero lives, thanks to you, Bob. To Genie Francis and Jonathan Frakes, for your friendship, and for providing me with a quiet place in Maine that got me over a writing hump. You are irreplaceable, and I love you.

James L'Etoile, a lifelong penologist (who happens to be one of the best Thriller writers around) opened a window into prison life and of ex-cons that I believe no one else could have. Alex Kenna, another legal professional who happens to write great crime books, guided me through the minutiae of courtroom procedure without boring the living hell out of myself, and (hopefully) the reader. Jerri Williams, a retired F.B.I. agent and current kick-butt crime writer, schooled me on the truths of major robberies. Thank you Jim, Alex, and Jerri. Anything I can do for you…

Jeff Ayers, who offered early reads and advice for improvement. You're an excellent friend, Jeff. Thank you. John J. York, who opened up about his medical challenges over the last few years to give me insight into that journey. I ultimately opted not to go that route in the story, but I sure learned a lot more about you, and myself, and my book is all the better for it. You're the best, my friend. I am in awe.

To Lynn Marie Latham. In addition to being one of the most accomplished writers in Hollywood, she's also been editing since her teens (her father was an author and she would proofread his work). Going line-by-line to spot every small point that could be improved—commas to cut, antecedents to add—Lynn found them all, and my book is immeasurably better because of it. I love you, Lynn. Thank you.

And last, but never least, to the readers. Thank you for choosing *Hollywood Payback*. I did everything I could not to waste your precious time. I hope you got what you came for.

With gratitude and respect,
Jon Lindstrom